ONE BY ONE . . .

"You fought the Horned One and killed it," Lokhra said. She was voluptuous and wore only a flower in her hair and a bracelet of grass.

Blade thought that she was beautiful.

"When the Horned One attacks our hunters, some of them always die. Four men now live who would otherwise be dead," Lokhra continued. "When a man of the Fak'si saves another, the man he saves must give him a woman for one night. The men cast the bones, and four of them were chosen—each sends you one of his women. I am the first."

To Blade it seemed a sensible way of showing gratitude. While she'd been explaining why she was here, Lokhra's fingers were moving gently but steadily over his body.

Blade found his breath coming harder and felt Lokhra's nipples hardening against the palms of his hands. Blade didn't know what Lokhra might expect, but he knew what he wanted, and he knew he wasn't going to wait any longer. . . .

* * *

After a while Lokhra, quite satisfied, but still naked, walked across the shelter and pulled open the curtain of leaves which served as a door.

"Come in," she said to the darkness outside. Blade started to rise—then three women were standing in the doorway. All three of them wore the Fak'si knee-length skirts, but before Blade could recover from his surprise they started pulling them off.

Blade was amused at the prospect of having to satisfy three more women tonight. From the way they were looking at him, they were also looking forward to the rest of the night.

Blade threw his head back and laughed, until his laughter drowned out the night sounds outside and the four women were laughing with him. Then he stood up and walked over to the first of the three newcomers.

THE BLADE SERIES:

HEROIC FANTASY SERIES

31

BLADE

GLADIATORS OF HAPANU
by Jeffrey Lord

PINNACLE BOOKS   LOS ANGELES

BLADE #31: GLADIATORS OF HAPANU

Copyright © 1979 by Book Creations, Inc.

An original Pinnacle Books edition, published for the first time anywhere.

Produced by Lyle Kenyon Engel

First printing, July 1979

ISBN: 0-523-40648-7

Cover illustration by John Alvin

Printed in the United States of America

PINNACLE BOOKS, INC.
2029 Century Park East
Los Angeles, California 90067

Chapter 1

Richard Blade walked alone down the underground corridor two hundred feet below the Tower of London. As he walked he tried to see the corridor as would a man who'd never seen it before and knew nothing about it.

The floor was large, close-set tile, a bland, neutral brown alternating with an equally bland gray in a sort of checkerboard pattern. The tile threw up echoes from Blade's footsteps for the walls and ceiling to catch and bounce back. The floor showed signs of wear from many fast-moving feet, but it was spotlessly clean. In fact it was not merely clean, it was as antiseptic as the floor of a hospital.

So were the walls. They were not tiled, but something solid covered with pale green semi-gloss paint, easy on the eyes and easy to wash. At intervals the walls were broken by plain metal doors. All of them opened by push buttons rather than knobs, and all of them had spy eyes in the middle, so that the people inside could see anyone waiting outside. The impression the doors gave was less a hospital than a top-secret military installation. These were doors which might hide the latest guided missile or experiments with a new and deadly nerve gas.

In other places the walls were broken by metal panels with EMERGENCY stencilled on them in foot high red letters. There were no conventional fire alarms or fire extinguishers in sight, and it was impossible to guess what might lurk behind the panels.

Overhead was a ceiling of pale white acoustic tile, broken every few feet by more metal panels, ventilating grilles, squares of translucent glass or plastic, and sometimes grids of small holes that might have been made by termites. At intervals a faded discolored line ran across the floor, up one wall, across the ceiling, and down the wall again. Something once stood across the corridor in these places. Now it was gone and

1

the corridor stretched unbroken from end to end, more than two hundred feet.

Even without the steady echoes of Blade's footsteps, the corridor wasn't entirely quiet. There was the distant hum of air-conditioners, the click of typewriters, muffled hints of human voices, and other sounds that might have been anything. The corridor itself was echoing, empty, and sterile, but there was life and activity on either side of it.

So much for seeing the corridor through a stranger's eyes. Blade turned off his imagination and walked faster. He enjoyed these mental exercises, and was good at them. When he'd been at Oxford a teacher said he would make at least a respectable novelist, though probably not a great one.

Blade hadn't become a novelist, but when he'd left Oxford he'd entered a profession where a good imagination was almost as important. He became a field agent for the secret intelligence agency MI6A. In fact, he was hand-picked by its chief, the graying man known only as J. J saw a particularly promising young man, and he was right. Blade became one of the agency's best men, carrying out missions few others could have handled and surviving dangers that would have killed practically anyone else.

One reason for his success and survival was that imagination of his. More easily than most, he could put himself into the mind of an enemy, thinking of what the man might do, sometimes before the enemy thought of it himself: This kind of imagination didn't win him any prizes, but it saved his life a good many times.

Then a brilliant, eccentric scientist named Lord Leighton conceived the idea of linking a powerful human mind with an even more powerful computer. He wasn't exactly sure what this would produce, but he hoped it would be something more powerful and complete than either the computer or the man.

He chose Richard Blade for the experiment, because he needed a powerful mind in a superbly fit body and Blade had both. The computer went to work on Blade's mind—and suddenly Blade was whirled off across nowhere into an unknown world they called Dimension X.

The same gifts that kept him alive as a secret agent now kept him alive to return to England. They went on to keep him alive many more times, for Dimension X was obviously a major scientific breakthrough. A breakthrough into what, even Lord Leighton wasn't quite sure, but certainly a breakthrough. Out there in the unknown lay human resources of raw material, knowledge, and living space. All of it might be put to use for Britain, all of it might become the foundation for a new British Empire.

So the exploration of Dimension X became a Project, with the support of the Prime Minister's office, a budget of millions of pounds, a staff of dozens of the most brilliant minds in twenty different fields. None of these hired geniuses knew what the Project was all about, because the Dimension X secret was the most closely-guarded in Britain's history. No one cared to guess what might happen if the secret got out, but so far they hadn't had to find out the hard way. J became chief of security for the Project, and so far he'd done his job there extremely well. Dimension X was still a secret.

All of this, however, rested on the shoulders of one man —Richard Blade. He was the only living human being who could make the round trip into Dimension X and come out alive and sane. They'd found this out the hard way, at the cost of a number of people dead or mad.

In spite of this, the search for a new Dimension X traveler still went on. Blade's shoulders were broad, but they could bear only so much of a burden for so long. Even more important than Blade's body was his mind. *That* was strained to the limit every time he was hurled off into Dimension X, and sometimes matters didn't stop there.

Blade remembered the time he'd encountered the Wizard of Rentoro, an Italian Renaissance nobleman who'd passed into Dimension X by pure mental powers. The Wizard was a master of telepathy, telekinesis, and teleportation, perhaps the most dangerous opponent Blade's mind or body ever had.

At least he *had* been the most dangerous, until Blade's most recent trip into Dimension X. Lord Leighton was introducing not only a new, incredibly more powerful computer, but also new techniques for sending Blade into the unknown. With the new KALI computer and a completely automatic main sequence, it might finally be possible to send Blade to the same Dimension time after time. That would have been as important a breakthrough as finding another Dimension X traveler, although not quite as big a help to Blade.

As a matter of fact, the new technique did send Blade into the same Dimension twice in succession, as reliably as the London Underground. So the theory behind KALI was sound enough. Lord Leighton's theories usually were. In practice, it was very nearly a case of "The operation was successful but the patient died."

3

Out in the unknown Blade met the Ngaa, the collective minds of an incredibly ancient race trapped on a doomed and dying world, once immensely wise but now grown evil with desperation. The Ngaa returned to England with Blade, driving him insane in the process—and that was only the beginning of the trail of destruction it left. By the time the whole nightmare was over, more than thirty people were dead. The Project was thrown into chaos and came within a few hours of being shut down for good by order of the Prime Minister.

In the end it was Blade himself who saved things. His mind restored, he pursued the Ngaa to its home, fought it, and destroyed it. Now Lord Leighton was free to continue the Project on a slightly less ambitious basis, and Blade was fit and ready for another trip.

Fit and ready, but with more scars than usual, including one that wasn't on his body and might be a long time healing. One of the victims of the Ngaa was Zoe Cornwall, kidnapped by the Ngaa and then murdered by it. Once Blade loved her and she loved him, in a past that now sometimes seemed as distant as the Middle Ages. They'd planned to marry, but the demands of Blade's work in the Project and the Official Secrets Act eventually drove them apart. Blade wasn't sure he'd ever stopped loving her. In any case, he hated to see innocent people of any sort dragged into the dangers he faced as a matter of professional duty.

Perhaps he was selfish in wanting Zoe alive, and certainly it would have been hard for them to start up a life together again. The Ngaa not only left her a widow but murdered her three children as well. She would have carried her own set of scars to the end of her life.

But it still hurt—terribly.

Blade had read the whole report on the battle against the Ngaa, a stack of paper as long as a best-selling novel. He'd marveled at the ability of bureaucratic prose to reduce horrors and disasters to the proportions of a leaky faucet. He'd also been reassured that every possible precaution was being taken to prevent such a disaster from happening again. To be sure, there'd been only one Ngaa, but it was far from certain that Dimension X didn't hold other and perhaps worse menaces. In fact, very little was certain about Dimension X, and the affair of the Ngaa had if anything increased that uncertainty. If Blade hadn't known these precautions were being taken, he'd have been forced to have second thoughts about another trip to Dimension X. Danger to himself was one

4

thing. Danger to the whole human race or even a few dozen innocent people was an entirely different matter.

These thoughts and memories carried Blade the rest of the way down the corridor and through the outer rooms of the main complex. J met him at the door to Lord Leighton's holy of holies, the room holding the master computer.

"Lord Leighton either hasn't arrived or hasn't noticed we're here," said J with a thin smile.

"That's no surprise," said Blade. The KALI computer which had caused much of the trouble last time no longer existed. A squad of strong men wielding sledgehammers and blowtorches had reduced it to unrecognizable electronic junk.

Fortunately the hardware of the previous master computer had survived, stowed away in a secret warehouse. Lord Leighton was a frugal soul at heart, in spite of his frequently extravagant ideas of what to do for the Project with the taxpayers' money. Once he'd been known for squirreling away copper wire and test tubes. Now he squirreled away entire computers.

So the old computer was back in place. Its installation was something of a tape-and-chewing gum job, though, and needed careful maintenance. Lord Leighton insisted that he was the best man for much of this maintenance, and he was probably right. He was quite possibly in the main room now, fussing with some components and as oblivious to the rest of the world as if he were on Mars.

Blade and J chatted for a few minutes—afterward Blade couldn't remember what they talked about—then the door opened and Lord Leighton's voice invited them in. J led the way. They passed into the familiar rock-walled room, with the equally familiar gray crackle-finished consoles back in place. They showed signs of neglect and hasty installation, though, and there were trailing wires all over the floor. J and Blade stepped over them as carefully as if they'd been poisonous snakes.

In spite of this J moved so fast that Blade found himself falling behind. J passed around a console and vanished from sight. Then a sudden, explosive, "What the bloody—?" echoed around the room, loud enough to make Blade break into a run. He came around the corner and stopped dead.

J was standing, glowering at Lord Leighton. The scientist was looking steadily back at J, refusing to be intimidated. In spite of his humpback and polio-twisted legs, there was something rocklike and enduring about his stance and manner.

5

Leighton was also standing beside a silvery metal object, about seven feet high and looking like a cross between a medieval Iron Maiden and a futuristic space capsule. It didn't look particularly sinister, but it made Blade start and he could understand why it made J angry.

It was the launch capsule used with the KALI computer, supposedly destroyed along with it. Its existence proved that Leighton had violated strict orders from the Prime Minister, with the cooperation of Project staff.

Blade said nothing, but headed for the changing booth. He wasn't sure this unexpected development justified canceling the trip, and if it didn't he'd need to strip as usual. He felt a trifle dubious about leaving J, because the older man looked quite genuinely on the verge of having a stroke. On the other hand, it was hard to believe he had anything to contribute if an all-out quarrel between J and Leighton was brewing. He had no illusions that either man would accept him as a mediator, even though J regarded him almost as a son and Leighton had great respect for his intellect and survival qualities. When the chips were down, both men were too stubborn to listen to anyone.

By the time Blade came back, wearing only a loincloth, the atmosphere seemed a bit less tense. Whatever was going to happen, it wouldn't be the sort of head-on collision that might make it impossible for the two men to work together again. That would be almost as final a disaster for Project Dimension X as another attack by the Ngaa!

"—radical reduction in the stresses imposed on the subject during the transition," Leighton was saying.

"Is this a fact, or simply an educated guess?"

Leighton must have been in a fairly good mood, because he didn't bristle at being accused of the obscene act of "guessing." He shook his head. "It's a hypothesis, but one supported by all the data we have on Blade's first transition into the Dimension of the Ngaa."

J nodded slowly. "That's true. The stress on Richard was so low that he was in the other Dimension before he realized it. That's basically how the Ngaa was able to take him over."

"Precisely," said Leighton, obviously keeping the triumph out of his voice with difficulty. "I'm not going to defend my bending of the rules, except that I've kept only the most useful and least dangerous part of the KALI system. In fact, I would say that using the old launching chair with this hastily-rigged computer installation could be much more dangerous than using the KALI capsule."

Leighton was capable of telling almost any sort of lie with a straight face. He would have made a superb politician if he hadn't had such a total contempt for politics. However, he seldom tried to lie to J on a matter of Richard Blade's safety. The old spymaster was too concerned about Blade and much too alert.

By now the snatches of the conversation he'd heard were triggering Blade's memories. Unlike the old system of wires and electrodes fastened in place by hand, the capsule made a circuit between him and the computer that was complete and identical each time. Leighton seemed to believe this might radically reduce the stress on the person in the capsule as he was shot off into Dimension X. That hadn't been in any of the reports, but it certainly sounded plausible. And if it was true —well, anything that reduced the danger of *any* part of the trip into Dimension X was a blessing.

For the moment at least Blade wasn't going to look a gift horse in the mouth. He cleared his throat, making the other two men pause, then asked Leighton:

"You'll be using the old manually-controlled main sequence with the KALI capsule this time?"

"Yes. The two are compatible, with a few modifications I've made."

"And there's no other KALI hardware plugged in anywhere?"

"None."

Blade turned to J. "Sir, I think I'd better take the chance. It doesn't sound like an unacceptable risk, as long as we're using nothing but the launch capsule. In fact, reducing the stress load on me won't do any harm at all. The faster I'm ready to fight when I reach the other side, the better. Most enemies there aren't so sneaky as the Ngaa."

J frowned. "The problem is, you *will* be taking a chance, and a bigger one than I like."

"That's possibly true," said Blade. "But either I take the chance, or the whole Project takes it. If I know anything about the way politicians think—"

"Assuming their mental processes can be described as thinking," put in Leighton.

Blade went on. "I suspect we're not out of the woods yet, as far as the Prime Minister is concerned. If we don't produce a fairly straightforward and normal roundtrip to Dimension X fairly soon, he may have second thoughts about keeping us going. We're still in the 'risky' category, and politicians like to keep that category as small as possible."

J managed to laugh. "Richard, telling me that is teaching your grandmother to suck eggs. I was dealing with politicians while you were in short pants. But you're basically right. Go, and you'll have my blessing." He raised his right hand, with the fingers firmly crossed.

Then he turned to Leighton. "Leighton, I don't particularly like this business of the hidden KALI capsule. But I'll let it pass on one condition. You tell me exactly how you managed to keep the thing hidden, and who helped you. I'm not questioning anybody's loyalty, but facts are facts. A network like yours could hide more disagreeable things than a piece of equipment."

"Yes, but—"

"No 'buts,' Leighton. I don't play games with your computers. In return, I'll have to ask you not to play games with the Project's security."

He took a deep breath. "If you won't cooperate, I'll have to do a housecleaning myself. Nothing brutal, you understand—just reassigning everybody I suspect of having had anything to do with hiding the capsule."

"That certainly won't speed up our recovery from the Ngaa affair," said Leighton.

"I'm willing to risk up to six months delay in the Project over this," said J firmly. "I'm also willing to put the whole matter before the Prime Minister if necessary. It's not just our enemies who could benefit from sloppy security. What about the CIA, for example?"

Leighton sighed. "All right. I trust you to keep your mouth shut and not get anybody in trouble."

The two older men shook hands, and after that things went swiftly. Leighton punched the button to initiate the Main Sequence. Blade climbed into the capsule, lay back, and relaxed. Leighton counted down, and as the count reached six, pressed another button to close the lid of the capsule. A *click* and darkness swallowed Blade. He felt the firmness of the capsule's inner surface against his skin.

Then in rapid succession:

A dazzling golden flash.

A soft, warm blueness, and a subtle sensation all over his

8

skin, like a dozen skilled masseuses all working on him together. It was pleasant, almost erotic.

A harder blueness, neither cold nor warm.

Complete blackness.

Chapter 2

Blade woke up in the middle of such a din that for a moment he thought he'd landed in the middle of a busy city. Then he recognized the chattering of birds and apes, the drone of insects, the rustle of leaves. Now he thought of a jungle instead of a city.

He opened his eyes—or at least he tried to. The world stayed dark. For a moment that seemed hours long, Blade was frozen by a gruesome question. *Was he blind?* If the KALI capsule had somehow destroyed his sight—

Before these thoughts could go any farther, Blade realized what was wrong. His face was covered from hairline to mouth with something like half-melted tar. It smelled and tasted like rotten vegetables, but it wasn't doing anything except completely covering his eyes. He raised one arm and began carefully scraping the muck off his face with his fingers.

Slowly the world around Blade came into sight. The noises hadn't lied—he was in the middle of a jungle. Above him the vine-grown trunk of a massive tree soared up until it vanished into a canopy of shaggy green leaves which left the ground in a sort of greenish twilight. In every direction the ground was covered with a nightmarish tangle of thorny bushes, creeping and climbing vines, and small trees, most of them bearing vividly colored flowers. It was impossible to take a breath without being half-choked by the smells of flowers and decaying vegetation.

It was also going to be difficult to move more than a few yards in any direction without getting caught in the undergrowth. This jungle was about the last place Blade would have chosen to land naked as the day he was born. He would have considered selling his left hand for a machete to wield with the right, as well as something to protect his feet and skin from thorns and insects.

He sat up and finished cleaning off his face. Then he realized that his chest and left arm and leg were also covered with the same saplike liquid. It seemed to be getting stickier, as if it were congealing on his skin. It was also beginning to itch. He started scraping it off as fast as he could, pulling handfuls of leaves off the vines to help him.

Eventually Blade got himself as clean as he could manage. There were streaks and strings of drying liquid all over his skin, itching like a mild attack of poison ivy. A good deal of it was also clinging to his hair, which now stuck out in all directions like the quills of a porcupine. Blade suspected he looked more like the Thing from the Bottomless Swamp than a human being, and hoped any natives he met wouldn't decide to shoot first and ask questions afterward.

Blade stood up and did a series of exercises to loosen up his muscles. He decided that his body had come through the transition into Dimension X in first-class condition. In fact, he'd never felt nearly as good this soon after the transition. Everything was in place, everything worked, and he didn't have the faintest trace of a headache.

The twilight seemed to be getting brighter. Blade looked up and couldn't tell whether the sun was rising or just coming out from behind some clouds. At least right now he had enough light for traveling.

He'd have to travel, unless he wanted to stay here by the tree until he took root along with it. Never mind the vines and thorns in his path. There was no water in sight, no fruits or fleshy plants, no birds large enough to be worth trying to catch. There was life all around him in the jungle—the uproar proved that. But he wasn't going to be able to get much use out of it here.

He also wasn't going to be able to find the human life of this Dimension, if there was any. Not that moving on would necessarily bring him to civilization, of course. In this jungle an army might pass half a mile away without his seeing it, and he might wander around until the computer drew him back to Home Dimension. A bloody lot of good that would do for the Project!

Or there might be no people at all—nothing but dinosaurs and birds. In that case Blade would finally end up, as he'd put it, "Playing Tarzan without any apes to help me." Pointless, certainly uncomfortable, but hopefully not too dangerous unless the wildlife was too wild! That was another thing to find out by doing some exploring.

So it was time to move out. Find water and food, get a weapon, then go hunting for the natives. It was almost a routine for Blade, but not boring. Each new Dimension held too many surprises to ever let Blade become bored, and more than enough to kill him if he left anything out of this "routine."

Blade broke a branch off a nearby bush to use as a flyswatter. He pulled a few leaves from the branch, tasted one, then started chewing it slowly for the moisture. Waving the branch ahead of him, Blade started off.

It was an hour before he was out of sight of the big tree. In another hour he couldn't have said how far he'd come, and only occasional glimpses of the sun told him he was traveling roughly northwest. Since he couldn't see that one direction was much better than another, he kept on in that direction. Sometimes he was even able to travel in a straight line for a whole five minutes.

After the first couple of hours, he'd learned to tell the places where he could push through from the places where he had to go around. He'd learned the hard way, and his skin showed a fine pattern of thorn gouges and pricks. The scent of blood attracted a swarm of insects, a few of them with stingers.

After another hour Blade was able to move faster, because the underbrush was thinning out. In places the ground was bare for fifty yards at a stretch, except for dead leaves and patches of moss and ferns. It was easy to see why. Overhead the trees now made such a perfect canopy that sunlight could barely reach the ground. Blade realized that he might be moving faster now, but without the sun to guide him he might also be moving in a circle. It still didn't matter too much, as long as he didn't have the foggiest idea of the best way to go. Meanwhile it was a great relief not to have thorns jabbing him every few yards.

There were plenty of the vines whose leaves Blade had chewed first. Every time he passed one he plucked a fresh handful of the leaves, to keep his mouth and throat moist. They didn't stop him from sweating buckets, though, or replace the water he lost in that sweat. By the time he'd been on the move for half a day, he knew he'd have to slow down if he didn't find water soon.

Only a few minutes later Blade came around a clump of bushes and found something almost as good as water. Along with it he found something else that sent him diving for the nearest cover.

On the other side of the bushes was a tall red-barked tree, with an unmistakable campsite at its base. The tree was half hidden by a thick vine winding up and around it like a boa constrictor. The vine was heavy with yellowish fruit. All around the base of the tree lay rinds, skin, seeds, and half-eaten fruit. That was about as good as a doctor's certificate for proving the fruit was edible.

Unfortunately the people in the camp had done more than eat fruit before they left. Two of them hadn't left at all. They lay on the ground, one on each side of the tree. Both were male. One lay on his back, legs stretched out and arms crossed on his chest, with leaves covering his eyes and piled on his stomach. Clotted blood swarming with insects covered one side of his face.

The other man was sprawled like an abandoned doll, arms and legs twisted and bent at impossible angles. Blade looked closer and swallowed hard as he realized large chunks of flesh were missing from the body. They'd been roughly hacked out —or perhaps bitten out.

Blade examined both bodies more closely. It became obvious that they were of two different peoples—possibly even two different species. The neatly laid-out corpse was almost completely covered with hair, the eyes were large, the ears set close to the narrow skull, and the arms and legs unnaturally long. Were this man's people even fully human? To Blade he looked more like an ape than a man.

The other seemed completely human, as far as Blade could tell from what was left of him. He was square-bodied, with thick-boned arms and legs heavy with muscle. One hand was missing, but the other was heavily callused, and so were his bare feet. His skin was unmistakably a dark blue, and in places Blade saw traces of whitish tattooes.

So there were human beings in this Dimension, and even in this jungle. Not just one race, either, but two—and apparently not on particularly friendly terms, either. For the hundredth time Blade wished he could see and hear in all directions at once. Both bodies were swarming with insects, but neither of them smelled particularly bad. In this damp heat decay would set in almost at once. Either or both peoples could still be too close for comfort. Blade didn't look like either one, of course, but would they be able to see this before they speared him or hit him over the head?

At least he could get food and liquid from the yellow fruit, and worry about the rest later. He walked over to the vine

13

and plucked a fruit, then peeled off the skin and bit out a chunk. The juice dribbled down his chin as he chewed. The flavor wasn't entirely pleasant—rather like overripe pineapple with a faint hint of sulphur—but he'd lived for days on things tasting far worse. A dozen or two of the fruit would hold him for several days.

Blade started picking, noticing that most of the fruit close to the ground was still on the vine. Higher up it was stripped almost bare. Either the fruit up there was better than lower down, or else somebody liked climbing trees for the fun of it.

Blade collected fifteen of the fruits, then pieced together a rough sack out of fern leaves and lengths of vine. He made himself an even rougher hat out of more fern leaves, then looked around for a weapon of some sort. Not far off he found a fallen branch the size of a small tree. Much of it was rotted, but one chunk was still sound enough to make a good club.

Blade saw no sign of any trail, and his hunter's sixth sense told him that no one was watching or listening from cover. He picked up the club, slung the sack of fruit across his shoulder, and moved on. He was not afraid, for Blade was about as incapable of fear as a sane man could be, but he would have liked a loaded pistol in his belt as well as that machete and some bug repellant.

Blade didn't get a pistol or a machete, but before nightfall he did find all the water he could possibly use.

The twilight was deepening steadily as Blade tramped along. It was time to start looking for a safe place to spend the night. Should he climb a tree or risk staying on the ground? Most of the trees here were solid and climbable, but their lowest branches were far overhead and he didn't know what might hide up there in the green-tinted shadows. On the ground he'd be vulnerable to anything that wandered by, but he'd seen no traces of anything large enough to be dangerous, not even snakes.

As he walked, Blade argued with himself and listened for the slightest sound that might help him decide one way or the other. The noises of the jungle now seemed to be fading away along with the light. The creatures of the day were falling asleep, and the creatures of the night weren't awake yet.

In this near-silence Blade suddenly heard the unmistakable splashing of water off to the left. He stopped, listening carefullly. Gradually he recognized the sound as a stream running over stones, rather than some large animal splashing in the water.

Blade turned toward the sound and moved forward, darting from one tree to the next, listening from behind each one like a soldier sneaking up on an enemy camp. He suspected he might be exactly that. If the hunting parties hadn't left this stretch of jungle entirely, the bank of a stream was the most likely place to find them camped for the night.

Finally Blade came out from behind the last tree onto the bank of the stream. What he'd heard was a short stretch of rapids, as a stream flowed out of one pool, plunged down a thirty-foot bluff, and spread out into another pool. Dead leaves and twigs covered the water close to the banks, but in the center of the pools it was clear, dark, and almost still. There was no sign that anything human had ever passed this way.

Blade felt like cheering. He could not only drink all he wanted, he could even bathe. The dried tree sap might not come off with just water, but the sweat and dirt certainly would. Tomorrow he could head downstream, sure of a water supply. If the stream widened enough, he might be able to build a raft of branches tied together with vines. Even if it didn't widen, following it would give him a much better chance of meeting the jungle tribes. In this kind of jungle, people lived by the water or at least traveled on it or along it.

Blade stepped forward, then halted. On the far side of the lower pool an animal was peering out from under a bush. It was about the size of a large dog, but it looked more like a pig with a faintly scaly skin, large ears, and a thick straight tail. It blended in with the bushes and ferns so well that it was hard to tell its color.

It was obviously coming to drink, and Blade tried to think of some way of catching it. If it was edible at all, it would give him a couple of solid meals and perhaps some strips of hide to protect his feet.

The animal's noise twitched, then it lowered its head to drink. As it took its first swallow, two scaly knobs popped out of the middle of the pool. Blade froze as a pale eye opened in each knob. The animal raised its head, then squealed in sudden fear and tried to hurl itself backward away from the water.

The animal's desperate effort only made its fate certain. Its hind feet slipped on the muddy bank and went out from under it. Before it could do more than squeal again, the creature

15

in the water was upon it. Six-foot jaws tipped with horns opened like a pair of scissors, then clamped down on their prey. Half the animal disappeared into those jaws with a final agonized squeal. The creature in the pool rose higher out of the water, showing a reptilian head with a second pair of horns jutting up behind the eyes. Its victim's hind legs thrashed wildly in the air, then there was a faint splash and nothing but spreading ripples and a little blood on the surface of the pool.

Blade decided that it might not be such a good idea to bathe in one of the pools after all.

Instead, Blade climbed halfway down the bluff, then slipped into the water. He'd underestimated the force of the current, and was promptly swept off his feet and down toward the pool. Rocks bruised him and scraped skin off his arms and legs, and for a moment he was afraid he was going all the way down into the pool and what waited there. Then he caught a projecting root, and with a desperate wrenching of all his muscles heaved himself out of the water.

At least he could drink safely from the rapids, and he drank until he could almost feel the water sloshing around inside him. Then he ate two of the fruits, scrambled up a tree, and made himself as comfortable a bed in its branches as he could manage. Blade didn't know how far the reptiles were willing to come out of the water, and didn't want to find out the hard way. At least he could be fairly sure they didn't climb trees.

His tree-bed wasn't really comfortable, but after his day's exertions Blade didn't care. He was asleep within minutes, drifting off as the night chorus of the jungle rose around him. The last sound he heard was an uproar of splashing from the direction of the stream.

Chapter 3

More and louder splashing woke Blade, along with whis-
tlings, hootings, and gruesome noises like the horns of gigan-
tic trucks. The birds and insects were lost in the uproar. With
a safe fifty feet between him and the ground, Blade watched
the reptiles heading for home.

He counted at least twenty of them lumbering through the
trees and splashing into the lower pool. They ranged from
comparative runts no more than fifteen feet long to one
monster who must have been well over forty. His skull alone
was a yard wide, and each of the jutting spikes along his back
was two feet high. Each scale on his belly was the size of a
man's hand. Like all the others, he was a greenish-black on
the back and head, and a dirty orange on the belly and the
insides of his four clawed legs. The creatures looked like
some nightmarish horned caricature of a crocodile.

Some of the creatures were smeared with dried blood and
shreds of flesh from their night's victims. All of them seemed
to be in a bad temper. They honked, hissed, slapped their
tails on the ground, and occasionally hurled challenges to
fight. Then two of them would go at each other with horns
and teeth, rolling over and over, clawing at the ground, lashing out with their tails hard enough to flatten bushes and
small trees. None of the fights seemed to hurt anything
except the undergrowth.

Eventually each of the horned crocodiles plunged into the
lower pool, briefly sank out of sight, then swam off downstream with only its eyes above water. Blade waited until the
last one was gone, then waited a little longer to be on the
safe side. By the time he finally climbed down, it was full
daylight.

He looked downstream as far as he could see, without
finding any sign of the creatures. Apparently they hunted
along the banks by night, then laired up in the water by day.
If he traveled by day and spent the nights in the trees, he

should still be able to follow the course of the stream without any unfortunate meetings with the crocodiles.

He'd still better have some sort of weapon against them. No matter how alert he was or how thoroughly the creatures stayed hidden by day, he didn't want to rely on luck and his ability to outrun them. But did he have any chance of making an effective weapon? The crocodiles were as long as small boats, they must weigh as much as large automobiles, and they were far more agile out of the water than any similar Home Dimension creatures. Their tooth-lined jaws could probably snap Blade in half at a single bite.

Their jaws—there was the key to the problem. Perhaps he couldn't make a weapon to hurt them, but he might make something to keep them from hurting *him*. If he could keep them from closing those formidable jaws on him—

Quickly Blade began searching the ground for sticks and lengths of vine. Again he wished he had a machete, but realized he probably wouldn't need one here. The fighting crocodiles had mangled the underbrush as thoroughly as a team of bulldozers, and bits and pieces of wood lay everywhere.

It took him less time than he'd expected to find what he needed, and almost no time to put the pieces together. Within a few minutes he had a length of wood, roughly straight, about two inches thick and two feet long. With lengths of vine he tied two more shorter pieces of wood crosswise to the longer one, about four inches from each end. He'd have liked to put a point on each end of the long piece, but there weren't any sharp stones in sight.

There was his defense against any crocodile. He would wait until the creature opened its mouth, then shove the jaw-bracer inside. As the creature tried to close its mouth, the ends of the longer stick would dig into the upper and lower jaws, holding them apart. The two crosspieces would help hold the longer stick in place.

At least that was the theory, and Blade couldn't see anything wrong with it. In practice, the jaw-bracer was going to need great speed, nearly perfect timing, and a certain amount of luck. Blade knew he had the first two, and could hope for the third. After that he wasn't going to worry. With its jaws braced open, the crocodile would have to chase him and try to knock him down with its tail. Blade was fairly certain he could outrun any of the crocodiles.

Blade made a belt of a longer piece of vine and hooked the jaw-bracer over it, where the weapon would be ready to hand. He considered making a second one, then decided to wait. He could pick up the pieces for the second one as he moved along, and he certainly wouldn't need more than two. It would take some luck to meet one of the crocodiles with the jaw-bracer, and really incredible luck to survive two of them. If he was attacked by three—well, his luck was going to run out, and there wasn't much he could do about it.

Blade ate two more of the fruits, threw away several which had started to go bad, and drank some water. Then he started off along the bank of the stream.

Swebon was the son of Igha of the Two Spears, chief of the Four Springs village among the Fak'si. Igha's wives bore him four sons who lived to manhood, but of these one was killed in a raid against the Yal the year before Igha's death from the Stomach Eater. Another was eaten by a Horned One in the very moon of his father's death. This left only Swebon and his brother Guno to be chiefs of the village, and most of the warriors felt that Swebon was much the wiser of the two. Guno was held in great honor for his strength and swiftness, but he had a hot temper which had made him enemies. In fact, his temper was so hot that some of the warriors who voted for Swebon also urged him to have Guno put to death.

"No," said Swebon. "Guno is a mighty warrior, as you have said. He is also wise enough to know that he can now do nothing against me. Since this is so, I will not kill him simply because he *might* do something. The Fak'si need all their warriors."

No one could deny that, with the Yal, the Banum, and the Kabi all seeming to make two raids for every one they'd made in years past. Not to mention the Treemen, and the slave-raiders of the Sons of Hapanu, who were worse than the other tribes and the Treemen put together! Swebon would have had to think hard before killing Guno, no matter what he might threaten against his brother and leader.

So Guno lived, and so far he'd done nothing to make Swebon regret letting him live. In the last seven months he had defeated twelve warriors of other tribes and taken three of their women. He'd also killed a Treeman and rescued a woman of the Fak'si from him. He'd even killed one of the

Sons of Hapanu, although in doing that he'd taken a sword wound in his thigh which nearly killed him. But he was healing now, and he would go with the Fak'si on the next raid. The warriors praised him, some were proud to call him friend, and all now thought well of Swebon for letting such a man live.

So Swebon was very much at peace with not only his brother but the rest of the world as well, as his canoe glided down the Yellow River. The sun was warm and bright, so the Horned Ones would not be out. His belly was full of meat and fish, and all the hunters with him were also well fed. They were bringing back much food, much stone, some metal, and even the hide of a young Horned One. Swebon decided that part of the hide would be made into a shield for Guno. He deserved the honor.

Best of all, out of the four canoes they'd only lost two men. One had died from the bite of a snake—what kind, no one knew for sure. The other simply vanished into the jungle like the smoke from a fire vanishing into the sky. That usually meant the Treemen had carried him off and eaten him. Swebon could only hope that the man killed at least one of the Treemen before they killed him.

They hadn't met any of the slave-raiders of the Sons of Hapanu, and that was almost unfortunate. Four canoes full of warriors might have been enough to destroy the raiders. Certainly none of the warriors would have been captured, to be taken as slaves to Gerhaa the Stone Village at the mouth of the Great River.

On the other hand, perhaps it was still good, not to meet the Sons of Hapanu. Their swords and bows, the metal they wore on their bodies and heads, and the way they stood together in a fight always gave them great power. Many warriors would have died or been wounded so they would not fight again, even if all the Sons of Hapanu died also. So much death and blood could never be good.

Swebon cursed under his breath. Nothing could ever be truly good, until the Sons of Hapanu were beaten—beaten so that they would never again come into the Forest or along the Great River, to take the firestone from the bottoms of the streams and the strong men and women from the tribes. When that day came every man and woman of the Forest People would be happy. But would it ever come? Swebon did not have much hope left. The Stone Village had squatted at the mouth of the Great River since the time of his grand-

20

father's grandfather or even before. It would probably be there in the time of his grandson's grandson.

But such thoughts might bring bad luck if he let them go on too long. Swebon forced himself to stop thinking of the Sons of Hapanu and looked at the banks of the Yellow River passing on either side. There was the tree struck by lightning many years ago, when Swebon had just been given the Hunter's Gift and become a full man of the Fak'si. That meant they were not far from the River of the Six Dead Hunters, and would be well past it before they had to stop for the night.

Good. Along the River of the Six Dead Hunters the Horned Ones were so thick that no wise man ever spent the night within half a day's walking of it. A large party such as Swebon's might not be in danger, for the Horned Ones seldom attacked large groups of men. Yet one could never be sure, and it would be foolish to lose men to the Horned Ones when they were no more than two days from home.

Swebon leaned back on the pad of leaves and rushes in the stern of the canoe and stretched his legs. From the rear canoe he could hear the Paddlers' Chant, but in the other three canoes they paddled silently, with no sound but the ripple of water alongside and the dripping from the paddles.

Suddenly half the hunters seemed to be shouting at once, in surprise or even in fear. Swebon remembered that he was in a canoe just in time to keep himself from jumping to his feet and falling overboard. He sat up, to see that men had picked up spears and were pointing them toward the bank.

A man was standing on the bank, where the River of Six Dead Hunters flowed into the Yellow River. At least he looked more like a man than anything else, although he looked like no man Swebon had ever seen before. The man's skin was almost hairless, so he could not be one of the Treemen. He was almost as tall as one, though—taller than any of the Forest People and most of the Sons of Hapanu. For a moment Swebon thought he might be one of the Sons, and reached for his bow. Then he got a closer look at the man, and realized this could not be.

The man's skin was covered with dirt and dried *kohkol* sap, but underneath it was pale, almost white. It was not the skin of any tribe of the Forest People that Swebon had ever seen or even heard of. It was certainly not the skin of any of the Sons of Hapanu, who were all dark brown, like the mud from the bottom of a river. Perhaps he was the son of a Treeman and a captured woman of the Forest People, who hadn't grown a hairy coat and so been turned out into the Forest?

Or perhaps he wasn't a living man at all? At the thought, Swebon's shout made all the paddlers bring their canoes to a stop. If what they saw on the bank was the spirit of one of the Six Dead Hunters killed by the Horned Ones here, what could they do against it? And what had they done to bring it forth now, in daylight? Swebon was not only confused, he was frightened—so frightened he might even have admitted it if anyone had asked him.

Then the "spirit" spoke. He put down the branch he was carrying as a club, cupped his hands around his mouth, and shouted, "Hallooooo! You people in the canoes! I am Richard Blade, of the English. I come in peace, and I want to speak to your chief."

He spoke the language of the Forest People as if he'd sucked it in with his mother's milk, although the accent was strange. Swebon had never heard of a tribe of the Forest People called the English, but perhaps they were so far away that they no longer met or spoke with the other tribes. That would explain why this Richard Blade of the English sounded strange.

Swebon waved at the English man. "Ho, Richard Blade! I am Swebon, chief in the Four Springs village of the Fak'si. I will listen to any words of peace you speak."

The English man laughed. "I speak only words of peace when there has been no war. I wish to ride in your canoes with you to your people, live among them, go where they go, and perhaps help them. Will you take me?"

Swebon frowned. He could not be sure that it was wise to bring a man of no known tribe among the Fak'si, but would it truly be dangerous? He looked at Blade again. The man had the body and muscles of a warrior and hunter. He wore only a belt with sticks hanging from it and a hat of leaves. The club and a sack of wisdom-fruit lay on the grass at his feet. That was not much to bring into the High Forest. Blade was either mad or very brave. He certainly did not sound mad, and he seemed to be ignoring all the spears and arrows pointed at him. He stood many paces from any shelter, and if Swebon spoke a single word he would look like a spine-fish from all the arrows and spears sticking out of him. Yet he was speaking as calmly as if he were sitting by the fire, picking his teeth with a fish bone. This had to be courage.

22

So here was Richard Blade, a strong, brave warrior and hunter of an unknown tribe called the English, who spoke the speech of the Forest People. He wished to come among the Fak'si, and said he might be able to help them. How? Swebon almost wanted to ask that out loud, but decided not to. He did not trust Blade enough to tell him about the troubles of the Forest People.

He would take Blade home to the village, though. The man was strange, but he did not seem dangerous. If he was watched carefully he could do no harm even if he wanted to.

"Richard Blade!" shouted Swebon. "One canoe will come to the bank for you. Get into it. Leave your club behind." The sticks hanging from Blade's belt looked somewhat like the spirit sticks the Yal tied to trees when they made sacrifices. No doubt Blade's sticks were used in the sacrifices of the English. It would not be proper to take them from him.

Blade nodded. "Thank you, Swebon. I will be happy to come among your people." He picked up his club, tossed it into the water, and stood with his arms folded on his chest, watching the canoe heading toward him.

Chapter 4

Blade wasn't quite as happy among the Fak'si as he told Swebon he'd be. So far they hadn't done anything openly unfriendly, and they seemed willing to follow their chief's lead in dealing with Blade. On the other hand, there were more than forty warriors in the four canoes. They carried either a spear or a bow and a quiver of arrows, most of them had heavy wooden clubs hanging at their waists, and all had crocodile-hide shields ready to hand.

They weren't particularly pleasant-looking, either. They all resembled the dead man Blade had seen in the jungle—about five and a half feet tall, stocky, well-muscled, and blue-skinned. Most of them had spectacular white tattoos all over their chests and arms, and a few had their faces tattooed into grotesque masks. The sides and backs of their heads were shaved, and the rest of their hair was fastened into a topknot with elaborate bone pins and ornaments.

The leader in the canoe made a space for Blake in the stern and he sat down. The paddlers backed water and the canoe slid out into the river again. Blade noted that the paddles were long, narrow, and balanced at the upper end with stones tied in place with vine. With nine pairs of muscular arms working steadily, the canoe rapidly gained speed.

Blade's canoe fell into line immediately behind Swebon's, giving him a chance to look at the chief more closely. Swebon was a trifle taller than most of the others, and his tattoos spread down onto his thighs. Unlike the others, who wore only plain hide loinguards, Swebon wore a loinguard of reptile hide and a bone bracelet around one ankle. Several scars crossed his chest and shoulders, and another cut across his forehead, stopping just above his left eye. At the moment he was leaning back almost lazily on a pile of leaves and rushes, but Blade sensed alertness and leashed power in the man. Swebon would clearly be formidable, either as friend or as enemy.

The day grew steadily hotter and the paddles splashed

monotonously. Blade felt himself growing drowsy and fought against it. He was a long way from being safe enough among these people to risk going quietly to sleep now. If they were really determined to kill him they could probably do so whether he stayed awake or not, but if he was awake they'd have a fight on their hands. The prospect of that fight might keep them from planning any hostile move in the first place.

All four canoes were heavily loaded, but with the current behnd them they seemed to be making a steady six or seven miles an hour without the paddlers really breathing hard. Their construction helped. From a distance they looked like ordinary dugouts, each hollowed from a single log. Seen close up, they turned out to be built in sections, the seams between each section calked with bark, grass, and some sort of dried sap. A line of branches bound end to end ran down the center of the bottom, linking all the sections together.

These canoes were remarkably ingenious craft, Blade realized. By building them up from a series of sections, they could be built in whatever length the Fak'si needed—twenty feet, thirty, fifty. If one section sprang a leak, it could be thrown away and replaced without having to dispose of the whole canoe. If a canoe had to be hauled across land for some reason, it could be dismantled into its sections, moved to the next riverbank, and put back together there. By accident or skill, the Fak'si had managed to reach something rather close to mass production for their canoes—amazingly close, considering the tools they had to work with. Blade's respect for them went up quite a bit.

The Fak'si paddlers seemed almost as tireless as machines. They made no stops all day, eating and drinking as they paddled and relieving themselves over the side when they needed to. The long shadows of twilight were beginning to reach out across the river before they even slowed down.

After that, they headed for the bank the minute they saw a clear spot for a campsite. The canoes were unloaded and each crew took a share of the campsite. Then all forty turned to and pulled each canoe in turn completely out of the water.

By this time twilight was turning into night. With strokes of an iron-headed hoe. Swebon cleared a patch of ground, chanting to himself as he did so. When there was a large enough patch of bare ground, two of the hunters used flint, dry grass, and twigs to get a fire started. Then wood was piled on the fire until the flames shot up six feet high or more.

Blade noticed that the men worked in silence, with almost

military precision. He also noticed that those with spears kept their weapons close to hand, the archers kept their bows strung, and everybody left his club hanging at his waist. He even caught one or two of the men casting doubtful looks at the fast-darkening waters only a few feet away, when they thought no one was looking at them.

"Swebon," said Blade. "I see that your warriors seem to be on guard against an enemy."

"This is so," said the chief. He didn't seem interested in saying more, but Blade wanted to draw him out.

"Are these enemies men, or are they—? I do not have your name for them, but—" Blade squatted down and with a twig drew the outline of one of the horned crocodiles on the ground.

Swebon smiled. "Yes, we watch for the Horned Ones. They are thick along the Yellow River at this time of the year, and they are always hungry. So we watch, but I do not think we will see them coming against us tonight. They do not often come against so many men, and the fire also protects us. The Horned Ones hate light."

Blade nodded. "I learned this quickly, after I met them."

"It is well to learn quickly, about the Horned Ones. Those who do not learn quickly seldom live to learn at all."

"I am sure of that," said Blade. "We have such creatures in England and in other lands where the English have traveled. But our—*crocodiles*, we call them—are not so large, and they have no horns."

"Did you see many of the Horned Ones as you came to the Forest?" asked Swebon. His curiosity seemed to be getting the better of his caution about Blade.

"Enough to learn much about them," said Blade. He thought of mentioning his jaw-bracer, but decided against it. The jaw-bracer might be considered a weapon and be taken from him, and in any case it hadn't been tested in action. "I reached the Forest by land, so I did not spend much time close to the rivers. When I spent the night close to one, I climbed a tree and slept in the branches."

"A strong one, I hope," said Swebon. "The Horned Ones can knock down trees with their tails if they are angry."

"Thank you for telling me that."

Swebon seemed to hesitate, then went on. "Did you meet any other—any others of the Forest People—as you came toward the Yellow River?"

No doubt he meant other, perhaps, hostile tribes. Fortunately Blade could not only reassure him but tell the truth at the same time. "No. I saw no other living men of any tribe or people, and only two dead ones. One was of the Forest People, the other—I do not know if he was truly a man, but—"

"Was he taller than you, and hairy like an animal?"

"Yes."

"Ah, then you found one of the Treemen. Where, and how did he die?"

Blade described his discovery of the two bodies and watched Swebon's eyes widen. Then the chief sighed. "I thank you for this news, though it is not good. At least now we know for certain that the Treemen took Cran."

"I am sorry to have been the bringer of bad news," said Blade. Then he decided that a small diplomatic lie might be useful. "I do not know the proper death rites of the Fak'si, so I said only the prayers for a warrior of the English over his body. We believe that no honorable warrior can be hurt by such a prayer, even if he is not helped by it."

"Cran was an honorable warrior," said Swebon quietly. "And so are you. Blade, I still do not know as much about you or the English as I must. But I begin to like you, and think well of your people."

"I am honored," said Blade.

Swebon laughed. "Good. And now that you have been honored, you will be fed. He waved one of his men forward. "Bring a chief's portion to Richard Blade of the English when the meat is ready. Until we are home he sits by me and is as my brother."

That put any fears of possible treachery out of Blade's mind. He was able to eat in peace, too hungry to care that the meat was half raw. After the meal, he followed Swebon's example in rubbing some of the grease into his feet and hands. Then he lay down and slept more peacefully and far more comfortably than he had the night before.

It was still well before dawn when someone shook Blade. He came awake with his fists clenched, and nearly knocked his waker into the ashes of the campfire before realizing that it was Swebon. The chief laughed.

"What did you think I was, Blade?"

Blade sat up. "I don't know, but I am a warrior on whom few men can lay a hand peacefully." That sounded pompous, but it was also a way to perhaps prevent "accidents."

Swebon nodded, apparently satisfied with Blade's explana-

27

tion. "That is proper and honorable for a warrior. But I swear I meant you no harm. I called to you, but you did not wake up. I feared your spirit might be sleeping as well as your body."

"Well, they are both awake now," said Blade, standing up and stretching. "Are we moving on?"

"Yes. I think that if we leave now, we can be home this day, before the Horned Ones come out."

Blade looked around. In the pale light he could see men gathering up their weapons and gear. One of the canoes was already afloat, and a gang was pushing a second back into the water. It was on the tip of Blade's tongue to ask, "What about the Horned Ones now, when they haven't gone to sleep for the day? But that might sound timid. Swebon was probably eager to get home, and he certainly knew the creatures' habits much better than Blade.

Nonetheless, Blade borrowed a knife from one of the men and cut points on the main piece of the jaw-bracer. When he climbed into Swebon's canoe, he unhooked it from his belt and laid it in the bottom of the canoe, ready to hand. Then all the paddlers started chanting together and the canoes swung out into the river.

As they'd done yesterday, the canoes moved in a single line. They moved more slowly, and the men sitting in the bows as lookouts seemed more alert. No doubt Swebon realized that moving in the twilight before dawn needed extra precautions. With nothing to do but listen to the chanting and watch dawn break, Blade leaned back and relaxed.

Slowly the river turned from black to golden-brown and the ghosts of trees on the banks turned solid. Sometimes Blade heard the Horned Ones calling in the distance, but mostly he heard only the water and the rising chorus of birds. The breeze rose until it was making ripples on the water and blowing away the insects. Blade saw the lookouts beginning to relax. In another few minutes it would be full daylight. If they hadn't run into any of the Horned Ones by now, they weren't likely to. Swebon seemed half asleep.

Then the lookout in the bow of the chief's canoe gave a shout that was almost a scream. The paddlers froze with their paddles in midair, unable to tell from the cry what they should do. Swebon lunged for his spear and Blade snatched up the jaw-bracer.

With a thud and a crunch of wood the canoe stopped so violently that everyone was thrown forward. Most of the men

28

lost their grip on paddles or weapons, and two went straight overboard with yells of surprise. Blade picked himself up just as the yells of the swimmers changed from surprise to sheer terror. One look over the side told him why.

The biggest Horned One Blade had ever seen was rising out of the water underneath the canoe. Its head was toward the swimmers and the jaws were opening. As the beast rose higher out of the water, Blade heard the seams between the sections of the canoe cracking. Then the canoe split in half, spilling everyone into the water.

As the canoe came apart, Blade leaped to his feet and sprang into the air like a diver taking off from a high board. He landed squarely on the Horned One's head. Blade weighed two hundred and ten pounds, and the impact of his landing forced the creature's head under the water and closed its jaws. The two desperate swimmers thrashed off in opposite directions, safe for the moment.

The Horned One swiftly got over its surprise. As if Blade was no more than a bird who'd foolishly landed on its head, it popped to the surface again. Water poured off its back and the river turned to foam as it thrashed its tail. It turned and at the same time raised its head. Blade gripped a horn with one hand and the jaw-bracer with the other, waiting for the creature to open its mouth and give him his opportunity.

An arrow whistled past, and another sank into the scaly skin inches from Blade's thigh. He swore, and heard Swebon shout, "Don't shoot, you'll hit Blade!" Then the Horned One reacted to the pain of the second arrow, hissed, and opened its jaws in a gape wide enough to swallow a cow.

Blade hurled himself forward, losing skin to the rough scales but reaching the creature's nose. With one hand he clutched a horn, with the other he shoved the jaw-bracer into place. The Horned One shook its head, and Blade slid sideways to hang in midair like a man on a trapeze, inches from the jagged six-inch teeth.

Then the Horned One snapped its mouth shut—or tried to. The points of the jaw-bracer dug into tender flesh, jamming the teeth a good foot apart. The creature hissed again at the sudden pain in an unexpected place, and Blade was nearly suffocated by the foul breath blowing past him.

Now all the Horned One's attention seemed to be on the jaw-bracer, and none of it on Blade. He swung far to one side, then swung back like a pendulum. Finally he hooked one leg over one of the horns behind the eyes and perched there. He didn't know what the creature was going to do next. He only knew that he had to do something first.

Without knowing if anyone would hear him, Blade roared, "Throw me a spear!" A moment later he was nearly knocked from his perch by a rain of spears coming at him from all directions. Several of them left bruises as they sailed past, and one sliced a shallow gash in the back of his thigh. That spear was the one he caught.

He didn't know for certain what a Horned One's vulnerable points might be. He did know that any animal, no matter how large or thick-skinned, was vulnerable in the eyes. Blade braced himself, raised the spear as high as he could, then thrust it into the Horned One's left eye with all his strength and weight behind the thrust.

The creature hissed like a bursting steam line and threw itself backward into a half-somersault. Blade flew high into the air and splashed down among the swimming men from the wrecked canoe. He went deep and thrashed furiously toward the bank as he rose. He didn't want to be anywhere nearby when the creature went into its dying convulsions, and if it wasn't dying—

It was. When Blade's head broke surface, he found himself in water slowly turning red. The Horned One floated on its back, tail still waving feebly and blood gushing out of its mouth. Blade couldn't tell if the jaw-bracer was still in place or not, but it no longer mattered. It had worked once, and that was enough.

Someone was calling him. He turned to see a canoe approaching with Swebon in the bow. He was smiling, and when he looked at Blade his smile seemed touched with awe.

"Blade, I did not understand why a warrior like you came through the Forest with only those weapons you had. Now I think I do understand. You did not need any others." He reached out to grip Blade's arms and help him into the canoe. Blade accepted the help, sat down, coughed some of the Yellow River out of his lungs, then shook his head.

"I could not have killed the Horned One without the spears your men threw me—though one of them threw a little too well," he added, rubbing the wound in his thigh. Fortunately it was so shallow the bleeding had almost stopped.

"You would not have lived to use the spear if you hadn't used your weapon first," said Swebon flatly. "The Horned Ones are always dangerous, and this one more than most. If it was out at this time of the day, it is a rogue, very old and very wise. Only nine men of the Fak'si have ever killed a Horned One alone. None of these men killed a rogue, or one so large."

Swebon put his hands on Blade's shoulders. "Blade, I do not know how you rank among the warriors of the English. But you will be great among the Fak'si of Four Springs village. Will you in return show us how to make and use your weapons?"

"Certainly."

Swebon gave his orders briskly. The men of the sunken canoe were divided up among the other three. As many of the weapons and as much of the gear as possible was salvaged. Then the canoes started off again, the paddling chant softer this time. Within a few minutes the floating body of the Horned One was out of sight astern.

Chapter 5

Thanks largely to Blade, none of the Fak'si had so much as a scratch, even those who'd gone for an unexpected swim in the Yellow River. All of them wanted to get home, and none of them wanted to run the slightest risk of being caught out on the river by nightfall and more Horned Ones. So the paddlers settled down to their work, chanting steadily as their paddles bit into the water. The canoes shot downstream as if they'd been propelled by outboard motors.

By early afternoon the paddlers were saving all their breath for their work and the chanting stopped. Somehow the rhythm remained unbroken—a little slower, perhaps, but otherwise unchanged as far as Blade could tell. By now that rhythm must be in the muscles and nerves of every paddler, so deep they didn't need the chanting to keep to it.

When a man in their canoe started swaying drunkenly, Swebon took over his paddle. The next time a man began to sway, Blade offered to take his place, but the chief shook his head.

"There is no need for you to work—not today." After a moment, Swebon added, "Also, you are not used to our canoes and our ways with them. You might slow us down, and that would not be good. My men will not be angry with one who has saved them from a Horned One. They will not be grateful, though, if you keep us from getting home tonight."

"Very well," said Blade, appreciating Swebon's tact. "But I admire your canoes and your ways with them. I would learn more of both."

"In time you shall," said Swebon. Then he turned back to his paddling.

About mid-afternoon the canoes swung around a last bend in the Yellow River and came out on a larger stream. Everyone was streaming with sweat, and several men were lying in the bottoms of the canoes, fighting for breath. Swebon called a temporary halt, and the canoes drifted on the slow current of the new river while everyone drank. When the water jugs were empty, they were filled with river water and poured over the exhausted men.

"Is this what you call the Great River?" Blade asked Swebon.

The chief laughed. "You have not see the Great River, or you would not ask that. On the Great River you could barely see the far bank from here. We would never let the canoes drift, either. It would take them in its jaws and crunch them like a Horned One taking a man.

"No, this is only the River of the Fak'si." He looked up at the sky, squinting to judge the sun's distance from the western horizon. "If our strength holds, we shall be home before nightfall."

The current of the Fak'si River was slower than the Yellow's, so the paddlers had to work harder to maintain the same speed. In spite of this, the knowledge that they were getting close to home seemed to give the men the strength they needed. The canoes glided steadily onward. As the sun dipped below the treetops, they passed the mouth of a small stream and all the paddlers stopped to cheer.

"We are now within the Home Trees," explained Swebon. "Nothing can keep us from reaching the village tonight, unless the river itself goes dry."

The river flowed on, the paddles splashed steadily, and as darkness fell Blade saw a yellow glow on the right bank ahead. The canoes swung toward it, the paddlers shouted and were answered from the bank, and more torches flamed into life. As they did, Blade got a good look at a village of the Fak'si.

He knew at once that these people lived all their lives in constant danger from floods, and took great pains to protect themselves. At least half the houses of the village might more accurately be called houseboats. They were huts of leaves and grass tied over reed frames, resting on light platforms balanced across two or three large canoes. Long ropes tied the canoes at the bow and stern to the trunks or exposed roots of trees on the bank. The houseboats could rise and fall with the river—or if the Fak'si wished, they could be untied and paddled off down the river to some place entirely new.

On land some of the huts were actually perched in the trees, if they could be called "huts" at all. They were more like canopies of leaves, tied in place over platforms of logs. Rope

33

ladders or wooden stairs led from the platforms to the ground, and women and children were scrambling down them to greet the returning hunters.

Other huts were raised high off the ground by complicated frames of logs and reeds. The frameworks also served as pens for the village livestock. Blade saw animals and birds scurrying around inside them. The only buildings at ground level Blade saw were simple tents of leaves or open stockades for more livestock. Everything meant to hold human beings could either rise with the river or stay completely out of its reach.

Swebon rose in the bow of the canoe and waved to the people on the bank. All of them, men, women, and children alike, waved back and a few shouted greetings. Swebon commanded them to silence and began telling the story of the hunting party's adventures. When he got to Blade's battle with the Horned One, he pointed at Blade and motioned the Englishman to his feet. Blade obeyed cautiously, realizing his legs were cramped from sitting all day. He didn't want to spoil Swebon's story by falling overboard in the middle of it!

Swebon finished his praise of Blade, and the people on the bank broke into wild cheering that drowned out the last few words of Swebon's story. There was nothing for the chief to do except stand, pointing at Blade and waiting for the din to subside. When it did, he signaled to the paddlers and the canoe glided forward until Swebon could leap from the bow onto the deck of one of the houseboats. Several old men threw ropes to the men in the canoes, and several more grabbed Blade by the arms and dragged him onto the houseboat. As his feet touched its deck, the cheering started again.

All day Blade had wondered if Swebon might be exaggerating the qualities of Blade's feat against the Horned One. The creatures were formidable, but the Fak'si weren't exactly weaklings. Also, Swebon was obviously a tactful man who wouldn't be above telling a few white lies to make a stranger feel welcome.

This cheering now suggested that Swebon had been telling the truth. Blade was a hero to the Fak'si. He grinned broadly at the cheers, but his feelings were mixed. Starting off as a hero wasn't entirely a blessing. It helped keep spears out of his back, as well as giving him more freedom of movement. On the other hand, it tended to make people expect a miracle from him every Thursday. When he couldn't produce the miracle, disappointment could spread and tempers grow short.

34

However, for the moment Blade was safe from everything except being trampled to death by the Fak'si greeting him. As he stepped off the houseboat everyone in the village rushed toward him, in such a crowd that a few people were pushed into the river. Fortunately none of them were hurt and all of them could swim. By the time they'd pulled themselves out of the water, Swebon's voice and fists were clearing a path for Blade.

Keeping close behind the chief, Blade strode up the main path winding through Four Springs village. The people let him pass, but as he did they reached out to touch him. All the men tried to pat his hair, and some of them were bold enough to try pulling out handfuls of it. Blade winced, told himself that hair must have some religious significance among the Fak'si, and managed not to punch any of the hair-pullers in the jaw. When he reached the top of the path, he still ran his hands through his hair to make sure he hadn't been plucked entirely bald.

At the top of the path stood three large trees growing so close together that their branches were intertwined. In those branches the Fak'si had built a positive mansion among tree-houses—seven platforms, some of them completely enclosed, each of them at a different level and all of them linked by light bridges of something like reddish bamboo.

"This is my house," said Swebon. "The farthest of the roofs—" he pointed "— is for the use of honored guests of the chief. To get to you, an enemy must pass not only me, but the men who watch in my house."

"I am honored, Swebon," said Blade. "But I do not think I need fear much from the Fak'si, at least tonight." He was tempted to add, "Except having my hair pulled out by the roots."

"Perhaps not," said Swebon. "But let us do you the honor you deserve for one night at least. After that you can sleep under the chief's roof, on the ground, or on the topmost branch of a *kohkol* tree if you wish."

"Very well," said Blade. The chief led him up an actual flight of steps, carved into the foot-thick bark of the largest of the three trees. Then they made their way from platform to platform, deeper into the branches.

On the third platform they found a tall man lying across the middle of it, head raised on one hand and the other hand lying across a spear. The man was about the same size as Swebon and looked like a slightly younger and much worse-tempered version of the chief. Possibly the bad temper wasn't natural—one thigh was heavily bandaged. The expression on his face still made Blade look at him carefully—and then wish he had a spear of his own.

"Hail, Swebon," said the man. "So this is the one they all cheer."

"They should cheer him, Guno," said Swebon. "So should you. You know what he has done, or if you do not, I will tell you."

"I know what he has done."

"Then why did you not come to meet us on the path?" He pointed to Guno's thigh. "There is pain in it, I know, but—" He broke off and said only, "It would have been good for you to come down and join us in honoring Blade."

"I know, my brother," said Guno, sitting up. "Blade, forgive me for this foolish wound that has kept me from doing you proper honor. I would not be your enemy because of this ill luck."

No, but you'd gladly be my enemy for some other reason, Blade thought. *"I'd better find out what it is, too.* If the chief's brother became hostile while Blade was living in the chief's house, things could get awkward.

"No, certainly not. We shall not be enemies at all, if I can do anything about it," said Blade. He gripped Guno's outstretched hand and patted his hair with the other hand, then let Guno do the same. After that Swebon led Blade on to the next platform.

It seemed that they'd been wandering among the branches for an hour when Swebon finally stopped at the end of a narrow bridge. At the far end was a platform completely enclosed in a beehive-shaped tent of leaves. Through a gap in the leaves Blade could see a small fire burning on a stone slab in the center of the platform.

"There is your place, Blade," said Swebon. "Food and drink are already there. Is there more that you wish? A woman, water, fish, or sticks to honor your gods, flowers—?"

Blade shook his head. "I would be greedy to ask the Fak'si for more tonight. I will pray to my gods tonight, but I can do that alone." He pretended to hesitate. "I would also like to join the prayers of your warriors and hunters. By the laws of the English I am allowed to do this when I travel. If the laws of the Fak'si permit me . . . ?" It was always possible to win friends among a people by joining in their religious rites.

Sometimes you could pick up important information as well.

"I understand," said Swebon. "I am sure you may join in some of our sacrifices to the Forest Spirit. The priests must say which ones, though."

"Of course," said Blade.

"Then be at peace this night, Blade, friend of the Fak'si," said Swebon. He patted Blade's hair, then turned away as Blade crossed the bridge to his sleeping quarters for the night.

Apparently the Fak'si were going to start honoring Blade by stuffing him like a Christmas turkey. Wooden plates and bowls were laid out on the floor all around the fire, along with wood-plugged gourds and bulging leather sacks. Blade sat down and started his meal.

There was fruit, porridge, and stews of leaves, roots, and herbs. There were several kinds of fish and two kinds of meat, one tasting rather like pork and the other tasting like nothing Blade had ever eaten or wanted to eat. He stuck to the pork. There were several kinds of fruit juices, two of them fermented until they were almost wine, and an overflowing sack of sour beer. There was enough food and drink for three men as hungry as Blade was, with enough left over for a few midnight snacks. When Blade lay down to sleep, he'd eaten all he could hold and drunk as much as he thought was safe.

His bedding was a thick mat of leaves held together by a net of woven-grass rope. There was a smaller pad for a pillow, but nothing like blankets. In this damp heat they were hardly needed. There were no insects inside the shelter. Blade noticed that some of the leaves woven into the walls had a peculiar odor, rather like overripe lemons. He wondered if they acted as a sort of bug repellant.

Blade moved his sleeping mat to the side of the shelter farthest from the door. Now the whole width of the shelter and the litter of empty dishes on the floor lay between Blade and any possible intruders. Anyone who barged in during the night was certain to make enough noise to wake him. Even if he couldn't fight, he could always break through the wall and drop to the ground. The woven leaves were no tougher than light cloth and the drop to the ground was less than fifteen feet.

Blade trusted Swebon, and perhaps Swebon's guards would do their duty. But if Swebon let his brother Guno live in the chief's house, and if Guno already saw Blade as an enemy or at least a potential rival— It might not be tactful to repay Swebon's friendship with suspicion, but Blade would rather be tactless than dead.

With this thought in his mind, he stretched out, rolled on to his side, and fell asleep.

Blade's instincts brought him awake, and his fighter's reflexes kept him motionless on his sleeping pad. The fire was dead and inside the shelter was utter blackness, but Blade knew he hadn't been fooled. There was someone in the shelter with him, standing by the door. He continued to lie still and resisted the temptation to challenge them. If he stayed quiet, they were likely to have more trouble finding him than he would have finding them. No doubt the Fak'si could hear and see in the dark much better than any civilized man, but so could Richard Blade.

The silence dragged on, broken only by the night birds and insects and by the faint scrape of the intruder's feet on the floor. He seemed to be a small person, moving slowly and cautiously around the edge of the shleter and only very gradually approaching Blade.

Suddenly there was a clatter of wood on wood, as the intruder tripped over a bowl and sent it rolling against another. A hiss of indrawn breath followed, then a sigh. Finally Blade heard fumbling motions, and then all at once a dim white light filled the shelter. Blade sat up and stared at the intruder.

Like most Fak'si women, she was only a little over five feet tall and built on generous lines, to say the least. This was usually obvious even in daylight, since the Fak'si women wore only a knee-length skirt. This lady wore even less—a flower in her hair, a bracelet of grass on one wrist, and a gourd on the other hand. The gourd was filled with something luminous—perhaps a phosphorescent moss—that gave off the white light.

Blade looked at the woman more closely. At first glance the pale light on her blue skin made her look like a long-dead corpse risen from its grave. A second glance showed that she was not only young but quite attractive. Her breasts were high and firm, the large nipples barely visible against the darkness of her skin. Her waist, unthickened by child-bearing, flowed down into smooth thighs. Her hair was shorter than usual among Fak'si women, but heavily decorated with bone ornaments. A reddish jewel gleamed just above her left ear. Her skin shone as if it had been oiled, and she smelled faintly of flowers.

At last she giggled and looked down at the floor. Blade realized he'd been staring at her in silence for several minutes. She sat down, folding her legs under her, and Blade laughed.

"All right," he said. "You know who I am. Who are you, and why are you here?"

The woman laughed. "I am Lokhra. Why I am here—Blade, do you not know the ways of women?"

Blade nodded. "I see. Yes, I know the ways of women. In fact, it is not wise to ask that of a man of the English. He might think it an insult."

"Good," said Lokhra. "We hoped the English were that way. The warriors of the Kabi must be lovers of men for three years. We would not have been happy to find you like them."

"Who is this 'we?' " asked Blade.

"Oh," said Lokhra. "It is I and the other three women."

"That doesn't tell me as much as you think," said Blade. "Remember that I've only been among the Fak'si for two days. Most of that time I spent among the warriors and hunters. So perhaps you should treat me as a child who must be told everything."

Lokhra wriggled across the floor to Blade and rested one soft-fingered hand between his thighs. "Blade, I do not think you are a child in all things. Or my eyes and hands are telling lies."

"They are not," said Blade, putting an arm around Lokhra's shoulders and resting one hand on a breast. "But I would like you to tell me the truth. You and the other three women—*who are you?*"

"You fought the Horned One and killed it," she said. "When such a Horned One attacks hunters, some of them always die. The men who saw you fight the Horned One met tonight. They decided that four of them would certainly have died if you did not fight the Horned One."

"Did they decide which four?" asked Blade.

"No. They only knew that four of them live who would otherwise be dead. Now, when a man of the Fak'si saves another, the man he saves must give him a woman for one night. The men cast the bones, and four of them were chosen to each send you one of his women. I am the first."

"I see," said Blade. It seemed a sensible way of showing

gratitude—and one he wouldn't find it at all hard to accept. While she'd been explaining why she was here, Lokhra's fingers were moving gently but steadily. Blade was finding it harder and harder to keep his mind on what she was telling him or keep his own hands from tightening on her breasts.

Now Lokhra's story was finished, and there was no more reason for Blade to hold back. He raised both hands to her shoulders and turned her until he could kiss her. Apparently kissing wasn't the most common gesture of affection among the Fak'si, because she was clumsy at first. Apparently she also had the right instincts, because the clumsiness didn't last long. Her lips turned warm under Blade's, her tongue crept out to join his, her free hand ran up and down his back. Blade found his breath coming harder, and felt Lokhra's nipples hardening against the palms of his hands.

Blade didn't know what Lokhra might expect, but he knew what he wanted, and also knew that he couldn't wait much longer for it. What Lokhra was doing to him was both marvelous and painful at the same time.

Blade released his grip on the woman, then pressed one hand against her forehead and the other against her stomach. Lokhra went over backward, wriggling sideways so that she lay on the sleeping mat. Her legs spread apart, then rose to lock around Blade.

After the excitement of what had gone before, the actual joining with Lokhra was almost a disappointment for Blade. She didn't carry him to any breathtaking, delirious heights. She didn't rise to any herself. She simply held him against her and within her until his body arched in the final spasm and all his breath went out in a choking cry. She went on holding him with his head nestled between her breasts, although most of his weight must have been on her.

She held him until he found the strength to enter her again. This time her cry echoed his own, and he felt the warm solid flesh under him writhing and twisting wildly. Again he relaxed, head between her breasts and the sound of her racing heart pounding in his ears. Again she held him until he found his strength returning. This time when they were finished he felt much too comfortable to even think of moving.

After a while Lokhra wriggled off the mat and crawled over to the remains of dinner. She returned with a gourd of fruit juice and a platter of sliced fish, then held both out to Blade. He ate and drank to please her, although he was more thirsty than hungry. When he'd finished, he reached for her again. She held him off with one hand while she held a drinking gourd with the other. She drank, and as she drank she seemed to be listening for something in the darkness outside.

Blade was beginning to get annoyed, and he was about to ask her what the devil she was doing when suddenly she jumped up. Stark naked, she walked across the shelter and pulled open the curtain of leaves which served as a door.

"Come in," she said to the darkness outside. Three shapes moved there. Blade started to rise—then three more women were standing in the doorway. All three of them wore the Fak'si skirt, but before Blade could recover from his surprise they started pulling them off. By the time he'd recovered, the three newcomers were as naked as Lokhra.

Blade was amused at the prospect of having to satisfy three more women tonight. He also found himself looking forward to it. Lokhra was the best-looking of the four women, but the other three were hardly ugly. All were young, well-fleshed, and firm-breasted. From the way they were looking at him, they were also looking forward to the rest of the night.

Blade threw his head back and laughed, until his laughter drowned out the night sounds outside and the four women were laughing with him. Then he stood up and walked over to the first of the three newcomers.

Chapter 6

Blade never could remember much about what happened during the rest of the night. He only knew that when he woke up, it was well after dawn and all four of the women were gone. The mat under him and the floor of the platform were soaked with sweat, and all the leftovers from dinner had vanished.

He suspected that whatever he'd managed to do had been enough, although he never learned any of the details. He only knew that Lokhra grinned openly at him whenever they met, and several of the men who'd seen him fight the Horned One always slapped him on the shoulder and patted his hair. "You have skill with other weapons beside those sticks, yes, Blade?" said one man.

Other than that, no one mentioned Blade's first night among the Fak'si. He was quite happy to let it be forgotten. There was just too much else to do, if he was going to learn about this Dimension and its people. He was also going to have to learn about them without as much help from the Fak'si as he'd expected. It wasn't that they were hostile, or even reluctant to speak when he asked them questions. It was just that he had to think up all the questions himself, find the people to answer them, then put the answers together into some sort of reasonable picture.

It wasn't really surprising that the Fak'si weren't experts at explaining themselves to outsiders. They probably didn't have much practice doing so. But it meant some delay, and it would have meant even more if Blade hadn't been a fairly good rule-of-thumb anthropologist. He wouldn't have been alive otherwise. He was better than any college professor at looking over a primitive people and learning their ways, particularly the ways which might be dangerous to him. It didn't take him long to learn his way around the Fak'si and learn about their world.

Exactly how large this Dimension was, Blade could never

even guess intelligently. The question always nagged at Lord Leighton, and also at J and Blade. Was each Dimension X something the size of the whole Earth, with many lands beyond the one Blade found? Or were they each only a *partial* alternate reality? Certainly some of the Dimensions were complete alternate Earths, or even complete alternate universes. But with many others there was no way of telling, and that was the case in this Dimension.

What Blade did learn about was what the Fak'si called the Forest—as though there were no trees anywhere else in the world. It spread many days travel in all directions, with mountains to the west, ocean to the east, and no man knew what to the north and south. Through the Forest the Great River flowed from west to east, fed by the rains and by dozens of tributary rivers and streams.

In the Forest lived the four Great Tribes—the Fak'si, the Yal, the Banum, and the Kabi. There were also minor tribes, mostly founded by men who'd fled from one of the Four Great Tribes. No one took these seriously. There were so many of them that no one could keep count from year to year, let alone from generation to generation. Also, some of them had the habit of changing their names whenever the whim took them, apparently so that the Forest Spirit shouldn't know who they were.

"I do not know if they confuse the Forest Spirit," said one warrior, explaining this to Blade. "But I know they confuse us. Think no more of the Little Tribes of the Forest, Blade. A warrior and friend of the Fak'si has nothing to do with them."

So Blade abandoned any hope of learning about these odd-men-out of the Forest and concentrated on learning about the four Great Tribes. The only one he had in front of his eyes every day was the Fak'si, but apparently the other three were very similar.

Each tribe lived in a part of the lower valley of the Great River, with villages scattered along the tributaries. No one lived permanently along the Great River itself, and only brave men with urgent business traveled on it at all.

"When it is in flood, Blade, no man can see from one bank to the other," said Swebon. "It rises so that trees higher than those where I built my roofs vanish beneath the water. We do not fear much in the Forest, but we do fear the Great River in its anger." Other descriptions of the river agreed with Swebon's. To Blade, the Great River began to sound

43

more and more like the Amazon—vast, powerful, and deadly.

However, the Forest gave a good life to those who kept their distance from the Great River. Each of the tribes had at least a dozen villages, and each of the villages could send out two hundred warriors without leaving itself defenseless. The Forest People had domestic animals and fowl for meat, plenty of fish, small garden plots in most villages, and everywhere around them the Forest with its leaves, fruits, seeds, roots, and game animals. Food was so plentiful in the Forest that a child might grow gray-haired without ever knowing an empty belly.

The tribes added their own skills to the Forest's offerings in making a good life for themselves. They were masters at working any sort of wood their tools could handle, as well as leaves, grass, animal hides, gourds, and anything else that came to hand. Blade was sure they could have built much more substantial dwellings than they had, except for the danger of flood and the need to keep cool.

Their weapons were adequate, though not particularly sophisticated. There were the shields made from the hides of Horned Ones and smaller reptiles, the spears, the bows, and the clubs Blade had already seen. The quality of the iron in the spear points was surprisingly good, but the bows were weak. Blade guessed they had perhaps a twenty-five or thirty-pound pull, half that of a Home Dimension hunting bow and a third that of an English longbow. The clubs were really beautiful pieces of work, perfectly balanced and weighted with stones or chunks of pig iron. They were the most popular weapon in the wars against other tribes.

This warfare hardly seemed to deserve the name. In some ways it was a wide-open affair—the tribes raided where they wanted, when they wanted, and against any other tribe it took their fancy to bother. There was nothing like permanent alliances, or for that matter permanent hostilities.

On the other hand, when warriors of the tribes did meet, the fighting was comparatively formal and restrained. Bows were often not used at all, and spears usually only when defending or attacking a village. Much of the fighting was done with clubs and shields, and this led more often to broken bones than to broken heads.

Accidents happened, of course, and people did get killed. Women and children were frequently kidnapped from one tribe and carried off to the villages of another. Livestock was slaughtered or stolen, canoes set adrift, and even houses burned.

Yet no raid ever destroyed more than a small part of any tribe's weath. Houses and canoes could be replaced within weeks. Even the kidnapped women and children found themselves at home in their new tribes within a year or two. Lokhra herself had been captured as a girl from the Yal, and one of Swebon's grandmother's had been the daughter of a chief of the Banum.

So the warfare among the tribes of the Forest People was really a sort of rough outdoor sport, occasionally bloody but hardly dangerous to the future of the tribes. No doubt the Forest People would start fighting more seriously if their population ever grew large enough, but right now there was a great deal of Forest and not very many Forest People.

The fighting against the Sons of Hapanu was another matter. Here the Forest People were deadly serious, and would have gladly killed much more often than they did. Unfortunately, the Sons of Hapanu were too strong.

The brown-skinned people who called themselves the Sons of Hapanu were from a land across the ocean to the east. They'd come to the mouth of the Great River about two hundred years ago and built a city there. By now the city was enormous—half the world lived in Gerhaa, according to the tales of the Forest People. To Blade, this meant at least fifty thousand people. It was also called the Stone Village, because it was strongly fortified with stone walls and towers. Most important, it was a deadly and growing menace to the Forest People.

The Sons of Hapanu raided up the Great River in search of two things—slaves and firestones. When they caught Forest People, all those too young or too old to be useful were killed. Warriors became gladiators who fought in the Games of Hapanu, and other able-bodied men became laborers. Women became household servants, unless they were young and beautiful. In that case they were trained as prostitutes.

The firestone was a jewel found in large chunks on the bottom of many of the smaller streams in the Forest. It had the rich blood color of the finest rubies, but it was considerably harder, too hard for the Forest People to work. The Sons of Hapanu could work the firestone, and valued it highly both as a jewel and for religious purposes. They eagerly sought it in the streams and carried it off to Gerhaa in large

45

quantities. They called it the Blood of Hapanu. The Forest People had no particular use for the firestones themselves, but they felt that the Sons of Hapanu were offending the Forest Spirit.

Unfortunately there wasn't much the Forest People could do. The Sons of Hapanu had powerful crossbows, which could kill at a much greater range than the bows of the Forest People. They carried short thrusting swords, which could penetrate the hide shields and were much handier than the spears and clubs. They wore iron helmets and shirts of iron scales sewn onto leather. Finally, they fought in disciplined ranks, while the Forest People fought every warrior for himself. So even when the Forest People had the edge in numbers, the Sons of Hapanu usually won.

In spite of this, their raids had been more of a nuisance than a menace until the last few years. The Forest was large, and although the soldiers from Gerhaa fought well there weren't too many of them. No tribe had lost more than a few dozen people in a year.

Now things were changing rapidly for the worse. A new ruler in Gerhaa was sending out more and larger bands of soldiers, and bringing still more across the ocean. The raids came more often, and last year the Kabi had lost a whole village. Did the new ruler of Gerhaa want to conquer the whole Forest and kill or enslave all the People? No one knew.

No one knew how to keep him from doing it, either, if that was his plan. This wasn't because everyone was paralyzed with fear. It was obvious to Blade that everyone desperately wanted to fight off the Sons of Hapanu. It was just as obvious that no one knew how. Weapons or tactics to meet the soldiers of Gerhaa simply weren't on hand. Blade decided the best thing he could do was come up with some, and keep his mouth shut in the meantime.

To make matters worse, the Forest People had to do serious fighting against another opponent beside the Sons of Hapanu. They had to fight the Treemen, and Blade soon learned all he needed to know about this enemy.

Blade spent several days in the Swebon's house, then suggested that it was time for him to move to a place of his own. He did not mention that one reason for this was Guno's increasingly open suspicion of him and what his coming might mean to Four Springs Village. In theory, Blade would be safe as Swebon's guest, but in practice any incident while Blade

46

was under his protection would be an embarrassment to the chief. That would be making a poor return for Swebon's trust and hospitality, and matters might go beyond that. Guno was a mighty warrior, with more victories to his credit than any other two men of the village. He had friends who might not be ready to make trouble for Swebon, but would certainly not hold back from making trouble for Blade.

Fortunately Blade had no trouble finding his own quarters. Everyone was glad to oblige a man who'd slain a rogue Horned One single-handed, and as it happened the carpenters had just finished a new houseboat for the eldest of the village blacksmiths. Unfortunately the blacksmith died the day before the houseboat was finished, so the carpenters were happy to offer it to Blade.

Blade moored his new home at the far north end of the village, and put on longer ropes to allow it to float well clear of the bank. He also made a rough "burglar alarm" in the form of a long stick with sharp nails sticking up through it. By day he kept it covered with a thick grass mat, but at night he removed the mat. Anyone jumping from the bank to the bow of the houseboat would land on the nails, and after that his yells would be enough to bring Blade out armed and ready.

"You are farther from the light of the village than I am happy to see," said Swebon. "I would not see you taken by a Horned One."

"It will take a strange Horned One to attack me so fast that I do not wake and leap to shore," said Blade. "In any case I do not fear Horned Ones as much as I do men—or at least one man." He didn't want to say any more, but judging from Swebon's expression he didn't need to.

Blade took his spear and club, pots and bowls, sleeping mat and water jug to the houseboat on his fifth day in Four Springs village. He passed a quiet night and spent the next day talking with the village bowmaker. The man had many complaints about the poor quality of the wood the carpenters were bringing him.

"Oh, if there was wood in the Forest to make a bow strong enough to send an arrow through a Treeman or the metal shirt of a Son—! But the carpenters say there is none, and perhaps they know. If there was such a wood in the Forest, they would have found it long ago."

"Very likely," said Blade politely. He'd been thinking about the bow problem ever since he heard of it. He didn't want to raise anybody's hopes, though, until he knew a good deal more. So he and the bowmaker talked of other things over a leisurely dinner, then Blade returned to his houseboat for the night.

He'd just fallen soundly asleep when an explosion of shouting and screaming jerked him awake. He grabbed his club with one hand and his spear with the other, then whirled toward the bow. Any attack would be coming from there. After a moment he realized that whatever was going on wasn't aimed at him, at least not yet. Keeping down, he crept forward and peered through the screen of leaves.

In the pale light of the campfires, people were running around as if flames were licking at their heels, shouting and crying out to one another. Mothers were clutching children, while stark-naked warriors with clubs, spears, and shields were herding clusters of weeping women ahead of them. For a moment Blade thought the village was being raided by another tribe. Then he heard shouts of "The Treemen! The Treemen! Gather by the river! The Treemen are upon us!"

Blade knew that the Treemen were seven-foot apemen like the one he'd found dead at the little camp on his first day in this Dimension. He didn't know much else about them, except that they were deadly enemies of the Forest People. He did know that he was going to need his weapons before long. He bent down and began pulling on the ropes to the bank. Slowly the houseboat crept toward the land.

Blade was no more than ten feet from the bank when a moving shadow in the branches of a tree caught his eye. The shadow froze as if it sensed Blade's eyes on it, then started moving again as three women and two gray-haired men came toward the base of the tree. Blade opened his mouth to shout a warning and raised his spear to throw, but the Treeman was quicker than Blade.

Like a pouncing lion he leaped down from the tree into the middle of the five people below. A sweep of one long arm knocked a woman and a man flat, while the other arm clutched another woman around the waist. She screamed, clawed, and bit. The Treeman tightened his grip, ignoring the woman's struggles until her teeth finally worked through the hair into his skin. Then he let out a roar more like an animal than a man and smashed his other fist into the woman's head. She went limp, either stunned or frightened into paralysis. The Treeman reached for a branch overhead with his free hand.

As he started hauling himself and his victim up into the trees, an arrow whistled from behind a hut. The Treeman roared again as the arrow hit him in the left shoulder, but didn't stop or drop the woman. With the arrow still in his flesh he hauled himself up into the branches and disappeared into the darkness.

Blade rose to his feet and leaped to the bank. As he landed, the fallen man and woman started struggling to their feet and the archer from the hut darted out into the open. Blade reached for the woman, then the roars of more Treemen made him turn.

This time there were three of them. Blade hurled his spear with all the strength of his right arm. It drove into a Treeman's thigh so deeply that the bloody point came out through his buttock. He took a couple of staggering steps forward, then dropped to his hands and knees and started crawling. Blood poured out around the spear and he roared with pain at every movement, but he kept on coming.

The other two Treemen swung to either side of their maimed comrade. The archer nocked an arrow to his bow and sent it squarely into one Treeman's stomach at close range. The Treeman howled, charged, plucked the arrow out of himself with one hand, and snatched the bow from the archer with the other. The archer gave a wild, wordless cry and raised his club.

Against the Treeman the club was no more use than a toothpick. The Treeman grabbed it and the hand holding it, jerking the archer off his feet and holding him at arm's length in midair. Then the Treeman started smashing his fist into the dangling man's face, throat, ribs, and stomach. The man screamed, spraying blood through smashed teeth, then choked and fell silent as his chest caved in.

That was all Blade was able to see before he had to meet the third Treeman's attack. He backed away, to give himself room and make sure the first Treeman wouldn't try grabbing him by the ankles. The Treeman followed, arms spread wide, hissing and rumbling in his throat, pale eyes and black-lipped mouth both wide open. The mouth was lined with broad but sharp-pointed yellow teeth.

The Treeman and Blade circled around each other twice, then suddenly the Treeman was coming at him. Blade leaped high and to one side, swinging his club as he did. The weighted head crashed down on the Treeman's left arm and Blade felt bone give under the blow. The Treeman roared and swung to clutch at Blade with his right hand, left arm now dangling useless. Blade feinted at the Treeman's head with

49

his club, and saw the right hand shoot out to grab it. Blade pivoted on one foot, kicking at the Treeman's groin and karate-chopping at the right elbow simultaneously.

The chop missed, the kick connected. The Treeman howled and doubled up, but not before his right hand clutched Blade's left wrist. Nails as long and sharp as claws gouged Blade's flesh. He knew that within seconds he'd be pulled within range of those teeth and decided attack was the only defense. He sprang forward, his legs and the Treeman's pull sending him high in the air. As he rose, both legs shot out and both feet crashed into the Treeman's ribs. This time he went right over backward, and the shock as he landed broke his grip on Blade's left wrist. Blade went down, rolled, came up hoping his left hand was still there, and discovered it was.

The Treeman struggled to his feet, but after his pounding from Blade he could barely stand. He blinked at Blade as he picked up his club, blinked again as Blade swung, then closed his eyes for good as the club smashed in his skull. Blade watched his victim fall, then jumped back just as the Treeman he'd hit with a spear tried to bite him in the leg. He stared down, hardly believing the Treeman could still be alive, let alone able to fight. The Treeman slumped down, eyes half-closed and one bloody hand plucking at the spear in his thigh. Blade raised his club to put the Treeman out of his misery— then screams and shouts behind him made him turn again.

A Treeman was running out from among the huts, a naked woman under his arm and several men with spears and clubs at his heels. The arrows that stuck out from his back didn't even seem to be slowing him down. Blade saw that the men behind were about to catch up, started to step aside to give them fighting room, then saw that the Treeman's victim was Lokhra.

Blade's cry was as animal as a Treeman's. Instead of stepping aside he leaped at the Treeman, his two hundred pounds of bone and muscle smashing into him at full speed. Lokhra flew out of the Treeman's grip, landed with a thud, and had enough sense to keep rolling after she landed.

Now Blade had all the fighting room he needed. Vaguely he realized that he might be preventing the Fak'si from closing in with their spears, but he didn't care. He was in a berserker's fury, and that made him more than a match for any Treeman. The Treeman was a foot taller than Blade, at least as heavy, and probably both stronger and faster. He still didn't have Blade's unarmed-combat skills, or Blade's rage driving him.

Blade punched the Treeman in the mouth, knocking loose half a dozen teeth. The Treeman spread his arms wide, then clutched at Blade, trying to embrace and crush him. Blade ducked under the arms and punched the Treeman hard in the stomach, one-two-three-four. The Treeman doubled up, gasping for breath. Blade stepped aside, grabbed the Treeman by one arm, and pulled him within reach. His other hand came down like an ax on the back of the Treeman's neck. The Treeman pitched forward, writhed briefly, then lay still.

The Fak'si warriors crowded forward, some to congratulate Blade, others to jab the Treemen with their spears to make sure they were dead. Blade was hardly aware of any of this. His berserk rage didn't really start passing off until Lokhra came running up and threw her arms around him. Then he was able to pat her on the shoulder and smile down at her. She was pale and covered with dirt and bruises, but apparently not hurt.

"Well, Lokhra," he said laughing. "You came to me after I saved your man. What happens now that I have saved you?"

Lokhra also laughed, then kissed him. "I am grateful, Blade, and you will find that out before long. But for now there is much else to do in the village." She sighed. "There always is, after the Treemen have come."

Chapter 7

Lokhra was right. It took a while to even measure the damage left by the Treemen, let alone repair what could be repaired.

The Treemen seemed to have come for blood, not destruction. They'd tried to kill every man and carry off every woman in their path. They hadn't wiped out half the village only because there hadn't been enough of them. Some people said there'd been Treemen perched in every tree around the village, but Swebon doubted there'd been more than twenty. Still eleven men were dead or dying and a dozen more hurt, some of them so badly they'd never be able to hunt or fight again. Four women were dead and seven more missing.

"Carried off by the Treemen, of course," Swebon explained bitterly. "I only hope most of them die before they have to mate with Treemen and bear their children."

So the Treemen and the Forest People were of the same race, in spite of their physical differences. "Why do the Treemen need to steal the women of the People?"

"Who knows?" said Swebon with a weary shrug. "They have done it as long as we and they have both lived in the Forest. Perhaps they have no women of their own. Perhaps their women bear few children, or few of the children live. No man has ever come close enough to the Treemen to find the answer and lived to bring it home."

Against the death and destruction in the village, only six Treemen were dead. Half of them were Blade's victims. Killing three Treemen in one night wasn't quite as rare a feat as killing a rogue Horned One, but it was rare enough.

The Treemen were faster than any true human and more than twice as strong. They were also extremely tough. Arrows from Fak'si bows they shrugged off like pinpricks, and spears only killed quickly if they struck a vital spot. Clubs were almost useless against the Treemen's immense reach, and those long arms could also tear a shield apart as if it were made of paper.

So a fight between the Forest People and the Treemen was usually a bloody shambles, in which the People got the worst of it. They'd been able to live with the Treemen's raids only because the Treemen were rare. They seldom raided in bands of more than five or six, so the larger villages had always been safe.

"But things may be changing for the worse," said Swebon. "This is the third time in the last year they have come twenty or thirty strong against a large village. They seem to be striking harder at us as the Sons of Hapanu also become more dangerous."

Blade frowned. "Do you think the people from the city could be causing the Treemen to attack you? I do not know how they might do this, but—"

"Neither do we," said Swebon. "And I do not think it is so. How could the Sons of Hapanu make the Treemen understand what they wanted? The Treemen have no language that even the wisest of men can understand."

Blade knew that there might be ways of communicating with the Treemen that didn't involve a spoken language. He also knew it would be hard to convince Swebon of this, and if he did, what good would it do? It would merely burden the chief with another worry for his people, without offering him any help against the dangers threatening them.

Besides, it didn't really matter whether the Treemen and the Sons of Hapanu were one problem or two. They were both becoming a serious menace to the Forest People. They both had to be met with better weapons and perhaps different tactics. Now all Blade had to do was invent these weapons and tactics.

He had no qualms about taking the side of the Forest People. The Treemen were an evolutionary dead end, too dangerous to be ignored as animals but too close to animals to be treated as men. They took and they would probably go on taking, without giving anything in return.

The Sons of Hapanu were a somewhat different matter. They had a well-developed civilization. No doubt they saw the Forest People the same way the People saw the Treemen, as an inferior race, hardly more than animals. Perhaps in the end they would win out and rule this Dimension, even the Forest.

Not now, though—not if Blade could do anything about it. The Sons of Hapanu might have all the virtues of civilization and a high opinion of themselves. That didn't give them the right to sweep through the Forest, killing or enslaving the People. The Forest People deserved at least a few more centuries to go their own way, and Blade would do everything he could to give them those centuries.

The only problem was that he still didn't know exactly what he could do to bring this about.

The village slowly recovered from the Treemen's raid. The dead were burned, their ashes cast into the river, and the proper rites performed in memory of the seven women carried off. The damaged huts were repaired, and the carpenters went to work on a whole squadron of new canoes. There were more than the village needed to replace the ones lost or set adrift by the Treemen.

"I am sending word to the Red Flowers village," Swebon told Blade. "I would like their chief Tuk and his best men to join us in a raid against the Yal. They do not have enough canoes of their own, so we must make some new ones to carry their men."

"Why a raid now?" asked Blade.

"We have lost women," said Swebon. "We need more, and so we shall go to the Yal for them. It is a good way to make sure the Treemen do us no real harm."

Blade thought it was also an even better way to make the wars among the tribes more dangerous. If every tribe who lost women to the Treemen promptly went out and raided its neighbors, the tribes would soon be fighting seriously. They would be weakening each other just at the time when they most needed to stand together against both the Treemen and the Sons of Hapanu.

For the tenth time, Blade wished he'd already come up with some new weapon or tactic to offer Swebon. Then he could not only point out how dangerous the raid on the Yal would be, he could offer an alternative. Unfortunately he still didn't have anything to offer.

Blade wanted to laugh and curse at the same time. Lord Leighton considered him something of a military genius for inventing so many new weapons in so many different Dimensions. His Lordship didn't know the half of it! It wasn't genius. It was just common sense, a good memory, and a keen eye for both detail and opportunities. None of this had done him a damned bit of good in this Dimension so far!

At least going out on this raid against the Yal would be a good starting point, whatever he thought of its wisdom. He'd be seeing the Fak'si in action, and while that might not help it certainly couldn't hurt.

"Swebon," Blade said. "I would like to go with the Fak'si on this raid. I am not of your people, only a visitor, so I do not know if I have the right to—"

Swebon clapped Blade on the back and slapped his hair so hard Blade's ears rang. "I was praying to the Forest Spirit that you'd ask! With two strong spears like you and Guno following me, the Red Flowers will have to send more of their own good men. Otherwise they will lose honor and some of their share of the women we take."

"Thank you, Swebon," said Blade. "I do not promise to fight any better against the Yal than I did against the Treemen or the Horned Ones. But I hope I shall fight no worse, either."

"Then may the Forest Spirit have mercy on the Yal," said Swebon, laughing.

The next day Swebon left for the Red Flowers village, while the warriors prepared their weapons and the women packed food. The new canoes were hastily finished, launched, tested, then tied up along the bank to the south of the village, hidden behind a screen of leaves. The tale around the village was that a hunting party was going out, into land where the Banum might be found. Only Guno and a few other leaders among the warriors knew the real target of the raid.

Swebon returned from the Red Flowers with a canoe filled with their warriors, another filled with dried fruit, and promises of much more of both. Guno was heard muttering, "I'm not going to hope for much more than promises from the Red Flowers until I see it."

He had to eat those words a few days later, when the Red Flowers showed up—five canoes and seventy warriors under their gray-haired chief Tuk. Swebon gave the Red Flowers three new canoes, and in return Tuk swore to follow Swebon as his chief until they all returned from their victory over the Yal. There was a final feast, and Lokhra spent the night being so grateful to Blade that he got very little sleep. Then the raiders set off, a hundred and fifty men in sixteen canoes.

They paddled up the Fak'si River, past its junction with the Yellow River, and on upriver for two more days. By the end of the third day they'd reached a point where a one-mile portage would take them to the river flowing down into Yal territory. Unfortunately, by the end of the third day it was also raining in buckets. The banks were rapidly turning into swamp and all the raiders were as soaked as if they'd been swimming. It was impossible to try hauling even the smallest canoe sections through the slimy ooze. It was impossible to even make camp and light fires to roast the fish they'd caught.

However, the rains gave with one hand what they took away with the other. It poured down so violently and so long that all the streams in the area were swollen to several times their normal size. One that was normally only knee-deep could now float loaded canoes. So instead of a mile of struggling overland, there was only a quick dash across a few hundred yards of ground high enough to be merely boggy, not liquid. Instead of costing them time, the rain ended up saving them two full days.

The banks of the new river rose more steeply, and there were fewer Horned Ones. Along the banks the trees grew taller, but their branches didn't make such a thick canopy as usual. The vines, creepers, bushes, and flowers of the jungle floor grew so thickly that the perfume of the flowers was sickeningly heavy and the cries of birds feeding on the fruit half deafened Blade.

The most common tree Blade saw was the same kind he'd awakened under, the kind with the ribbed trunk and the sticky sap. The sap oozed from the bark and collected in great puddles at the base. Swebon called it the *kohkol* tree.

"The sap has many uses, apart from decorating the skins of English warriors who fall asleep under the trees," said the chief. Blade laughed, remembering the mess he'd been when he first met Swebon. "We pour it on the leaves when we put canoes together. We also use it for other things, which you will see in time." Blade didn't ask what the "other things" might be; he suspected they were religious.

The river swarmed with fish, which had to be eaten raw, since fires might be sighted by Yal hunters. The Fak'si were skilled at cleaning their catch, and raw fish was considerably better than going hungry. After the first few meals Blade found himself almost looking forward to sampling new varieties.

There was one kind of fish all the Fak'si seemed to value, judging from the way they cheered when one broke surface. Why anyone would cheer about it was more than Blade could see. The smallest of these fish was six feet long and two feet thick, with bony spines all down the back, poisonous green and purple mottling on the sides, and a corpse-white belly. Instead of a proper mouth it had a circle of sucking discs rimmed with small teeth around a foot-wide black gullet. Blade wasn't sure how it fed and was sure he didn't want to find out. He mentally labeled it the "uglyfish," and couldn't understand why anyone cheered when one appeared. It looked unappetizing, if not actually poisonous.

About noon on the third day in Yal territory, Swebon and Tuk made hand signals for the canoes to head in for the bank. All sixteen canoes were grounded and the whole raiding party climbed out. The four priests, two from each village, stood by the water's edge and chanted what were apparently questions and answers in a language Blade couldn't understand. As usual the computer had altered his brain during the transition into Dimension X, so that the language of the Forest People reached him as English and his speech reached them in their own language. Yet for some reason his brain hadn't been altered quite enough to grasp the language the priests were using. If it was a purely ritual language it didn't matter too much in practice, but it might be an ominous development if it continued. Being tongue-tied in each new Dimension would be nothing less than a disaster!

The priests took turns asking and answering questions for about half an hour. Then one of them drove a wooden stake into the ground, a second killed a bird, a third held it up so that its blood dripped down on the stake, and a fourth sprinkled dried herbs from a bag onto the blood. This took another half hour. By that time Blade was getting impatient. Proper rites or not, did they all have to stand here on the bank like a lot of bloody statues, easy targets for any Yal who came by. A single flight of arrows could hardly miss hitting a dozen Fak'si.

Fortunately the rites came to an end before Blade's patience did. The raiders climbed back into their canoes and headed off downstream more slowly than before. Blade saw a man with a fishing spear squatting in the bow of each canoe, ready to throw.

The river wound back and forth, and the line of canoes stretched out. Only half the raiders were in sight when the man in the bow of the canoe just ahead of Blade's leaped to his feet. Ignoring the rocking of the canoe, he braced himself and raised his spear. The paddlers backed water until the canoe was almost stopped. Then the fisherman's arm snapped forward, the harpoon flashed down, the line hissed out, and suddenly an uglyfish broke surface in a shower of foam.

It was a real monster, nearly ten feet long, and for a moment Blade wasn't sure who'd caught whom. The fish charged the canoe and smashed into the bow so hard Blade heard wood crack. The impact half-stunned the fish and it was slow to turn away. As it presented its side to the fisherman, he snatched up another spear and drove it in deep. The fish leaped completely out of the water, knocked the fisherman overboard with a final blow of its tail, then fell back dead.

No one even tried to get the uglyfish into the canoe. There wouldn't have been room. Instead two men helped the fisherman back into the canoe while others looped a rope around the uglyfish's tail. Then the canoe started off again, towing the uglyfish tail-first behind it.

In two hours Blade saw the raiders catch at least seven uglyfish. No one said a word to him about what all this was supposed to mean. He had gruesome visions of a banquet of uglyfish, or some sacrificial rite that went on long enough to use them all. Neither idea appealed to him.

Another hour, and then Swebon suddenly signaled four canoes to follow him toward the bank. Blade saw that here the bank was lower and the *kohkol* trees grew so thickly that their branches kept the ground in shade. The vines and shrubbery were no longer thick enough to clutch a man like the tentacles of an octopus.

By the time Swebon's canoes were firmly grounded on the bank, the others were out of sight. Swebon turned to Blade, "You must be quiet, and try to understand all you see this day without asking questions. All the priests and Tuk wish it so, and you must do as they wish."

"May I ask why they wish it?"

"You are not of the People, not one who has beeen given spear and shield with the Forest Spirit watching. The Forest Spirit will tolerate your presence at—at what we do this day only if you show it respect by your silence."

"I will be silent, for it is the way of the English to honor those who watch over other peoples." He was perfectly happy not to participate in the upcoming religious rites, if they involved eating uglyfish.

"Good." Swebon sprang to the bank and motioned the other men to follow him. They scrambled up to the edge of the trees, spread out, then vanished into the jungle. Blade noticed that each one was carrying a large gourd, hollowed out and stoppered, and a small knife of iron set in bone, shaped somewhat like an old-fashioned straight razor. Swebon and half a dozen men armed with bows spread out along the bank to keep watch on the canoes, the river, and the Forest behind them.

Whatever took place in the trees took place in silence. All Blade knew was that in about half an hour the men started reappearing. Their knives were stuck in their belts and the gourds were not tightly stoppered and apparently full. As carefully as if they'd been handling eggs, they laid the gourds in the bottoms of the canoes and climbed in. Swebon was the last man aboard, then the canoes shot off after the others.

Before twilight they caught up, at a place where the river spread out through the Forest in a wasteland of marsh and bog. The four canoes turned into the widest channel through the marsh and followed it until the river was out of sight behind. Half a mile inside the marsh they came to the rest of the raiding party, the canoes drawn up in a circle with their bows grounded on a patch of dry land. The patch covered several acres, more than large enough to hold the four priests, four warriors to help them, and a large iron kettle hung on a tripod over a wood fire. One of the warriors was feeding the fire carefully with handfuls of moss that burned with a thin gray smoke, quickly lost among the branches overhead.

One at a time, the stoppered gourds were handed to the priests and emptied into the pot. Now Blade recognized what the gourds held. It was *kohkol* sap, freshly tapped from the trees. While one priest poured, another stirred the sap continuously with a wooden paddle. When he raised the paddle, long strings of the thickened sap trailed from it, like strings of glue.

By the time the last gourd was empty, the sap had thickened and turned whitish-gray. Now warriors came splashing through the waist-deep water, towing the uglyfish behind them. One fish after another was hauled up on the bank, to the feet of the man who seemed to be the chief priest. With a long saw-edged knife he made two quick slashes, one under each eye. Then he reached into the wounds and pulled out two dripping reddish glands, each about the size of a grapefruit. Finally he held the glands over the pot of *kohkol* sap and squeezed them until they burst and spurted reddish fluid. Blue fumes rose from the iron pot as the fluid fell into the sap. From the whiff he got, Blade wondered why the priests and their helpers didn't drop dead on the spot. The fumes smelled as if they came from something not only long dead but horribly diseased before it died.

Blade sat as more than twenty uglyfish were butchered, then dumped back in the water. By the time the last one was gone, the pot was nearly full and the blue fumes hung like a revolting fog over the land and the canoes around it. From the faces of the men around him, Blade knew he wasn't the only one suffering from the smell.

There was more, however. One by one the empty gourds were picked up and filled with the mixture from the pot, then handed back into the canoes. As the gourds were filled, the fumes slowly died away and Blade no longer had to fight to keep his stomach under control. Finally the nearly empty pot was overturned, dousing the coals of the fire with the sludge in the bottom, then loaded aboard the priests' canoe.

"Now the Shield of Life is ready," said Swebon. That didn't tell Blade much. It sounded more like a medicine than a weapon, but that was about as much as he could guess. He didn't really care, just as long as he didn't have to swallow anything which gave off the fumes he'd just smelled.

It was nearly dark, so Blade expected they'd stay in the marsh, camping on the dry ground or even sleeping in the canoes. Instead they returned to the river, then headed downstream again almost as fast as in daylight.

Blade leaned forward and tapped Swebon on the shoulder. "I should not question the judgement of Fak'si chiefs, but this night journey makes me wonder. What about the Horned Ones?"

Swebon's teeth were a white flash in the darkness. "Tuk had an idea. If we went down the river to the nearest Yal village in the darkness, we would not be seen before we struck. So we are going to do as Tuk said.

"We left all the *grashta*—" Blade assumed he meant the uglyfish "—in the marsh. Their blood flows into the water and it will draw all the Horned Ones of this river. They will be too busy fighting over the fish to attack us."

Blade mentally crossed his fingers, then laughed. "Why didn't you tell me this before, Swebon? Then I could have made jaw-bracers for each canoe, just in case."

"Tuk only spoke as we made the Shield of Life," said Swebon. He seemed slightly embarrassed. "He knows more of this river and of the Horned Ones than I do. There might not be peace with him if I did not follow him in this, for he is proud."

Blade shrugged. It could have been much worse, and certainly no people and no Dimension had a monopoly on proud old generals who got brainstorms. He relaxed, and gradually he began to enjoy himself.

Now it was completely dark, but sometimes luminous patches glowed as paddles and prows broke the oily surface of the water. There was no wind, but they were too far from either bank for most insects. The water dripped from the paddles and gurgled at the prows, the paddlers murmured to themselves, and night birds called from the distant banks.

It was hard to tell that a hundred and fifty men were moving swiftly down the river within a few hundred yards of Blade. He knew it, though, and knew that he belonged among these men. When everything that civilization put into him was stripped away, what remained was an adventurer and a warrior. That was the true Richard Blade, but that was also a man who had no safe or easy place in the Home Dimension of the twentieth century. Luck and the genius of Lord Leighton sent him to Dimension X, where he was usually far more at home than most men could ever have been.

Chapter 8

At dawn the Fak'si raiders were already within striking distance of their target. The gamble of the night journey had paid off. One canoe rammed a floating log and sprang an unstoppable leak, but its men scrambled safely into other canoes. A second canoe got lost in a side channel and for a while Swebon thought it might have fallen victim to the Horned Ones. But as the two chiefs were choosing men for the two attack parties, the missing canoe paddled up. So the chiefs had all their men for the attack on the Yal village.

It was actually four villages lying so close together that an attack on one had to be an attack on all. Among them the four villages had more than twice as many warriors as the raiders, so the two chiefs came up with an ingenious plan. Half the attackers would approach the villages in canoes, attacking them in succession. The other half would slip across country and take position in the Forest behind the first village.

As the attack from the river struck the first village, its women and children would run into the Forest and the warriors of the other villages would dash to its rescue. The attackers waiting in the Forest would catch the fleeing women and children and ambush the warriors coming to the rescue. The men in the Forest would also give warning if the Treemen came.

"Sometimes the Treemen come when they see us fighting," said Swebon. "They think to steal our women while we are too busy to protect them. But they have to be very quick. Otherwise we call the Truce of the Treemen and stop fighting each other to fight them."

That was what Blade might have expected from a people whose wars were hardly more than a rather bloody sport. On the other hand, the plan for the attack on the Yal villages was not at all what he'd expected. It was subtle, sophisticated, and implied a great deal of thinking by the chiefs and good discipline by the warriors. It might be "every man for himself" when the fighting actually started, but until then they seemed to follow orders as well as many Home Dimension troops.

So the Forest People might know a great deal about war, in spite of their primitive weapons. With better equipment, they might be able to hold their own against the Sons of Hapanu, or even drive them into the sea. But if the People had better weapons, would they be able to resist the temptation to use them on each other?

That was a difficult question, and it would have to wait. Swebon was counting off the warriors of his party, the ones to go overland. He signaled to Blade to join him. Blade picked up his weapons and walked over to stand by the chief. A few more men joined the circle around Swebon, then he raised his hand in farewell to Tuk and led his men into the green darkness of the Forest.

The Yal village lay quiet in the early morning sunlight, but it was not asleep. Its people were hard at work, but none of the work made much noise. Smoke rose straight from cooking fires and forges. Bare-breasted women and naked children pulled weeds from a field of yellow-leaved plants. Two men with armfuls of grass thatched a hut. Somewhere in the village somebody was pounding something, and every so often a child laughed or cried out. There was nothing else for Blade to hear, as he lay beside Swebon under a concealing bush.

The sun rose higher, sweat poured off Blade, and insects came to whine and nip. Swebon lay like a statue carved from blue granite and there was no sign of the river attack party. Blade tried to tell himself that if they'd been detected, the village would hardly be so still. A root under him began to painfully gouge his ribs—then suddenly the village was no longer quiet.

Three men in a canoe came paddling furiously up the river, one of them waving a bloody arm. A fourth man was slumped in the bottom of the canoe, a spear in his thigh. As they turned toward the bank, the paddlers began shouting.

"Raiders, raiders! The Fak'si are coming! Raiders—!"

That was all Blade heard from the men before the uproar in the village drowned them out. War cries and women's screams rose, followed by the thud of drums and the crash and clang of people beating on cooking pots and anvils. Someone tossed a handful of leaves into a fire, and instantly the smoke rising from it turned a repulsive green. Then four armed men appeared, herding women and children ahead of them into the field. Blade looked at Swebon, but the chief shook his head. A moment later the first canoe of the river party appeared around the bend. Tuk was standing up in the bow, waving his war club.

If there'd been confusion before in the village, now there was chaos. Or at least it looked like chaos, until Blade saw that everyone seemed to know where they were going. Many warriors were hurrying down to the riverbank, some standing in the open shouting defiance, some concealing themselves behind huts or trees. Other warriors were escorting more women and children inland. A steady stream of them was passing no more than fifty feet from Blade and Swebon. Some of the women were carrying pots, sacks, and baskets. Craftsmen were picking up their tools and handing them to women to carry to safety. The younger ones then armed themselves and joined the warriors, while the older ones went inland with the women.

Now the raiders' canoes were swinging in toward the village. Tuk was still standing in the bow of the lead canoe. Two warriors aimed spears at him and threw. Age hadn't dimmed his eye or slowed his arm. His shield snapped up and both spears thudded harmlessly into it. But the impact knocked him off balance, and as the canoe ran aground Tuk went overboard into the water with a tremendous splash. He could easily have been speared or filled with arrows as he struggled to his feet, but everyone on both sides was laughing too hard to use a weapon. Then the other canoes were pulling up alongside the first, the Fak'si warriors were splashing ashore, and suddenly there was nothing to laugh at in the fighting that exploded through the village.

Tuk rose out of the water and took a club blow on his shield. He swung at his opponent, got under the man's shield, and hit him in the thigh hard enough to stagger him. Tuk followed up his advantage so fast that he got out ahead of his men. Two of the Yal tackled him, one from each side. He beat down a spear thrust, but took a gash in the leg from a knife. The man with the knife didn't pull back in time and Tuk's club came down on his shoulder. He dropped and lay writhing. Blade noted that Tuk could easily have smashed the man's skull, but deliberately struck his shoulder instead. Then Tuk's men were all around him again, Guno among them, and the Yal were so badly outnumbered they had to retreat.

Or at least it seemed that way to the attackers landing from the canoes. Blade and Swebon had seen the Yal warriors seeking hiding places. They knew that the attackers were being led into an ambush. Unfortunately there was nothing they could do about it. If they broke out of cover now, they'd be finished before they could shout a warning.

The Fak'si from the canoes came on, and suddenly the air around them was filled with spears and thrown stones. The range was so close that everything hit hard, and the Yal were in too much of a hurry to aim carefully. Blade saw one warrior go down clawing at a spear deep in his chest, and another with his thigh gushing blood. Both would be dead within minutes. Other Fak'si also took bloody wounds, and in return they began to stop pulling their own blows. Blade saw Tuk smash a man's knee with his club, while Guno dropped both spear and shield to grip an opponent with both hands and choke him to death.

Then a wild chorus of screams and shouts erupted from behind Blade and Swebon. The refugees from the village had run into the overland raiders. Swebon signaled to Blade, then leaped to his feet and gave his war cry.

A warrior escorting the women turned, saw Swebon, and hurled a spear. Swebon deliberately lowered his shield, then snatched the spear out of the air with his free hand. He whirled on one foot, then threw the spear back at its owner. It sank deep into a tree. The other man pulled it free and raised it in salute to Swebon.

By now the Yal in the village had also seen Blade and Swebon. Several spears thudded into the ground around them, then an archer sent two arrows at Blade. One missed his head by inches, another struck the head of his spear with a metallic *tak!* Blade decided that the safest place around here was in the middle of the enemy's warriors, where the Yal couldn't shoot arrows or throw spears at him without hitting friends. He ran toward the nearest enemy and Swebon ran beside him.

Two Yal seemed to sprout from the ground at Blade's feet. One held a spear, the other a long-handled ax with a stone head edged with iron. Blade took the spear on his shield, then swung his own spear sideways at the axman's raised arm. The shaft smashed across the man's arm as his ax started down and Blade heard the bone crack. Somehow the man held onto the ax, but his blow was wild and harmless. For a moment he was wide open, and Blade kicked him

65

smartly in the stomach. He gasped and crumpled up, while Blade turned to face the spearman.

The man thrust at Blade twice more. The second time the thrust went through Blade's shield. As the man tried to pull free, Blade swung the shield violently. The swing jerked the man off balance before he could let go of the spear and Blade thrust at him. The man raised his own shield, then Blade hooked his shield around the edge of his opponent's and jerked, leaving the man wide open. Instead of thrusting the man through the chest, Blade jabbed him lightly in the shoulder. Then he dropped his spear and punched the man hard in the jaw. The man went over backward so violently he nearly somersaulted, then lay still, groaning, cursing, and out of the fight.

Beside Blade Swebon was also finishing off his second opponent. Now the Yal seemed to forget about their women and concentrate on Blade and Swebon. Suddenly the two big men found themselves surrounded by what seemed like a dozen opponents. They stood back to back and let the Yal come at them.

Blade successfully used the trick of hooking an opponent's shield aside with the edge of his own twice more. The Forest People didn't seem to have developed this particular fighting technique. Then too many enemies were coming at him too fast for him to risk having his own shield out of position for a single moment.

His battered spear broke off in someone's shield. He used the broken end of the shaft to beat aside someone's club, then thrust over the shield into the man's forehead. As the man staggered back with a bleeding scalp, Blade dropped the spear shaft and unslung his club from his belt in time to meet his next opponent. He struck one blow so hard it caved in the top of a Yal shield, and struck another blow that caved in the man's skull. Then he took a glancing blow that half-numbed his shield arm and crouched down, so he could rest his shield on the ground and still stay behind it.

Unfortunately this slowed Blade down, and three Yal closed in around him. One came too close and Blade swung his club in a flat arc, breaking the man's leg and knocking him down. A second Yal thrust a spear violently across Blade's shoulder. Blade's club swung, breaking the man's spear, then he drove his shield into the man's face and broke his spear arm with another blow of the club.

For a moment Blade had a clear space around him and

enough time to catch his breath and examine his shoulder. Fortunately it was only a simple flesh wound, one that should heal all right if it didn't get infected. But it wasn't so light because the Yal had pulled his thrust. The man had been doing his best to kill Blade, and he'd have gone on trying if Blade hadn't disabled him. It looked to Blade as if the bloody sport of war among the Forest People was sometimes more "bloody" than "sporting."

Then suddenly Fak'si warriors seemed to be dropping from the trees and springing out from among them all around Blade. Blade's opponents scattered, except for one man who stumbled and went down. Two Fak'si warriors clubbed him unconscious before he could rise.

Swebon greeted his men, then turned to Blade. "You did as I hoped, Blade. The Fak'si will not soon forget your fighting this day."

"Neither will the Yal," said Blade. Then he realized this sounded like a boast, rather than a warning of Yal anger and possible vengeance. He shrugged. "I will teach your warriors my skills with a shield, if they are willing to learn."

"They will be," said Swebon. "But you are wounded. Do you wish to go to the canoes?"

"Not yet," said Blade.

"Good," said Swebon. "By custom only the chief and those warriors he chooses may enter the chief's house in a captured village. I choose you to come with me."

"I am honored," said Blade. He was also feeling much less ready for another full-scale fight than he'd implied, but he could hardly drop out now. Swebon seemed ready to fight all day, although he looked as if he'd been wrestling a bear, with cuts and gouges in a dozen places.

The chief led the way toward the village, and a score of warriors fell into line behind them. They found the village firmly in the hands of the men from the canoes, except for the chief's house. This was on a single large triangular platform, supported by a tree at each corner. Tuk, Guno, and several more warriors were standing at the foot of the stairs up to the platform. All around them captured women and children were being tied up and dead and wounded Yal warriors laid out.

The two chiefs led the way up the stairs, shields and spears ready, with Blade following Swebon and Guno following Tuk. Guno was covered with blood, none of it apparently his, and glowered at Blade as they climbed.

There were four rooms in the chief's house, separated by light walls of reeds. The floor was covered with rush mats, some of them torn up. Bowls, gourds, and bedding were scattered all over. The two chiefs probed each piece of bedding with their spears.

"Sometimes the Yal will leave snakes in such places, to give us evil surprises," said Swebon. "In my father's time, none of the People did such things, but ways change."

Yes, thought Blade. *Ways change. They change, and war becomes more bloody at a time when the People need their strength against the Sons of Hapanu.*

Guno laughed harshly. "Swebon, is this Englishman a child, that you must explain such things to him?"

Blade saw the chief stiffen, but his voice was light as he spoke. "Ask the Yal who fought him today. If they call him a child I will eat my own shield for dinner tonight."

Blade smiled. "I think Swebon will eat meat tonight, Guno. Among the English, snakes have not been used in war for many years, so I did not know what Swebon told me. Among the English it is not the sign of a child to be told things— only to think or say that one knows everything."

With their picked warriors the two chiefs searched the captured house. They found no snakes, but a fair amount of valuable loot—carved bowls, ornaments of iron and bone, a decorated shield and several spears. Swebon gave one of the spears to Blade, who found it much better-balanced than any other he'd handled in this Dimension. It was a bit light, but it would certainly throw easily and accurately.

They searched the whole house without finding a living soul. They returned to the first room, and were piling the loot by the door when suddenly Blade heard a faint sneeze. He stiffened and looked around, then saw Swebon doing the same.

"Who sneezed?" the chief said. Everyone looked blankly at him, then at their friends, then up at the ceiling and down at the floor.

"Ghosts," someone muttered, and Blade saw some of the curious looks change to fearful ones. He shook his head.

"Living men, I think," he said. "Perhaps we should pull up the matting?"

Swebon nodded. Several warriors dropped their weapons and started tearing at the mats. Blade and the chiefs held onto their spears and kept watch.

The mats came up swiftly. Guno seemed to delight in showing off his immense strength, not only pulling the mats up but ripping them to pieces. At least he gripped a section that seemed to bulge slightly in the middle. He gave a tremendous heave and the mat tore free so suddenly that Guno sat down with a thump. Where the mat had been was a neat wooden box between the beams of the floor. In it were two cloaked human figures.

Before anyone could stop him, Tuk stepped forward and prodded one of the figures with the point of his spear. There was a sudden animal screech of rage that froze everyone, and the figure suddenly exploded into a young woman with a knife in one hand. She grabbed the shaft of Tuk's spear and heaved. Caught by surprise, the chief was jerked forward, tripped over the edge of a pulled-up mat, and landed flat on top of Guno.

The young woman leaped out of the box, looking ready to fight the whole roomful of warriors. Someone raised a spear. Before he could throw, Blade stepped forward. He dropped his own weapons and closed in bare-handed. The woman struck at him with her knife but he sidestepped the thrust and chopped her across the side of the neck. She went down, but struck again as Blade reached for her. He gripped her knife hand in both of his and twisted until the knife dropped to the floor.

He knelt beside her, holding her down, while Tuk and Guno got to their feet and came over to look at the captive. She glared up at them, and Blade saw that she was not only young but quite lovely, slimmer than the usual full-figured woman of the Forest People. She didn't say anything, but she didn't need to. The look in her eyes said enough.

"For what she has done to a chief, she should be turned over to the men," said Guno. The woman's expression didn't change, but Blade saw her shudder. "Then she should be—"

"She is Blade's captive," said Swebon. "It is he who must say what is to be done with her."

"Thank you, Swebon," said Blade. He pulled the woman to her feet and held her hands firmly. "In England, a woman who thrusts herself into matters of war is not raped or slain. We think she is no more than a child, and punish her as a child." He released the woman's right hand and started to turn her around.

She promptly bit him on the wrist. Guno laughed and started forward. "Are English warriors also children, that they cannot do with a woman as a man does? Here, Blade, let me help you, since—"

Blade was just about to release the woman in order to have both hands free for fighting Guno, when Tuk swung his club. It caught Guno squarely in the groin. He gasped, bit off a scream, and started to raise his spear. Then he saw four other spears already raised and pointed at his chest. He gave everyone a look as ferocious as the girl's, then hobbled off to a corner and sat down with a groan.

Blade used this moment of confusion to pull the girl close enough to whisper in her ear, "If you bite me again I'll have to knock you out. You're in no real danger as long as you don't make it impossible for me to protect you." The woman's eyes widened and for a moment Blade thought she was going to spit in his face. Then she nodded, so slightly that Blade was the only one who saw it.

Blade jerked the cloak over her head and threw it aside. Then he sat down, pulling the naked woman across his lap on her stomach. He took a firm grip with his left hand, and with his right began spanking her bare bottom as hard as he could.

She didn't scream, but even if she had Blade might not have heard her. Everyone else in the room except Guno was laughing too hard.

Chapter 9

Blade went on spanking the woman until his arm was tired and her buttocks were dark and swollen. He didn't like hurting her even this much, but he couldn't afford to be so easy on her that anyone would get suspicious—particularly Guno.

Toward the end the woman was quivering all over and trying to hold back her tears. When Blade released her and stood up, she rolled limp onto the floor for a moment, wincing as her battered rear end rubbed against the mats. Then she crawled over to Blade on hands and knees, kissed his feet, and burst into loud sobs.

Blade wondered if he'd hurt or humiliated her worse than he'd intended. Kneeling at his feet was about the last place he liked to see a woman, particularly if she was young, lovely, and naked. He started to bend down to her, she raised her head, and for a second time their eyes met. No one else in the room saw the look that passed between them, but it told Blade all he needed to know. She'd understood the game they both needed to play and her part in it. In spite of everything that had happened to her or might still happen, she was keeping her head. Blade found himself looking forward to getting to know her better.

"What is your your name?" he asked.

"Meera Ku-Na—" followed by a long string of syllables Blade couldn't understand at all. The other men in the room did seem to understand. Both Tuk and Swebon stared hard at the woman, then at Blade, their eyes widening.

Swebon shook his head. "Blade, you have made a great prize, if . . . No, you have made a great prize. This woman—she is the daughter of the chief of these villages. He is second among all the chiefs of the Yal. She is also by blood kin to the very first priestess of the Forest Spirit among the Yal."

"Is she a priestess herself?" asked Blade.

71

"No, but she has learned many of the rites, and she is a virgin. Her being captured here and now—I think it is a sign. Perhaps the priests will tell us what kind."

"Perhaps we should ask Meera herself why she stayed behind when all the other women were fleeing," said Blade. "Perhaps it is no sign at all, just her bad luck." He could hear in Swebon's voice and see on his face a reluctance to take Meera with them unless the priests approved. Swebon might be willing to just leave her behind, but Guno at least would probably want to rape and kill her.

Meera answered by pointing at the other figure in the box under the floor. Blade looked closer and saw that it was another young woman, now writhing slowly and moaning as if in a fever.

"Jersha was sick," said Meera. "If she went into the Forest she might die. If she stayed here alone she also might die. I thought that if I hid her and stayed with her, we would not be found. She was my friend, so I knew I had to do this for her."

"Very true," said Blade. He looked around the room, stroking Meera's hair as he did. "I say that Meera has been brave and wise. The capture of such a strong woman is a good sign. Do we need priests to tell us that?" Some of the Fak'si apparently wondered, but none of them seemed quite ready to argue the point with Blade.

"Good. Then Meera shall come with us, as my prisoner. But we shall also reward her. We shall give her friend Jersha water and what medicines will do her good. Then we will leave her here, among her own—" Blade had to stop, because Meera was clasping his ankles, kissing his feet, and crying again. This time she wasn't acting.

By this time Guno had also recovered enough to stagger to his feet and join the others. He glared at Blade and looked with interest at Meera, her body bent into a graceful curve. Her breasts were perfect cones with small dark nipples, the muscles of her thighs were firm, her skin had a faint sheen of sweat or oil—in fact, she seemed lovelier to Blade each time he looked at her. He didn't blame Guno for being interested, but he also hoped the man would leave Meera alone. Any trouble over her would bring the simmering quarrel between Blade and Guno into the open, perhaps dividing Four Springs village into hostile factions.

Blade pulled Meera to her feet. "I will take you to one of

our priests," he said. "He will give you water and medicine for Jersha. Then I—"

Before Blade could finish several warriors came running up the stairs. Their leader knelt briefly to the two chiefs, then said in a breathless voice, "The Yal of the other villages are coming against us by land. They are very many."

"How many?" said Tuk.

"Three hundred, maybe more," said the man. "Our people lay in wait and took the ones who came first. They told us how many followed."

Swebon frowned. "I did not think the other villages had so many warriors."

"Perhaps some from other Yal villages were here for a feast when we came," said Guno.

"Perhaps," said Swebon. "They are too many, however they came here. It is time for us to be on the river and on the way home."

Blade untied a water gourd from his belt and handed it to Meera. "Give this to Jersha, and hurry. I fear we will not have time to take you to a priest."

"It does not matter," said Meera. Then she said very softly, "I already have much to thank you for."

The Fak'si were as efficient in retreating from the Yal village as they'd been in attacking it. Since the Yal were all coming by land, Swebon decided the Fak'si would retreat by water. There weren't enough of their own canoes to take them all, but there were plenty of Yal canoes drawn up on the banks or tied to houseboats and trees. Instead of simply setting these canoes adrift, the raiders would paddle off in them.

Swebon and twenty warriors went out to reinforce the rear guard, while Tuk led the men in loading up the canoes. There were about forty women and children beside Meera, and an entire canoe-load of loot. Seven of the raiders were dead or dying and twenty more wounded, half so badly they couldn't walk. The bodies and the crippled were loaded into the canoes first, then the walking wounded, then the prisoners carrying the loot. By that time the noise of the fight against the Yal counterattack was rising to an uproar.

Just as it seemed the rear guard might need reinforcements, a horn sounded and the men came running along the bank to the canoes. They were carrying their dead and wounded with them, and Swebon brought up the rear. Tuk shouted an order, and all the archers in the canoes nocked arrows and crouched, ready to let fly. The rear guard scrambled aboard and everyone who wasn't holding a bow grabbed a paddle. The canoes slid out from the bank, as some of the prisoners began to wail and cry.

The last canoe was just out of spear range from the bank when the first warriors of the Yal counterattack ran up. Some of them took cover behind huts and trees, other bolder ones dashed out onto the open bank and hurled spears after the retreating Fak'si. Tuk shouted another order, and the archers let fly almost as one man. Most of the Yal in the open went down, and some of them didn't get up again. The Yal behind the huts replied with arrows of their own, but most of these fell into the river and none of them hit anyone. Then the canoes were rapidly pulling out of range, and all the surviving Yal could do was shake their fists and scream curses and threats.

Blade turned to Swebon, wincing at the pain in his shoulder. In the excitement of the last half hour he'd almost forgotten that he'd been wounded. He examined the shoulder again. The wound had stopped bleeding, but he'd have to boil some water and wash it out when they stopped for the night.

Swebon saw Blade's concern about his wound. "Do not worry, Blade. You will receive the Shield of Life along with our own wounded—unless it is against the laws of the English?"

"No. I do not think it will be." It might be against his stomach, if taking the Shield of Life meant having to swallow that revolting brew the priests had cooked up. But who could tell? It might do some good.

"When will it be given?"

"Tonight, when we can stop and give proper care to our dead and wounded."

"What about the Yal coming after us?"

Swebon laughed. "How are they to do that, Blade? We took all the canoes from the first village. They must run back to the other three before they can come after us on the river. By the time they do this, we will be so far ahead that the Yal cannot hope to catch up with us before dark. They will not risk the Horned Ones to chase us by night. Our victory has good strong roots, Blade. The Yal will not pluck it up."

Blade was inclined to agree. The whole raid had been a little masterpiece, well-planned and carried out with speed, skill, and good discipline. Swebon and Tuk would have made first-class commando leaders in World War II. Unfortunately the victory was also a waste of skill, strength, and lives the Forest People could put to better use against the Sons of Hapanu. The Yal might accept their defeat for now, but sooner or later they'd try to avenge it. The petty warfare among the Forest People would go on, until it ceased to be petty—and then the Sons of Hapanu would advance and the Forest People would be swept away.

Blade found that thought a good deal more painful than the wound in his shoulder.

Chapter 10

Swebon's canoe was the last one in line as the raiders withdrew, but Blade saw no sign of pursuit. The whole area was certainly alarmed and alert, since arrows were fired from the banks several times. Only two men in the canoes were hit, neither of them seriously. By mid-afternoon the raiders were nearly out of Yal territory.

They still kept on going after that, but more slowly, with only half the paddlers in each canoe at work. The rest drank water, ate dried fruit and seed cakes, and tended the wounded. Fractures were splinted, sprains were bandaged with dampened cloths, and men with head injuries got compresses of wet leaves. Minor wounds like Blade's were left entirely alone. More serious wounds had wads of leaves stuffed into them. The results looked ghastly, and Blade was very happy his own wounnd was so light. The seriously wounded men were doomed to agonizing pain at the very least, and possibly to fatal infections from bacteria carried into the wounds by the leaves.

By late afternoon they'd reached the marsh where the Shield of Life had been prepared. By the time Swebon's canoe reached the patch of dry land deep inside it, the lead canoes were already pulled up on the bank and their men were ashore. The priests were unloading iron pots and the gourds filled with the Shield of Life. Warriors scurried about, bringing moss and twigs, cutting up fallen logs, and clearing spaces for fires.

When the fires were blazing nicely, the iron pots were filled with water and put on to heat. "Now begins the healing of wounds with the Shield of Life," said Swebon. "You may ask to be first among those healed, for what you have done this day and on other days."

"Thank you for the honor," said Blade. "But I'll wait. There are many others with worse wounds than mine." This was true, and apart from that, the more Blade learned about

76

the Shield of Life before it was applied to him, the happier he'd be.

"So be it," said Swebon. He signaled to the priests, who picked up a pot and two gourds and went over to a wounded man lying at the base of a tree. He had a long spear gash in his leg, running almost from hip to knee, and was nearly unconscious from the pain and loss of blood. One of the captive women sat by him, fanning the insects away from his face. In the twilight Blade didn't recognize her until he stepped closer, then saw it was Meera. She looked up at him and smiled.

"The Fak'si will now be my people. It is a woman's duty to care for the warriors of her people. Is this not so?"

"Yes." That attitude did credit to both Meera's cool head and her warm heart. Blade wondered if she'd be feeling so charitable if she'd fallen into Guno's hands instead of his.

Meera rose and backed away as Swebon and the priests approached the wounded man. First they poured hot water over the blood-caked leaves until they were soft, then picked them all out of the wound. Mercifully the man was so nearly unconscious that he hardly seemed to feel what must have been agony as the leaves came out.

When the leaves were all out, the priests went on pouring water over the wound, washing away all the caked and clotted blood until the wound was bleeding freely again. For a moment Blade wondered if the poor man was going to bleed to death before the Shield of Life could do anything for him. Then the first priest opened a gourd and poured the Shield of Life out onto the wound. Almost as it struck the raw flesh, it started to congeal. The second priest worked it vigorously with his fingers to spread it all over the wound. Within a minute the wound was completely covered by a glazed layer of the Shield of Life, looking vaguely like gray plastic. It smelled as ghastly as ever, but at least Blade knew now he wasn't going to have to drink it.

The wounded man seemed to relax as the Shield of Life hardened over his wound. His breathing slowed and became more regular, and his eyes drifted shut. Instead of tossing half-conscious in a red haze of pain, he now seemed to be sleeping naturally. Meera came back, moistened a rag, and mopped the sweat off the man's face and the blood off his lips where he'd bitten them.

The priests did the same thing with each wounded man—clean the wound, pour on the Shield of Life, and make sure it completely covered the wound by the time it hardened.

With each man the effect was the same—a calming, a soothing, an apparent easing of their pain. One man had the Shield of Life poured on a maimed hand and recovered so quickly that he grabbed one of the captive women with his good hand and tried to pull her down to the ground beside him.

Swebon laughed at that and lifted the woman to her feet. "Enough, Fror," he said. "We Shield your life, not your manhood. Save your strength until you can do this woman some justice. Or would you have her believe that the Fak'si are less than men?" Fror smiled and let Swebon lead the woman away.

It was nearly dark by the time the priests finished with the last of the seriously wounded. By then several more fires were blazing merrily, and fish were broiling on spits over them. Fat hissed cheerfully as it dropped into the flames.

Blade lay down and let Swebon and the priests go to work on him. The hot water stung as it flowed into the wound, washing away the clotted blood. Then the Shield of Life came down on his flesh, and it was as if a cool, soothing oil was touching every part of the wound. The touch was so gentle that Blade's senses barely registered it, but under that touch all the pain vanished as completely as if he'd never been wounded. Blade felt a faint prickling on his skin as the Shield of Life began to dry, but nothing else. The most advanced Home Dimension anaesthetics couldnt' have done a better job.

Of course killing the pain of his wound wasn't the same as curing it, but he was willing to take his chances. The wound had been at least partly disinfected, and the hardened Shield of Life seemed to be sealing it as well as any bandage. Meanwhile he was getting sleepy, and he was incredibly thirsty.

He lay back, and was vaguely aware of Swebon calling for the sentries to take their positions. Meera appeared suddenly out of the darkness and held a gourd of cool water to his mouth. He drank until the gourd was empty, but satisfying his thirst didn't clear his head. It only seemed to make him sleepier. He felt slim, muscular limbs against his and soft hair brushing his cheek, then he felt nothing at all.

They were on the move again the next morning, as soon as there was enough light to make out the channel back to the main river. "It would be best to stay here another two days," said Swebon. "The Shield of Life is a great blessing, but the Forest Spirit asks a price for that blessing.

"However, we can do only the next best thing. We have

78

struck the Yal a mighty blow and they will be in a mighty rage. To wait here two more days would be as foolish as throwing a stone into a hive of wild bees and standing by, waiting for them to swarm out."

Blade saw what Swebon meant by the "price for that blessing" before they'd been on the river an hour. One by one, all the wounded who'd received the Shield of Life became feverish. How feverish they became depended on how badly they'd been wounded. Those with light wounds like Blade's merely became uncomfortable—confused, tired, and continuously thirsty. Those who'd been seriously wounded burned with fever, and many of them became delirious. One man went into convulsions and died just before noon. Swebon, Tuk, and the priests said the death rites for him and his body was slipped overboard as the raiders paddled on.

Blade spent the day paddling as well as he could with one shoulder half immobilized and the rest of his body hot and aching with fever. Meera was always on hand with drinking water, except when she was needed to pour water over one of the more seriously ill men. She worked hard, and by the end of the day Blade wasn't the only man who looked at her with respect and even affection as she moved up and down the canoe. She was still as naked as a baby, but didn't seem to care.

By the time they made camp that night, Blade and the others lightly wounded found their fevers were passing off. The more seriously wounded were slower to recover. They tossed and turned and moaned all night, and a second man went into convulsions. Swebon and the priests let Meera take charge of him.

"The Forest Spirit has blessed her greatly," said Swebon. "Young as she is, she knows as much of caring of the wounded as any of our priests or women. She also seems not to care whether the man before her is Yal or Fak'si. That gift is even more rare than the skills of healing."

Swebon shook his head. "I no longer can doubt it. That both you and Meera have come to the Fak'si at this time—it is a sign. I think it is a sign of some great change coming to the Fak'si. I only hope it is a good change."

Blade nodded. "I do not know much of signs and omens. But I know I have found a home among the Fak'si, a friend in you, and a strong woman in Meera. This says to me that things will change for the better."

Blade was quite sincere in hoping that all the changes

coming to the Fak'si and the Forest People would be for the good. They had enough problems already. He was also glad to see Swebon in a mood to look for omens and expect changes. That should make him more open-minded about any new ideas Blade might offer. Those ideas were now beginning to take a definite shape in Blade's mind.

Thanks largely to Meera's nursing, the convulsing man didn't die. His fever broke just before dawn, and so did all the other fevers, both high and low. The seriously wounded were sleeping like exhausted children when the able-bodied and the lightly wounded loaded them into the canoes for the day's journey. They slept most of the day, and only awoke when they were being carried out of the canoes into the night's camp.

When they did wake up, they were clear-headed, but weak as kittens and ravenously hungry. The hunters and fishermen were kept busy catching dinner, and the cooks kept even busier preparing it. Blade found that his own appetite was returning. He also found that the Shield of Life over his shoulder was beginning to prickle and itch. The wound itself no longer hurt at all, but the itching rapidly became uncomfortable, then positively maddening. From the strained expressions of the other wounded, Blade guessed they were all having the same trouble. He decided to leave the Shield alone. He still had his doubts about Fak'si medicine, but interfering with a wound that seemed to be healing fairly well was never a good idea, no matter how weird the treatment you'd received for it.

Because of the wounded and the prisoners, the raiders returned home by a different route than they'd used coming out. This one was considerably longer, but didn't involve any overland portage. It did involve passing along a stretch of river swarming with Horned Ones, but Blade was able to help out there. He showed how to make and use the jaw-bracers. By the time they reached the dangerous stretch, there were half a dozen carefully-made jaw-bracers in each canoe. Blade's status among the Fak'si went up another notch.

Meanwhile all the wounds were healing with amazing speed and practically without complications. Within five days Blade's Shield of Life turned from gray to brown and started cracking and peeling around the edges. One of the priests examined it and decided the time had come to remove it.

With a knife he picked away most of the dried Shield, then washed away the rest.

The wound underneath was going to leave a scar, but that didn't worry Blade. He already had more than his fair share of scars, picked up in one Dimension or another. What impressed him was that the wound was almost completely healed, with no sign of infection.

This wasn't an isolated miracle, either. One by one over the next few days the Shields of Life came off the wounds, and one by one all the wounds appeared as clean and well-healed as Blade's. By the time the raiders returned home, eleven days after the raid, only tthree men were still wearing their Shields.

Blade still found it hard to believe, but after a while he thought he understood what happened with the Shield of Life. The combination of *kohkol* sap and uglyfish gland made a powerful compound with several different effects on the human body. First, it acted as an anaesthetic, numbing damaged nerve tissues. Second, it acted as a purely natural disinfectant by stimulating the body's own defense mechanisms—specifically, stimulating the production of white blood cells. That accounted for the absence of infections, at the inevitable price of the fever as the white blood cells multiplied and fought their battle. Finally, the Shield of Life seemed to stimulate cell growth in general, and therefore the regeneration of damaged tissue. That explained the rapid healing of all the wounds, with a minimum of scar tissue.

In short, the Shield of Life was nearly the ultimate treatment for any sort of wound. No wonder the Forest People had been able to indulge in their tribal wars for so long with so little damage! Not only did they keep the bloodshed down, they had a reliable method of dealing with many of the wounds that did happen.

When Blade realized what the Shield of Life really was, he would have made any sort of bargain at all to be sure of getting a large sample back to Home Dimension. With a gourdful to analyze, the biochemists there should be able to synthesize it. After that many things could happen, most of them good.

He was also going to be able to pay the Forest People for their gift of the Shield of Life. There'd been some sleepless nights in the riverside camps, and during those nights he'd finally realized what the Forest People needed to fight the

Sons of Hapanu and the Treemen. He'd also figured out how to make the weapons, although he'd need to make some private experiments before he could be absolutely sure. He'd have to start by talking to Swebon, who should be in a mood to listen. Then he'd go to work—and see what happened.

Chapter 11

Blade was so busy working out his ideas that he didn't join in the celebration of the raiders' victory. He wandered about, mostly watching the carpenters and bowmakers at work. He not only ignored Meera, he ignored all the village women who wanted one of the great heroes of the raid against the Yal to take them to his sleeping mat. Lokhra put the doubts he was arousing into words.

"If the Yal woman had you in her grip, we would understand. She is very beautiful, wise, and strong. She is a good woman for you. But you do not take her either. She serves you only as a little girl or an old woman might do. Yet you still look at no other woman. Did you take a wound to your manhood, Blade?" The question might have been insulting, except for Lokhra's tone of voice. She seemed really worried about Blade's strange new habit of ignoring women.

Blade decided he was going to have to come up with some sort of explanation. "You do not need to praise Meera to me," he said. "I know the kind of woman she is. But that does not matter. I have had a vision." Visions and dreams played a large part in the religion of the Forest People, so this would seem a plausible explanation.

Lokhra's eyes opened wide and she made a gesture to turn away bad luck. "May you say what kind of vision it was?"

"I can say what I have seen so far. It was very clear. I saw that a great change might soon come to the Fak'si, perhaps to all the Forest People. I saw also that if the change came it would come through me."

Lokhra's eyes opened even wider. "What kind of change?"

"This I did not see. I saw clearly that I would have to wait for a second vision to know. I also saw even more clearly that I should not lie with a woman or drink beer until the second vision came."

Lokhra moaned faintly in awe and pressed her forehead

against Blade's feet, then against the floor. When she rose, she asked, "May I speak of this to others?"

Blade laughed. "Yes. It is no secret. Be particularly sure to tell the women. I would like them to know that my manhood is still with me. In time I will prove it."

Lokhra must have told half the village that same day. By the next morning Blade found himself being looked at with awe as well as admiration. All the women wanted to press their foreheads against his feet, and all the men wanted to pull his hair. Such crowds gathered every time he went out for a walk that he finally had to stop going out during the day. He stayed aboard his houseboat and let Meera bring him food and water, as wall as the charcoal and pieces of bark he needed for making drawings. No one seemed to think there was anything suspicious about Blade's vision.

At least none of the ordinary people seemed to think so. Blade now realized he should probably have mentioned his vision to the priests first. Home Dimension bureaucracies weren't the only place where it was a good idea to "go through channels." It was also a good idea among primitive peoples with possibly jealous priesthoods.

However, any damage was already done. He would just have to go ahead and hope the priests wouldn't mind this strange Englishman stealing all their thunder! Blade didn't know whether to be optimistic or not. The priests *should* have the interests of their people at heart—but it was quite possible they'd think their own power more important.

In any case, Swebon was certainly the best starting place.

It was a week after the raid before Blade asked Swebon to meet him in a place where they wouldn't be overheard. Early the next morning they climbed into a small canoe and paddled out into the middle of the river. Swebon threw the anchor stone overboard, and they sat while the sun rose and Blade explained his plans for helping the Forest People defeat their enemies.

"What you need more than anything else is a strong weapon," he said. "Strong enough to slay the Treemen and the Sons of Hapanu."

"We have known this for a long time," said Swebon wearily. "But our wisest men have found nothing. Perhaps the Forest will give us nothing, and the Forest Spirit is turning away from us."

Blade shook his head. "No, Swebon. That was not my

vision. The Forest Spirit has already given you all you need to win these battles. It merely asks you to see them in new ways." Blade wanted to make this point very clear from the start. It would answer the objections of those people who were simply afraid of anything new. Swebon wasn't one of them, but not all the Fak'si would be that intelligent.

"And—your vision has shown you these new ways?" asked Swebon. He didn't sound completely convinced, but he did sound ready to listen.

"Yes. The second vision that I was promised has come."

Blade started explaining. The best weapon the Forest People had against their two great enemies was the bow. It could strike from a distance, and it could strike with enough power to kill. Or at least it could if it was changed.

The bows the Forest People had now were weak. They could not shoot an arrow far enough or hard enough. They could not reach a vital organ of a Treemen or penetrate the armor of a Son of Hapanu.

"A stronger bow is all you need," said Blade. "I have looked at your arrows. They are as good as you need. I have also seen your archers shoot, and know they can shoot well.

"I know there is no one wood in the Forest that can make such a strong bow. But I saw that if a man used several *different* woods, he might make such a bow."

With the help of his sketches, Blade continued his explanation. He was proposing a *laminated* bow, built up by gluing together layers of different kinds of wood, and perhaps bone and sinew as well. The present bow of the Forest People was like the English longbow, carved out of a single piece of wood. Unfortunately the Forest had no tough but flexible woods like ash, elm, or yew, so the single-piece bows were weak. Blade was proposing something more like the Turkish or Mongol horsebows, which could penetrate mail at two hundred yards.

Making a laminated bow required choosing materials carefully, and then gluing them together so that they stayed together under stress. The only way to pick the right woods was by experimenting, but Blade already knew what glue he was going to use.

"*Kohkol* sap should do very well," he said. "It must be boiled longer, so that it will be stronger than it is now. But that should not be hard to do."

The laminated bow was Blade's most important idea, but not his only one. "It will be some time before all the Forest

People can have strong bows," he said. "Also, even the most powerful bow will not kill a Treeman if it does not hit him in a vital spot. I know how to make any arrow you may shoot hurt a Treeman, no matter where it hits him." Blade hesitated. "I now speak of matters which perhaps belong only to the chiefs and priests," he went on. "If I speak wrongly, will it remain between us?"

Swebon nodded. "I swear not to be angry at anything you say. I also swear that no priest who would be angry shall hear any of this from me."

"Good." Blade explained. If the Shield of Life could act as an anaesthetic, it might also act as a tranquilizer. Made much stronger and smeared on the point of an arrow, the Shield of Life could numb the muscles and slow the movements of a Treeman. Then the Forest People could close in and kill him.

Blade was rather surprised that the Forest People hadn't long since developed poisoned arrows and darts on their own. The natives of the Amazon basin used such weapons freely. On the other hand, the Forest People had plenty of metal for weapons and their bows were powerful enough for hunting birds and small game. They hadn't needed a really *deadly* weapon until recently.

Swebon's frown deepened as Blade explained this new use for the Shield of Life. When Blade was finished, the chief lay back in the bottom of the canoe and stared up at the sky. He was silent for so long that Blade thought he'd gone to sleep. At last he sat up.

"It is not our custom to let a man who is neither chief nor priest work with the Shield of Life. The priests will not like this change." He held up a hand as Blade was about to speak. "I do not like it myself. But—the Forest changes. Perhaps the ways of the Forest People must change also."

"I think so," said Blade. "I would not ask this if I did not think so."

"I know you would not," said Swebon. "Therefore I say— go and do what you will with the Shield of Life. But go into the Forest and do your work where no one can see you. Then no priest can say a word against you until your work is done. If you do what you promised, so many will speak for you that no priest will be brave enough to speak against you."

Blade wasn't surprised to find that Swebon's common sense and shrewdness extended to politics, but he was glad.

One point remained to be settled, though. Blade knew it was the most important point of all. He also knew it was the one where he and Swebon would be most likely to quarrel.

"Do you wish me to go entirely alone into the Forest?" Blade asked.

"No. You will need other hands to help you, and other eyes to watch your back. I would go with you myself, if I could leave the village for so long. But I do not think that would be wise. My brother—he still looks at your Meera with desire . . . ."

"I understand. But he will not be able to do anything against her. I am taking her into the Forest with me, to be my other hands and eyes."

Swebon started so violently he set the canoe rocking. By the time it steadied, he was staring at Blade as if the Englishman had suddenly grown a second head. Finally he sighed. "Blade, I do not understand this. You have not lain with the woman since you made her your captive. Yet you will take her with you into the Forest, to learn your secrets. Then perhaps she will stick a knife into your back and run away to her people with all she has learned." Swebon's voice was rising almost to a shout. "Blade, I must ask it—are you mad?"

"Not mad. I only follow my vision. It has told me—"

"Curse your visions!" growled Swebon. Then he sighed. "Go on. What tricks have they told you to play on the Fak'si now?"

"No tricks," said Blade quietly. "My second vision only told me that I should not worry if other tribes learn my secrets. In fact, the vision told me to give the secrets to them. So it does not matter what Meera learns or where she goes. I hope—" He broke off, because Swebon's face was twisting violently in both rage and surprise. For a long moment Blade wasn't sure the chief wasn't going to attack him.

Then Swebon took a deep breath. "Why, Blade? I ask only that. *Why?* The Fak'si have taken you in, been your friends—"

"I do not hate the Fak'si, Swebon. Do not think that. But I cannot hate the other tribes of the Forest People either. I cannot give the Fak'si the strong bow and the strong Shield of Life to help them fight the other Forest People. I must give these things to *all* the Forest People, so that they can all fight the Treemen and the Sons of Hapanu. Otherwise the wars among the Forest People will destroy them even faster

87

than the Treemen or the Sons of Hapanu. What will happen if every raid like ours kills fifty people instead of a dozen? Do you want to see that come, Swebon?"

The chief seemed not to be listening. He sat with his head in his hands and his heavy shoulders sagging. Then at last he raised his head and looked at Blade. To Blade's great relief Swebon was smiling.

"Blade, I had a vision of my own, one that gave me much pleasure. I had a vision of the Fak'si coming to rule the Forest People, and myself coming to rule the Fak'si." He shrugged. "But it seems that I cannot bring my vision to be without killing you. I will not do that.

"Also, you could be right. Certainly our raid against the Yal shed more blood than we often did in the past. In the future, with the new bows—who can say how much blood might be shed? And who would gain from it, except the Sons of Hapanu?

"Perhaps the time is here for the Forest People to become one tribe instead of four. Certainly that would be a better fate than the Sons of Hapanu and the Treemen killing all our men and making slaves of all our women. If we must be one tribe to live, then I will work beside you for this."

They shook hands and patted hair to seal that promise, then paddled back to the village.

Blade had to let Swebon gather the equipment for the trip into the Forest and the experiments there. The chief could go anywhere and pick up anything without arousing the suspicions of the priests or Guno, or drawing questions from anyone else. Blade trusted him to work fast and keep his mouth shut.

Guno was another matter. Blade couldn't trust the chief's brother—or rather, he could trust the man to do something against him. It was too bad that Guno was Swebon's brother, with his own reputation and circle of friends and allies. Otherwise Blade would seriously have tried to find some way of provoking a fight with the man and killing him. As it was, there was nothing to do but hope to succeed quickly and then come out into the open. After that he'd have more people to guard his back than Swebon and Meera.

Since there was nothing else for Blade to do, he returned to his houseboat and slept peacefully through the hottest part of the day. When he awoke, the shadows outside were getting long, but Meera wasn't back yet. This was a mild surprise.

Usually she spent the morning getting fresh food and water and the afternoon cleaning the houseboat and preparing the evening meal.

It was twilight before Meera returned, and by then Blade was beginning to wonder. Suppose the secret was out and Guno had struck at him through Meera? He was just about ready to arm himself and go out to turn the village upside down for Meera when she appeared on the bank. She held a bulging sack under one arm and two filled gourds in the other hand.

He helped her aboard the houseboat and unloaded her, then asked, "Meera, where have you been?"

"Beyond the village, getting food for us."

"Isn't there enough in the village?"

"Not—not the kind I wanted."

"What kind did you want?"

She looked up at him, her eyes meeting his so steadily that he had the feeling she could look right through him. It wasn't a sensation Blade particularly enjoyed, certainly not when it involved someone he was planning to trust with his life.

"I saw Swebon while I was in the Forest," she said.

"Ah." That syllable never gave anything away.

"He said you and he spoke together this morning."

"We did."

"He would not tell me why you talked, but I think he wishes us well." She smiled shyly. "He said—you had your second vision."

"So?"

"Blade, please! You said that after your second vision, you might take a woman again. Have you forgotten that?"

"No."

"Then—Blade, I thought—it seemed to me that . . . ." She pointed with an unsteady hand at the sack on the floor. "That is the *minya* root. To eat it makes a man and a woman—"

Blade laughed. "I see. You thought that even after the second vision, I might not want you because I *could* not want you. So you went and—"

She nodded, her eyes on the floor. "Or—you had been long without a woman, and sometimes then a man cannot—"

Blade laughed again, so loudly that Meera's head jerked up and she stared at him. "Meera, Meera, Meera, I ought to spank you again for doubting me. I will not need any *minya* root."

Her face was sober as she replied. "I would rather be spanked by you than beaten by the priests or their women. If you did not take me soon, they would wonder if I was a witch who cursed your manhood. Then they would beat me, or worse." She pushed her skirt down over her hips until it slipped to the floor, then stood naked before Blade.

Blade was already naked. Now there was a warmth in his groin that didn't come from the hot weather. The warmth grew as his eyes ran up and down Meera's body and he thought of not only looking but touching. He imagined his lips on her eyes and mouth, then moving down her throat and across her breasts, teasing her nipples into hard points, while his hands stroked her hips, crept to the inside of her thighs, felt the triangle of dark hair between her legs turning damp—

Meera laughed softly. "I see you do not need the *minya* root after all."

"Not when you are here in front of me, and I have imagined—"

"I know what you have imagined. Now—do it?" It was as much a question as a request, and Meera's voice was shaking. Her eyes were on the floor again. "Blade, do not make me beg. For—a virgin—this is not fit—but—I desire you."

"And I desire you, Meera," said Blade quietly, stepping forward to put his arms around her. She stiffened at his touch and her head jerked upward like a puppet's. For a moment he thought fear might have wiped out her desire. Then her lips were seeking his, found them, and drove out all his doubts.

Blade did everything he'd imagined, slowly, tenderly, making it last in order to give Meera time to awaken and accept him. After a while he realized that her breath was coming fast, her eyes were half-closed and staring at nothing, her nipples were solid against his hands, and she was pressing her belly steadily against his thigh. If Meera wasn't awake and aroused by now, no woman ever had been.

Blade took her by the shoulders and gently pressed her down onto the sleeping pad. Her eyes were now completely closed and her thoughts seemed to be elsewhere. Her legs spread wide at Blade's first caress of the inside of her thighs. By the time his hand was resting lightly on the dark, damp hair, she was lifting her legs and twisting her head from side to side. Her hair hissed softly on the matting, and sometimes she moaned.

90

Blade balanced himself above Meera—then suddenly her arms and legs seemed to coil around him like serpents and drag him down. He was deep inside her almost before he realized it. He felt her stiffen, heard her cry out at the first moment's pain, then heard her give a great sigh of relief. For a moment she lay still under him, then slowly her hips began to move in time with his own thrusts.

It should have been impossible for Meera's passion to rise as fast as Blade's. In fact, she seemed to be fully blazing within seconds. Her fingers raked Blade's back and her lips roamed over every part of his face and throat she could reach. Then her teeth clamped down on Blade's ear, and in the same moment as the pain stabbed at him both he and Meera exploded in a whirlwind of a thousand flaring colors. That whirlwind swept away the rest of the world, and it was a long time returning.

Somehow Blade found himself lying on the sleeping mat beside Meera. A hand cupped one of her breasts while her arm trailed across his chest. Blade felt relaxed and contented. He thought the feeling was going to last until they both fell asleep.

Instead Meera's arm suddenly began to move, and soon slim fingers with natural talent were playing games along the insides of his thighs. Things took their inevitable course, and this time when they were finished Blade found he couldn't even think of sleep.

Meera was obviously in the same mood. She pulled Blade's hands onto her body and smiled at him. He kissed her and said, "Meera, if you're this curious about being a woman, perhaps I should have some of the *minya* root after all." Meera nodded and jumped up. Even when she squatted down by the sack of food, she looked graceful.

The *minya* root was dry and powdery, with a sharp and not particularly pleasant flavor. Blade couldn't imagine anybody eating it for anything but its aphrodisiac qualities.

Whether it really had those qualities or not, Blade never knew. All he knew was that it was a long time before his strength ran out, and by that time Meera's curiosity was satisfied—at least for the night. They fell asleep in each other's arms, and it was noon before they woke up.

Chapter 12

Blade's search for a way to give the Forest People new weapons started off well. In fact, it started off so well that as he said afterward, "I should have known something was going to go wrong."

Swebon gathered all the equipment Blade expected to need, telling people that an exploring party was going out, searching for land for a new village. Such a party would need much more equipment than ordinary hunters or raiders. As far as Swebon could tell, this "cover story" went over quite well.

Blade couldn't use the patch of *kohkol* trees where the villagers normally drew their sap. It was visited at least twice a week, and there was always a priest with the tree-tappers. There would be too much danger of someone stumbling on Blade and his experiments.

So Blade and Meera would have to plunge deep into the Forest and seek out a *kohkol* grove two days' march from the village. Swebon was able to give Blade detailed directions for finding it, but few others in the village even knew of its existence.

"I send you into danger by sending you there," said the chief. "The Treemen seldom come as close to the village as the first *kohkol* grove. At the second, you will be in the High Forest, where the Treemen have been strong since the Forest began. I would do otherwise if I could, but I think you have more need to fear the priests and Guno than the Treemen."

Blade nodded. "Then we shall just have to make the new bows before the Treemen find us." He didn't particularly look forward to such a race against time, but he agreed with Swebon. The Treemen might be savage fighters, but they couldn't make the village dangerous for him.

By the time Blade and Meera had all their gear loaded on their backs, Blade was carrying close to a hundred pounds and Meera about half as much. Yet they couldn't reduce the load by another ounce without leaving out something Blade was sure they'd need sooner or later. Swebon would have been glad to send a trusted warrior with them, but Blade refused.

"We don't know that *anyone* except the three of us can be trusted in this," he said. "Besides, why drag anyone else into this and put them in danger?"

Swebon shook his head. "Blade, if you ever wish to be chief of the Fak'si—well, a man who thinks of danger to those who might follow him, who will face it himself instead —no one will easily stand against him."

"I do not wish to be chief of the Fak'si," said Blade. "Only the maker of new weapons for all the Forest People."

They were standing just out of earshot of the farthest tree-houses of the village. It was early morning, with dawn still only a hint of light beyond the treetops. Blade was leaning against a tree, while Meera sat cross-legged among the ferns. Both were carrying their full packs.

"May the Forest Spirit bring you to success," said Swebon, patting Blade's head and then Meera's. "And may it bring you back to us."

"May it keep you also, friend Swebon," said Meera. Blade gripped his staff with one hand and with the other helped Meera to her feet. Then they were gone into the darkness under the trees and Swebon turned back toward the village.

It took Blade and Meera three days to cover the two day march to the second *kohkol* grove. With the loads they were carrying, even Blade was slowed down and only sheer determination kept Meera on her feet. Blade was also careful to avoid leaving a clear trail for anyone to follow, and that slowed them down even more.

Eventually they came to the grove, with *kohkol* trees rising in a solid wall a hundred feet high across their path. A stream of clear water flowed out of the grove, and there was plenty of fruit, edible roots, and small game. They could live well here, for as long as they needed or at least as long as they could before the Treemen found them.

Blade was determined they'd also live safely, even if the Treemen did stumble across them. He set to work with ax and digging tool, cutting seven-foot poles and driving them into the ground. He sharpened the ends, bound them together with vines, then tied more poles across the top. When he was finished, they had a shelter six feet high and eight feet across, large enough to hold them and their gear. It was also tough enough to keep out any Forest animal and delay even an angry Treeman long enough for Blade and Meera to wake up and grab their weapons.

They had plenty of weapons. Each of them had a bow and quiver of arrows and a spear. Meera's spear was the one Blade had taken as a trophy from the chief's house in the Yal village. Blade also had the biggest war club Swebon could find in Four Springs village, a monster three feet long with a head bound in iron. He and Meera would be a match for three or four Treemen even without any new weapons, and in small bands the Treemen usually didn't press attacks on difficult or dangerous prey. It would be another matter if twenty Treemen showed up all at once, but such huge bands were still fairly rare.

When the shelter was finished, Blade lost no time going to work on his experiments. He tapped two *kohkol* trees and filled four gourds with the sap. With Meera's help he built a fire, then hung their iron pot over it, filled the pot with sap, and left it to boil.

Blade had guessed right about the *kohkol* sap. Boiled long enough, it became a remarkably tough and strong adhesive. It would stick almost anything to almost anything else, including Blade's fingers to each other. He discovered this while trying to retrieve a spoon which had fallen into the pot. He had to cut away the *kohkol* glue with a knife before he could use his left hand again, and he took a few pieces of skin along with the glue. After that Blade was more careful about handling it.

Once he knew he could make any amount of glue any time he wanted it, he started looking for wood to make the bow. He wasn't entirely sure wood was all he'd need—the famous Mongol bows used sinew and horn as well. Wood was certainly the most common material in the Forest, though, and the Forest People knew at least a hundred different kinds. Among them should be at least a few which could be laminated into a powerful bow.

Blade spent several days cutting samples of every kind of wood he thought might be useful. Meera's help saved him much wasted time and effort. She knew which woods might be completely useless because they were too soft, too brittle, or too quick to decay. She knew which parts of many trees had the best wood. She was also handy with a knife and vine cords, trimming and bundling up branches as Blade cut them.

Blade never felt the slightest need to watch her or any fear of turning his back on her. To be sure, this was partly because they were deep in the High Forest and Meera's chances of survival would not be good if he were killed. More of it was because Meera knew what he was planning and thought it was a good idea.

She said so plainly when he asked her. She went on to say, "I do not know if I trust Swebon as much as you do. It will surely tempt him, when he has weapons that could make him ruler of the Forest. But he is a strong man, so perhaps it will not tempt him enough.

"Also, I do trust you, Blade. I trust you to let me go home to my own people if Swebon tricks us. If I go home to the Yal with our secrets, Swebon will not be able to do them any harm."

It was surprising how Meera's mind and his seemed to run along the same paths when it came to the future of the Forest People. "I was planning on taking you home myself when we finished our work here and in Four Springs village."

"Leaving me there?" she said, apparently surprised.

"Only long enough for the Yal to learn everything we can teach them," Blade said. "I will not ask you to leave me, unless you want to."

Meera shook her head. "I am happy with you. You are good to a woman, and that is good for a woman." While Blade was trying to figure that one out, she put both hands on his chest and pushed him over backward. Then she climbed on top of him, pulled aside his loinguard, and there was no more talking for quite a while.

When the woodcutting was finished, Blade started slicing the wood into strips, while Meera trimmed and shaped the strips according to his instructions. She wasn't an expert carpenter, but again her willing help saved Blade many hours of work. He quickly discovered that once you started trying to laminate anything, the Forest was full of suitable woods for the job. In fact, Blade started by making his first two bows too strong.

These two were made of four layers of wood, glued together and then wrapped with glue-soaked leaves. They were incredibly ugly, more like clubs than bows, and impossibly stiff. Blade could hardly bend the first one, and in Home Dimension he'd easily handled a monstrous longbow with a hundred and twenty-pound pull.

Blade could bend the second bow, but it snapped every

bowstring he tried to use on it. Obviously the second bow was nearly as useless as the first one. Fak'si bowstrings were made of dried animal sinew and were much tougher than their bows. A bow that was going to be too strong for such bowstrings was going to be too strong for the average Fak'si warrior to handle easily.

So much for brute force. Blade started systematic experiments with various combinations of woods in two, three, four, and even five layers. He worked from dawn to dark and would have worked into the night if he'd thought it was safe. Unfortunately, having a fire blazing in the darkness could only be an invitation to the Treemen. So Blade banked the fire each evening and retired to the shelter, where Meera would bathe him and massage the day's kinks out of his muscles.

Eventually Blade's experiments got down to five, then four, then three different kinds of wood. He discarded one more because Meera said it was fantastically rare. This left him with two. He discovered that if he used a length of one kind, reinforced on each side with thin layers of the other, he had a basically good bow. Further reinforced with a wrapping of leaves, it came out with about an eighty-pound pull. That was the same as a heavy Home Dimension hunting bow or a good longbow. It was more than twice as powerful as any bow Blade had handled in this Dimension.

After finishing the bow he tried it out on several different targets, and saw it sink arrows deep into all of them. At last the Forest People would have a weapon able to hit the vital organs of a Treeman from a safe distance. The armor of the Sons of Hapanu made them a more difficult target, but Blade was also optimistic there. An arrow from an eighty-pound bow would inflict painful wounds through everything but the heaviest mail. With arrows raining down on them, some of the Sons of Hapanu would surely die and many would be wounded. That would break up their disciplined formations, then the Forest People could safely close in to finish the job with spears, clubs, and point-blank archery.

The new bows were still going to be hideously ugly, and even Meera said so. She also said, "The Forest People are going to be too happy with the new bows to worry about how they look. The Treemen are not wise enough to tell when a thing is ugly or not. The Sons of Hapanu are going to be too busy dying from the arrows to worry about how the bows look. So who is there to care?"

Blade now wanted to try out his idea for turning the Shield of Life into a powerful tranquilizer. With luck, it wouldn't matter whether the new bows pierced armor or not. Even if they only scratched a Son of Hapanu in the leg, he would soon be slowed down—and a man slowed down in the middle of a battle doesn't last very long.

This meant moving to a new camp. The *kohkol* sap for the Shield of Life didn't have to be fresh, but the uglyfish juice had to be. So Blade and Meera were going to have to sit down on the bank of a river and go fishing.

Blade made five more bows, one for himself, one for Meera, one spare, and two as gifts to Swebon and Guno. Then he and Meera plucked a sack of fruit as food for the journey, packed up their gear, and set off for the Fak'si River.

Chapter 13

Blade left behind in the shelter everything they weren't going to need by the river. Both he and Meera could now walk through the Forest like human beings instead of staggering along like pack mules, and they pushed south as fast as Meera could go. When they awoke on the morning of the fourth day, Meera saw water birds above the treetops. She told Blade that they would probably reach the river before nightfall.

The good news made Blade eager to move on. So they started off at once, eating the last of the fruit as they marched. By the time it was full daylight they were almost ready for their first rest stop. As always when they stopped, Blade walked back along the last hundred yards of their trail. He hoped to discover anyone or anything following them too closely. Twice he'd found the footprints of Treemen, and once he'd seen two of them leap into the trees and vanish.

This time Blade saw nothing until he'd nearly covered the hundred yards. Then he stopped abruptly, as his eyes picked out something moving fifty yards farther on into the Forest. It was a branch, but it was moving jerkily and irregularly, as no branch should—particularly when there wasn't enough wind blowing to even stir the leaves. Blade raised his club and spear, then moved toward the jerking branch a step at a time, prodding the vegetation ahead with the spear point as he went.

The moment he saw what was making the branch jerk, Blade went flat on the ground and started scanning the trees. It was a Fak'si hunter, one side of his face a mask of blood and his hands and feet bound crudely but effectively. Half-conscious, he was rolling back and forth. With each roll his shoulder caught the branch and made it jerk.

Treemen! That was Blade's first thought. Then he remembered that he'd never heard of the Treemen binding a victim. No one even knew if they could tie a knot. This man had to be the victim of human enemies. Or *was* he a victim? Blade examined the man more closely. Apart from the blood on his head, he showed no signs of any injury, not even a cut or a bruise.

It was just possible that an enemy raiding party could surprise a lone Fak'si warrior and take him prisoner without doing him much harm. It wasn't likely, though. Blade's thoughts moved on, steadily and grimly, from doubt to open suspicion.

Was this man bait? If he was, who'd put him out, and who was he supposed to trap?

As Blade asked himself these questions, he was studying the trees ahead again. This time he was expecting human silhouettes, and he found what he expected. Deep inside the branches of a squat, spreading tree, two men were waiting.

Now to turn the tables and ambush the ambushers. Blade got down on his belly, as flat to the ground as any snake. He crawled through the shrubbery, trying hard not to disturb a single leaf, until he had a clear shot at the men. He couldn't recognize them or even their tribe, but that didn't matter. It was hard to believe they were Fak'si, and if they were, there was only one reason for them to be here. They were on his trail, to put an end to him and all his plans for helping the Forest People. They were going to kill him in the name of the priests, or tradition, or the Forest Spirit, or plain simple fear.

It amused Blade to think that servants of the priests might be the first victims of the new bows they'd tried to prevent. He smiled, and was still smiling as he rose from cover, nocked an arrow to his bow, drew, and shot.

His sudden appearance made one of the men shout. Then the arrow struck and got a second shout that turned into a scream. Another scream, the sound of cracking branches and rustling leaves, and Blade's victim thudded to the ground. The arrow was deep in his side, and as he rolled about in agony the shaft snapped off.

As it did, the second man came cracking down through the branches, leaping wildly with weapons in both hands. Blade's second arrow whistled over his head, and Blade didn't have time to shoot again. He had to drop the bow, snatch up his spear and club, and meet the man's rush. It was Guno.

Guno's face was twisted with rage and desperation, and his attack was that of a madman. He came in recklessly, swinging wildly but so hard that Blade knew he couldn't let even one of Guno's blows connect. Blade gave ground and let Guno's first half dozen swings land in the air. Then suddenly he turned halfway around and took a few quick steps, as if he was starting to run off in fear. Guno's spear came up as he got set to throw. For just long enough, he was a stationary target. Blade wheeled, hurled his warclub with all his strength, then ducked. Guno flinched as the spear left his hand, and it flew harmlessly over Blade's head.

Guno's flinching didn't save him. The club's ironbound head smashed jaw and one cheek into bloody flesh and bone. Guno staggered, tried to scream, tried to raise his own club, then collapsed as Blade came up and struck him in the stomach with the butt of his spear.

Blade washed some of the blood off Guno's face with water from the gourd at his belt, then waited for the man to catch his breath enough to talk. Blade had a fairly good notion of what was in Guno's mind, but he badly wanted to know more. He and Meera might be out of immediate danger, but what about Swebon? Any plots aimed at Blade would sooner or later also strike at the chief.

Slowly Guno seemed to recover his wits, at least enough to glare up at Blade with the look of a trapped, furious animal. He said nothing, only clasping his shattered jaw with one hand, the blood slowly trickling between his fingers.

"Can you talk?" said Blade sharply.

Silence.

"If you want a clean death, Guno, you'd better talk. Your two friends can't help you, and I'm certainly not interested in keeping you alive. But there are different ways of dying." He pointed his spear toward Gino's loinguard. "Now—how did you come to follow me, and why?"

Blade had to rip off Guno's loinguard and draw blood with the spear before the man started talking. Then fear of dying like an animal instead of a warrior seemed to loosen his tongue. He was half-incoherent with rage, frustration, and pain, but with prompting from Blade's spear he told his story clearly enough.

One of the priests of the village saw Swebon collecting tools for Blade and guessed at least the most important parts of the chief's plans. He didn't dare challenge Swebon openly, since the chief was much too popular. Instead he went to Guno.

With two trusted comrades, Guno trailed Blade through the Forest to the first camp. He'd planned to attack Blade there, but then had second thoughts. It would be better to wait until Blade finished the work on the new bows, *then* kill him and Meera. After that he could hide the new bows and return with a tale that Treemen had killed Blade and Meera. No one would doubt him except Swebon, and with the help of the priest Swebon might disappear some night. Then Guno could retrieve the bows, claim them as his own invention, become chief of Four Springs village, and in time hope to rule all the Fak'si—and reward the priest.

Guno expected Blade and Meera to return straight to the village, and was planning to ambush them on the way. Instead they went off toward the river, and it took him a while to pick up their trail. He'd just caught up with them this morning, and Blade knew the rest.

Apparently the priest who'd put Guno on Blade's trail wasn't a simple-minded "Better the Fak'si die than the old ways change" man. He was a much more dangerous sort of opponent—a schemer who wanted to make sure that if the old ways changed, he would get part of the new honor and power.

Blade couldn't help wondering how long the alliance would have lasted. It made him think of an alliance between two rattlesnakes. It would probably have lasted just as long as neither man could figure out a reliable method of eliminating the other. Without Guno as an ally, the priest would be much less dangerous. But he would still be much too dangerous to leave alive in Four Springs village, free to seek new allies against Blade and Swebon.

"Who is your friend the priest?" asked Blade. "You cannot save him by silence. Swebon will cast down all the priests if he does not know which one, and—"

The sudden widening of Guno's eyes and the pad of feet on the grass behind him warned Blade with precious seconds to spare. Blade leaped aside as the man who'd been lying on the ground charged with a knife in one hand. The "binding" of his hands and feet had been as much of a trick as his "head injury."

As the man charged, Blade caught him in a judo hold and used the man's forward momentum to flip him head over heels. The man was lighter than Blade expected, flew higher, and came down head-first. His neck snapped with a sharp, dry sound and he sprawled with his head at an impossible angle to his shoulders. As he stopped twitching, Guno made a desperate leap for the weapons on the ground and came up holding a spear.

The weapon nearest to Blade was the dead man's fallen

knife. He snatched it up, dropped to one knee as Guno rushed in, and thrust upward. He'd meant only to disarm the man and drive him back, but Guno came on and suddenly Blade's knife was deep in his chest. The spear fell from limp hands, blood gushed out of a gaping mouth, and Guno toppled. The rest of his secrets were gone with him, but at least his ambitions and plots would never be a problem for anyone again.

Blade tried to wipe off some of Guno's blood with a handful of leaves, then walked over to the man he'd hit with the arrow. The arrow was in so deep that the man was already mercifully unconscious from loss of blood. Blade was bending over to give him a quick death when he heard Meera screaming in the distance.

"Blade! Treemen! Treemen! Help!"

Blade whirled, snatched up a spear with one hand and his bow with the other, and ran toward where he'd left Meera. The quiver bounced on his back as he plunged through the Forest at the speed of an Olympic sprinter. Speed was everything now—the Treemen had no way of ambushing him as he moved, but they could easily carry Meera off into the Forest. Then he'd have the nearly impossible task of trailing them.

Meera didn't scream again, but as Blade got closer he heard the sound of branches snapping and leaves rustling as bodies thrashed about. Then a Treeman bellowed, just as Blade burst into the open.

One Treeman was picking Meera up under his left arm. A second was guarding the first one's back, arms spread, teeth bared, apparently ready to fight the whole world. A third was lurching to his feet, face twisted in pain. Meera's spear jutted out of his belly. It wasn't in far enough to kill, but it must be slowing him badly. As Blade appeared, the Treeman reached down to pull the spear out, then froze with his hand on the shaft. The other two Treemen also froze where they stood.

The Treemen's surprise gave Blade all the time he needed. His arms were a blur as he nocked an arrow, drew, and shot the Treeman holding Meera. The arrow went deep into the Treeman's back. He staggered, dropped Meera, took two lurching steps forward, then fell and lay writhing.

As Meera hit the ground she rolled, gripped the shaft of the spear sticking out of the Treeman's belly, and pushed with all her strength. He weighed three times as much as she did but she caught him off-balance. He bent over backward and Meera leaned on the spear, driving it through him until the point dug into the ground. He howled, thrashed wildly, and tried to grab her, but she always managed to stay out of his reach without letting go of the spear.

The sudden attack on his two comrades kept the third Treeman too paralyzed to move. Blade nocked another arrow and put it squarely into his heart. As he hit the ground, the first Treeman Blade hit stopped writhing and lay still on the bloody grass. The Treeman with Meera's spear in his belly was still struggling, but more feebly with each moment. Blade walked over, gently pulled Meera away, then brought his club down on the dying Treeman's skull.

As the last Treeman went limp, Meera sank to her knees at Blade's feet, shaking all over. She pressed her face against him and threw both arms around his waist. As tenderly as if he'd been handling a child, Blade lifted Meera to her feet and held her against him until she stopped shaking. Finally her breathing slowed. She even managed to smile as she wiped her face and tied her clothes together as well as she could.

"Your new bow—it does what you promised!"

Blade nodded. "I was hoping for the best, but I'm surprised things turned out this well. I know how to make such bows easily enough with English woods, but the woods in your Forest are new to me. I couldn't have worked so fast or done so well without your help."

Blade told her about his battle with Guno. She listened, saying nothing but obviously not much surprised. Blade finished with, "Now let's collect the bodies and make things look right, in case anyone should come along this way. I don't want anyone to know this wasn't just another battle between hunters and Treemen."

The job of covering their tracks was long and bloody. The bodies of Guno and his men had to be brought to where the Treemen lay. Then all the wounds had to be altered with knife and spear until they looked normal. Finally all the bodies had to be arranged naturally, as if they'd fallen where they lay in the fighting.

By the time the job was done, Blade was covered from head to foot in blood and sweat. Meera told him he looked gruesome and smelled worse. Unfortunately the nearest water was the river, still a few hours away. The insects were already swarming around, impartially settling on Blade and the dead bodies. The only thing to do was move on as quickly as possible.

They started picking up their equipment. Most of it had

survived the fight, although the iron pot was cracked from being thrown against a rock. Blade thought he might be able to fix the pot, and if he couldn't there might be villages or hunting parties where he could find another.

"If I can't do anything else, I can always try hollowing out a section of log. I can fill it with what we want to boil, then heat stones over a fire and drop them into the liquid. I've seen it work with soup, so maybe it will work with the Shield of—"

Wssst-whunk! An arrow stood vibrating in the trunk of a tree a yard to Blade's right. It was short and thick, with a blue shaft and elaborately carved fins. Blade had never seen one, but he'd heard enough descriptions to know what he was seeing.

The Sons of Hapanu were within bowshot.

Blade's eyes met Meera's and he knew that she was thinking the same thing he was. *If we get deep into the Forest, we're safe. Otherwise—*

Blade didn't like turning his back and running from any opponent, but he liked even less fighting when he didn't know the odds. They turned, and as they did five more arrows hissed out of the trees. All of them flew low, at no more than knee height, and four of them missed. The fifth drove through Meera's left calf, making her jump and scream in surprise and pain. She went to her knees, and Blade turned to help her. *I'll have to carry her,* he thought, *and that will—*

Before he could complete the thought, armed soldiers of the Sons of Hapanu swarmed out of the trees. At first glance there seemed to be hundreds of them, and even at a second look there were at least forty. *Too many to fight,* said Blade's common sense, but Blade's fighting instincts weren't listening to his common sense. He and Meera couldn't hope to get away, so the only thing to do was kill as many of these bastards as possible before they went down themselves!

Blade hit the ranks of the Sons of Hapanu like a battering ram, so hard and so fast that he would have done damage if he'd been completely unarmed. As it was, he carried a spear in one hand and a club in the other, and he killed a man with each one in the first moment of the fight. Another man came at him now, shield up and sword thrusting. Blade struck the shield down with his club, crippled the man's sword arm with one spear thrust, then drove the spear into his throat. The man jerked so violently the spear was torn out of Blade's hands, then reeled away, dying on his feet. Blade tried to follow the man to retrieve his spear, found a soldier with elaborately-decorated armor in his path, and started fighting the man with club against sword.

The man's sword opened a gash along Blade's ribs as Blade's club came down on the man's shoulder. He dropped his sword, Blade raised the club to smash his skull, then what felt like half a dozen men tackled Blade around the legs. He went down on top of them, still lashing out with his fists as he fell, satisfied to feel his fists connect and hear men grunt and cry out.

Then there were more men looming over him, hoisting a stark-naked Meera into the air. She plunged down out of sight among the men and screamed as if she was being torn apart. Blade echoed her screams with a bull's roar, then something came crashing down on his skull. Blackness filled Blade's eyes, then his ears. Pain roared through him and tossed him like a wind. Then at last the blackness swallowed him.

Chapter 14

Blade came awake lying face-up on a prickly mat of some kind. Overhead the sky showed through a lacework of branches and leaves. Close by he could smell wood smoke and roasting meat, and a little farther off water plants and the mud of a river bank.

His head throbbed, his scalp itched, and his mouth was as dry and painful as if it were filled with thistles. He was bound hand and foot with lengths of chain fastened with heavy locks. He turned his head to get a better look at his captors and the world around him. Someone took two quick steps toward him, then a boot toe smashed into his temple. Someone else shouted in anger or surprise, and the boot came in a second time. Blade felt blood flowing from his scalp and suspected he'd lose consciousness if he was kicked a third time.

Then a man was looming over him—no, two men, one with his sword out, pointing it at the other's stomach while he held the man by the arm.

"Cha-Chern, get back, or Hapanu help me, I'll—"

"You and how many others?"

"Push me, and you may find out."

The man with the sword pointed at his stomach wore the same kind of elaborate armor as the man Blade had wounded. He seemed to consider the warning worth taking seriously. Slowly he backed out of Blade's sight, but the conversation went on.

"What's he to you, anyway?"

"Only my share of what we'll get for sending him to the Games, that's all. So keep away from him. That's an order."

"You can't—"

"I can. I just did, and I'll do it again. You may be one of the Protector's—people—but I've served much longer than you. Kra-Shad isn't going to be commanding again before we get home, so that leaves me over you. And if I get any more of your waving tongue about it, I'll have you tied up along with the prisoners."

The other voice—Cha-Chern's—came sneeringly. "So holy, and yet you had her along with all the rest of us."

"A woman is one thing," said the man with the sword, sheathing it briskly. "Getting us all home alive and unspeared is another. That's what I'm thinking about now. You'd do better to do the same."

"Oh, I will—for now." Blade heard receding footsteps, then the man who'd been defending him squatted down beside him. Blade saw a lean brown face with extraordinary gray eyes on either side of a beak-like nose. The face was heavily lined, and the hair falling over the scarred forehead was mostly gray.

"Do you need anything?" the man asked. He spoke the language of the Forest People, but with such a heavy accent that Blade would have understood him much better if he'd been speaking his native language. The computer's work on the language centers of his brain didn't always make allowances for accents and dialects!

"Water," said Blade. The gray-haired man nodded, reached out of Blade's sight, and brought up a bulging leather sack. He uncorked it, tilted it up, and let Blade drink until the thistles were washed out of his mouth.

"Thank you."

The man nodded, corked the sack, and stood up. "You go to the Games, I know. But even there—remember that you can choose to live or die. I think you are a man who will choose to live." Then he was gone.

If his head hadn't been aching too much, Blade would have laughed at the man's words. Not in derision, but because the man's words so closely matched his own thoughts on what came next. He was going to be a slave in Gerhaa, a gladiator in the Games of Hapanu. Gladiators were usually privileged slaves, with weapons in their hands. That wasn't a bad starting point for a man who could keep his wits about him. It would probably be enough to save Blade, and perhaps it would be enough to save Meera.

Meanwhile there was the gray-haired soldier, who was apparently willing to see that Blade reached the city and the Games alive. Now if the man could just be brought to do the same for Meera—

Blade didn't see Meera until the next morning, when they

were both being loaded into the slave raiders' canoes. He was awakened by two men, who shaved his head and washed the cuts in his scalp with something which stung painfully, then slapped on a rough bandage. After that his hands were unchained and he was fed a breakfast of coarse bean porridge with bits of salt meat and all the weak beer he could drink.

Then they chained his hands again, unchained his feet, and led him down to the canoes. As he sat down, he saw four soldiers coming down the bank, carrying Meera on a crude litter. He was shocked at her appearance. She was naked, and apart from the wound in her leg, her face, breasts, and thighs were swollen with bruising. At first Blade thought she was unconscious, then saw that she was simply half-numb with shock or fear. Her eyes stared blankly upward, and she didn't blink even when the bearers dropped one end of the litter. It was hard to believe from looking at her that she was still completely sane.

Blade didn't blame Meera. There could be no doubt what she'd been through yesterday—mass rape and probably a beating as well. It would be hard to save her, though, if she couldn't lift a finger to help herself. She might even be killed outright, if the slave raiders decided she wouldn't bring them enough money in the slave markets to be worth carrying to Gerhaa.

Blade could think of only one thing to do. He was going to have to speak to the gray-haired soldier, and ask to be allowed to care for Meera during the trip downriver. No doubt the man would then realize Blade cared for Meera, and that any threat to her would bring him under control. Blade refused to worry about that. He certainly wasn't going to abandon Meera without doing everything he could to save her. Any danger to himself was small, compared with the danger to her.

The gray-haired soldier didn't appear until the canoes were nearly loaded. Four soldiers appeared, carrying the officer with the smashed shoulder on another litter. The man was only half conscious. Behind him came a slim young man wearing an elegant and intricate outfit of dyed leather instead of armor. When he spoke to the bearers, Blade recognized the voice of Cha-Chern, the man who'd kicked him and quarreled with the gray-haired soldier.

The man Blade wanted brought up the rear. As he stopped to take a final look around, Blade raised his hands and rattled his chains loudly. "Captain! I have something to ask you."

The gray-haired man turned, hand on his sword hilt but apparently not angry. "Yes, slave?"

"The woman—the woman who was with me—" Blade pointed as well as he could.

"Your woman?"

"Yes."

"Not any more," interrupted Cha-Chern. "She goes to the—"

"Cha-Chern, you will be silent," said the gray-haired man, drawing his sword. "Your woman goes to the Happy Houses. Surely you know this?"

"Yes, but—can you not allow us these last few days . . . ?"

Cha-Chern opened his mouth, then shut it as a gesture from the other allowed Blade to continue. "Captains—consider that if she does not heal, you get only a poor price for her. You may get none at all. If she and I have these last few days together . . . "

Blade spoke in the language of the Forest People, although it required a conscious effort to avoid slipping into the language of the Sons of Hapanu. However, neither officer seemed to suspect he was anything unusal, in spite of his pale skin. Speaking to them fluently in their own language would be sure to arouse those suspicions and make his situation and Meera's more difficult, perhaps more dangerous.

He was also letting a whine creep into his voice, the whine of a slave willing to beg. Blade hoped it was convincing, and that the officers would agree before the disgust rising inside him spoiled the act. He wouldn't have done this beggar's act for himself, not in a hundred years. But if it would help save Meera, he'd try it.

Both officers were silent for so long that Blade almost gave up hope. Then the gray-haired one nodded. "Yes, Cha-Chern, I think the slave has wisdom. If the woman is sold as she is, the Happy Houses won't pay us nearly what she's worth. I can tell when a woman has promise, and she has much. So I say let him have her as he wishes, until we reach Gerhaa."

"But, Ho-Marn—" began Cha-Chern, then stopped as the other's sword twitched.

"It shall be done," said Ho-Marn, sheathing his sword and turning his back on Cha-Chern. He scrambled down the bank toward the canoe, leaving the younger officer to run after him. Blade fought not to laugh. He also fought to keep an expression of humble gratitude on his face. That wasn't easy, when what he really wanted to do was pick up Cha-Chern and throw him into the river, fancy leather outfit and all.

The trip downriver was always high on Blade's private list of Experiences I Wouldn't Repeat for a Million Pounds. Fortunately it gave Meera time to slowly return to something like health and sanity.

Blade never knew whether it was his care, Meera's natural toughness, or simply the passage of time that healed her. It was probably some of each. By the time they'd been on the river five days, Meera began to recover her health and spirits. The bruises were fading, the leg wound was healing without any complications, the aches in her joints no longer kept her awake at night, and even the nightmares no longer woke her screaming.

"I cannot forget," she whispered one night. "I will not forget. I do not want to forget until I have killed Cha-Chern with my own hands. After that I may forget. For now, I will do anything you say must be done."

Blade kissed her gently and held her for a moment in silence. That was all he could do without the guards noticing and Cha-Chern making lewd jokes. In that case Blade didn't completely trust himself to keep his own hands off Cha-Chern's throat.

Cha-Chern not only made lewd jokes, he caressed Meera and struck Blade whenever he thought Ho-Marn wasn't looking. That wasn't too often, as Ho-Marn was the kind of officer who seemed to be in about six places at once. When Cha-Chern did get his opportunities, the other soldiers who saw him said nothing. Cha-Chern was an officer of the Protector's Guard, whatever that was, and this seemed to make everybody but Ho-Marn afraid of him.

From overhearing the talk of the soldiers, Blade was able to reconstruct the events leading up to Meera's and his capture. The soldiers were part of a raiding expedition coming up the Fak'si River from a temporary base at the point where the Yellow River flowed into the Great River. They'd been stopping to repair some leaky canoes when they heard the sound of the fight against the Treemen in the distance.

In the hope of capturing the survivors of the fight, the soldiers promptly set off in the direction of the noise. They arrived just in time to capture Blade and Meera. The bodies lying around and the fight Blade put up convinced them that a large party of Forest People was close at hand. There would be no slaves to be taken along this stretch of the Fak'si River this time, at least not without a savage fight. So the raiders were now on their way home, almost empty-handed.

Blade got a grim laugh out of this story. If he and Meera hadn't stayed around to arrange the bodies naturally, they would have been gone before the Sons of Hapanu arrived. On the other hand, by arranging the bodies they'd prevented the Sons of Hapanu from carrying out a slave raid and perhaps killing or carrying off many of the Forest People. Blade and Meera's bad luck had been good luck for others.

As far as Blade could tell, none of the soldiers had noticed the new laminated bows. Hopefully these were still a secret. If Blade or Meera could escape, they might still be an unpleasant surprise to the Sons of Hapanu.

The raiders paddled down the Fak'si River and then the Yellow for six days before reaching their base camp. Meera's face set into a grim mask when she saw the camp. It had the look of an American frontier fort, with log walls, solid huts and barracks, and a fleet of canoes and small sailing ships.

"The Sons of Hapanu grow bold, and think we in the Forest grow weak. They have never built so strongly this far up-river. The raids we have seen before now will be nothing to what we shall see when they raid from this place." If looks could have started fires, Meera's expression would have burned the enemy camp to the ground.

As the canoes approached the camp, Ho-Marn squatted down beside Blade for a few private words. "It would be best that you and your woman do as the other slaves do now. Otherwise, you will attract the notice of the Protector's men. Here I can no longer guard you from them."

"It shall be as you wish." He still wanted to know who the Protector was, but this wasn't the time to ask. If most of the Protector's men were like Cha-Chern, it was certainly best to play things safe.

"Good. If I do not have to risk myself against the Protector's men, I can do much for you later. I can see that you go at once to the Games. I can also see that your woman goes to a Happy House where there are women of the Forest like her."

Again Blade nodded. Sending Meera to a brothel would be an unpleasant business at best, but if she went to one where some of the other women were Forest People, she would at least find it easier to stay alive and sane.

There might be a catch, of course. For a slave there usually

111

was. He didn't know why Ho-Marn was offering this protection, or whether the man could be trusted. He did know that without Ho-Marn's protection he and Meera would be very badly off indeed, so they had practically nothing to lose by trusting the officer, at least for now.

When they reached the camp, Blade and Meera were separated. Meera was led off to what seemed to be the camp kitchen, while Blade was taken to a low-ceilinged, reeking barracks and chained to the wall. He stayed there for ten days, except for two hours each day when he was taken outside for a meal and exercise. He kept his eyes and ears open while he was out, and he also spent a good deal of time watching and listening at the chinks in the wall of the barracks.

There were about three hundred men in the camp. Raiding parties went upriver and convoys with captured slaves or men returning to Gerhaa went downriver at regular intervals. Otherwise the men seldom left the camp, and most of them drank, gambled, or quarreled to fight off boredom.

Many of the quarrels were between what appeared to be the regular soldiers such as Ho-Marn and the Protector's Guards such as Cha-Chern. The Protector's Guard seemed to be an elite military force under the direct orders of the Protector of Gerhaa. Their officers all wore leather outfits like Cha-Chern's, and even the common soldiers had enameled mail shirts and swords with gilded hilts.

In spite of their privileges and fancy equipment, Blade wasn't impressed by the "Protector's Pets." Their weapons were dirty, their discipline was poor, many of their officers were usually drunk, and the rest seemed to spend half their time perfuming their hair and applying cosmetics. Blade heard it said that the best way to become an officer in the Guard was by sleeping with the Protector.

The hostility between the Guardsmen and the regulars was as thick in the camp as the smell of the river. Blade realized that here was a weakness in the apparently invincible Stone Village of the Sons of Hapanu. So far the two factions of the city's defenders had been willing to stand together against the Forest People. Could that be changed?

Perhaps. And even if it couldn't, the rivalry might increase Blade's and Meera's chances for survival and escape. Ho-Marn had been willing to let Blade and Meera be together simply to annoy Cha-Chern. Other regular officers might be willing to do even more.

On the eleventh day, Blade and Meera were chained with

forty other slaves and loaded aboard a small sailing ship. It had two masts with lateen sails, a long bowsprit, a high castle on the stern, and twelve long sweeps on each side.

Amidships was a stinking black hold, and in that hold Blade and Meera sailed down the Great River to Gerhaa, the Stone Village of the Sons of Hapanu.

Chapter 15

Blade expected that the Forest People's tales exaggerated Gerhaa's size and strength. After all, they weren't used to cities, fortresses, or stone walls. He found that they hadn't exaggerated very much. The city was at least a mile on a side, its gray stone walls studded with towers and each tower mounting a huge catapult. On the land side, the walls rose thirty feet above a twenty-foot ditch. On the river side the walls were only half as high, but below them rocky cliffs dropped almost vertically fifty feet to the river. There were cranes and pulleys on the walls for hauling up heavy cargo from the quays along the river, and in three places winding wooden stairs. Otherwise there was no way up the cliffs.

The slave ship furled her sails at the entrance to the harbor and came in under her sweeps. The harbor lay along the city's southern side, between the bank of the Great River and a long narrow island. The island was not only narrow, it was so low that at high tide or during the spring floods it was hardly more than a chain of sandbanks. Most of the time it protected the harbor from both the current of the Great River and storms coming up from the sea. Three stone forts, perched on the highest points of the island, kept the Forest People's canoes from slipping in through the channels at high water and raiding shipping in the harbor.

Inside the harbor at least two dozen sailing ships lay at anchor or tied up to the quays. Dozens of small boats scooted about like irritated waterbugs, carrying people and freight. At each end of the island a galley packed with archers lay at anchor, checking ships in and out.

Blade's ship anchored in the middle of the harbor and a large flat-bottomed barge came alongside. The slaves were loaded into it and rowed to the nearest quay. From there they were marched up one of the flights of stairs to a gate in the wall.

Inside Gerhaa Blade and Meera were driven at a trot

through streets as dark and narrow as alleys, their ankle chains scraping on pavements crusted with garbage and filth. Gerhaa didn't seem nearly so impressive from the inside, and it smelled far worse. No doubt Gerhaa had to be crowded together this way. Without those stone walls the Forest People or even the Treemen could easily become a menace, and those walls would not be cheap or easy to build. Still, it was easy for Blade to see that while the city might easily be defended as long as its walls were intact, after that matters could easily take a very different course.

At the iron-gated entrance to a massive stone building, the slave chain was split up. Meera and the other women were led off one way, Blade and the men another. The gate opened with a squeal, then closed with a clang. Blade was alone, a slave in Gerhaa at the mercy of the Sons of Hapanu.

Actually no man is ever at the mercy of another, even when he's a slave, as long as he keeps his strength and his wits. At the very worst, he can always force those who call themselves his masters to kill him, rather than submit to something intolerable.

The stone-walled chamber where Blade and fifty other male slaves lay was so far underground that it was impossible to tell day from night. It was damp and the stones were slimy to the touch, but otherwise it was clean, almost free of rats and lice, and heated by a charcoal brazier. There were tubs for water and human wastes, and plenty of porridge and salt meat twice a day. Once each day the slaves were unchained from the walls, led into another chamber, and forced to exercise for an hour. Then they were rubbed down with warm oil and led back to their prison.

A third of Blade's fellow slaves were Forest People. The rest were apparently Sons of Hapanu or other races from across the ocean. Most were tall and all looked tough and robust. Some had impressive displays of scars and missing fingers or even missing eyes. This was obviously a roomful of men intended for the Games of Hapanu, and their strength had to be preserved. The keepers were quick enough to deal with anyone who rebelled openly, but otherwise left their charges alone.

The men of the Forest People mostly seemed too stunned to do more than go through the motions of living. Except for one or two who'd apparently been slaves for a while, they sat staring at nothing, seldom speaking. The Sons of Hapanu talked more. Some talked of drinking, women, fights, and what they'd like to do to the guards or soldiers. Others talked of homes, families, what they'd seen in Gerhaa, or what crimes they'd committed. Among them, they said more than enough to give Blade a rough picture of the people called the Sons of Hapanu.

Gerhaa was a colony of the Empire of Kylan. In fact, it was mostly settled and maintained by the nobles and merchants of one city, Mashom-Gad. They were the boldest explorers and adventurers in Kylan, the first to take their ships out across the ocean and reach the lands of the Forest and the Great River. The first settlement was small, but then the firestone was discovered. The priests of Hapanu decided that the god's worship demanded a steady supply of it. From that moment Gerhaa's prosperity was secure, as the leaders of Mashom-Gad bribed the Emperor to give them a monopoly of importing the precious Blood of Hapanu. Every temple in Kylan needed the jewels, and all the nobles and merchants also demanded them.

So Gerhaa grew, and as it grew it acquired its own class of nobles and wealthy merchants, with time and money to indulge their vices. The most popular of these vices was the Games of Hapanu—gladiatorial combats that would have made any ancient Roman feel right at home. Apparently these Games were far more popular in Gerhaa than at home in Kylan. The slave merchants of Gerhaa always bid high for condemned criminals and others sentenced to the Games, and even then they couldn't get enough men.

So the slave raiders began their work among the Forest People. It was so longer a case of simply bringing back any men or women captured while digging the Blood of Hapanu from the river bottoms. It was systematic raiding to supply the Games and the brothels of Gerhaa.

About five years ago a new ruler came to Gerhaa. His official title was "Protector of the City," but more and more he protected only those willing to join or at least support his faction. The Protector's Guard were almost openly a private army, obeying only their master's orders, recruited from anyone who would join. They weren't completely useless in battle, but they were certainly no match for the regular soldiers of the Imperial garrison. Much of their fighting was against their fellow soldiers or even against their fellow citizens. One of the men in the room with Blade was there because he'd attacked two Guardsmen. They'd been carrying off one of his sons for their officer's amusement.

116

The Protector himself was a young nobleman from Mashom-Gad, apparently less than thirty years old. But he had vices and viciousness enough for ten men twice his age. His homosexuality was the most respectable of them. At the same time he was shrewd in choosing friends and allies and open-handed in rewarding them. He also had the support of his powerful family and their allies among the nobles of Mashom-Gad and elsewhere in Kylan. So he was in a position where he could do more or less as he pleased. ,

"The only way we'll get rid of him is if he drops dead going at it with one of his pretty-boys," said one of Blade's fellow slaves. "And the bastard's young yet. We could have him forty more years." He spat on the floor at the idea.

One thing the Protector did with his Guard was to increase the slave raids. They went out more often, went farther, and burned villages as well as bringing back Forest People. No one knew for sure why the Protector was doing this, although there were a few guesses, most of them obscene.

Blade didn't bother guessing about the Protector's motives. They weren't important, compared to what he now knew for sure. There was more than narrow streets and foul smells hiding behind the stone walls of Gerhaa. There was a city full of intrigue, perhaps ready to explode into civil war if the right man gave it a well-timed push in the right direction.

Blade also knew that for the time being both he and Meera were in the power of an able, ruthless, thoroughly evil, and deadly dangerous man. It was just as well he knew this, because after about a week in the prison Blade was brought before the Protector of Gerhaa.

Chapter 16

The guards who came to take Blade to the Protector's palace were two regular soldiers and two Guardsmen. They hustled him up the stairs as if hungry wolves were chasing them and broke into a trot once they reached the street.

After the first few corners the Guardsmen began to pant, then they started to slow down. As they did, the regular soldiers seemed to catch their second wind. Their muscle-corded, tanned legs pounded as steadily as the pistons of an engine. It amused Blade to keep up with them easily, and it amused both him and the soldiers to see the Guardsmen struggling more and more desperately to keep up. By the time they'd reached the palace, halfway across the city, the two Guardsmen were gasping and coughing like a couple of tuberculosis patients. The two soldiers couldn't help winking at Blade as they turned him over to the Guardsmen at the palace, and he trusted them enough to wink back.

The Guardsmen who took charge of Blade obviously resented that little victory over their comrades. For a moment they looked at him so fiercely he was afraid they were going to take out their resentment on him. Before they could move two officers appeared at the top of the stairs and called them off.

One of the officers was Cha-Chern. He looked Blade up asd down with what could only be called a leer on his face as they climbed the stairs. "The Protector may indeed find you interesting, barbarian. You would not be to my taste, but our master's tastes are not mine."

Blade was happy he didn't have to reply to Cha-Chern's remarks. Then they reached the top of the stairs, the bronze doors of the palace swung open, and for a moment he couldn't have replied even if he'd wanted to. The spectacle of the palace was too staggering.

Beyond the door was a room five stories high, with a balcony across the rear, stairs curving up to each end of the

balcony, and a quadruple archway under the balcony. Everything was on a colossal scale, dwarfing human beings to the
size of ants.

It wasn't just a matter of sheer size, either. As Blade stud-
ied the room, he couldn't find a single square inch of wall or
floor that wasn't decorated. The floor was inlaid with marble
and other polished stones, separated by silvered metal bands.
The columns of the arches were carved from something like
blue jade into the forms of Horned Ones, birds, and snakes.
Each step of the stairs was made of a different kind of stone,
except for a few made of carved and polished wood. The
railings of the stairs and the balcony were complicated metal
lattice-work, all enameled or gilded. Everywhere Blade saw
Blood of Hapanu, some faceted stones the size of a man's
fist, others as fine as dust.

The walls were covered to twice the height of a man with
paintings and mosaics. Some were landscapes or river or
forest, others were abstract, but most were the most explicit
erotic scenes Blade had ever seen. Absolutely nothing was
left to the imagination. Every possible act that men, women,
and animals could do with or to one another was set down
in loving detail.

Along the walls stood more of the Protector's Pets, the
leather of the officers brilliantly dyed and tooled and the
armor of the men silvered. There were also a few servants
scuttling back and forth, as nervous as mice passing under the
noses of cats. None of the servants wore anything except
makeup and heavy perfume. More perfumes floated out into
the chamber, so overpowering that Blade was fighting not to
cough.

The only thing in the whole chamber that wasn't part of the
display was the ceiling. That was plain stone, painted or
whitewashed to a pale ivory color. Blade found it a relief to
look upward and rest his eyes and brain with the ceiling. Then
his escorts prodded him toward the stairs. He went up them,
his escort falling back as he approached the top. In a chair of
plain white wood in the middle of the balcony sat the Protector of Gerhaa.

Blade stopped as the Protector's eyes met his, then examined the man. The ruler of Gerhaa looked hardly more than a
boy, except for his eyes. They were large, dark, luminous, and
full of hints of more knowledge than any three sane men ought
to have. Otherwise the Protector was short and not particularly handsome, although well-muscled. He wore only knee-

length breeches embroidered with gold and a belt with a curved sword, and his skin shone with scented oil. He'd shaved the top of his skull and let the hair on the sides of his head grow down into long trailing sideburns, stiff with grease and heavily scented.

Across his lap rested a truly awe-inspiring badge of office —a staff four feet long, with a gold shaft and silver tips. The gold and silver were both almost hidden, though, under masses of Blood of Hapanu, forming swirling patterns up and down the shaft. At each end the silver flared into a mounting for a stone nearly the size of a hen's egg.

The Protector rose gracefully, putting his staff aside. Liquid fire seemed to flow up and down it as the light danced along the stones. The man beckoned to Blade. "Come to me, my fine barbarian friend." Blade took one stiff step forward and stopped. The Protector laughed. "I said—*come.* To those I call friend, I give pleasure, not pain. May I hope to call you friend?"

The voice was low, smooth, and polite. To someone who wasn't looking at the Protector, it would have sounded like the voice of a civilized man making a reasonable offer. To Blade that voice completed the picture of the Protector he'd started building when he saw the man's eyes. He had to force himself not to take a step backward and raise his fists. This man was *unclean,* from head to foot and from his oily skin inward to whatever lay at the heart of him. It wasn't just his sexual vices—they were probably the least important thing about him. It was everything about him—more than Blade could have found words to describe.

The Protector sensed Blade's hesitation. He came toward the Englishman, cooing like a dove, hand outstretched to pat Blade comfortingly. Then abruptly he stopped, fingers inches from Blade's skin, as if a bear trap had closed on his leg. He'd seen the look in Blade's eyes and read their message.

If you touch me, you will die. Nothing you can do will stop me. Whatever you use for brains will be splattered all over your expensive interior decorating.

The Protector of Gerhaa had more than his share of bad habits, but stupidity wasn't one of them. He sensed that the man facing him was ready and able to kill him bare-handed, even if he died in the process. The Protector also sensed that even if he avoided a confrontation now, he'd never be safe or at ease with this man loose in the palace, or indeed

120

within a hundred yards of him. There were other things to be sought beside pleasure.

So the Protector's hand froze in midair. Then he slowly lowered his arm and turned his head without stepping back. "Heh! Take him away. He is magnificent, but I should not be selfish. He will do as well in the Games, and then all can enjoy him." Then he shrugged and sighed elegantly, as the two Guard officers came up the stairs to lead Blade away.

After the diseased decadence of the Protector's palace, the underground barracks of the gladiators in the Games of Hapanu came as a positive relief to Blade.

The barracks were a series of caves and tunnels far underground, on the west side of the city. More tunnels led from the barracks out to the Island of Death, where the Games of Hapanu took place every ten days, as well as on the various sacred holidays and every day during the week of the High Feast of Hapanu. This added up to about forty rounds of Games during the standard Kylanan year, more than enough to demand a steady flow of gladiators. Some of the fights were to the death, and even those that weren't often left men crippled for life or disabled for months at a time.

The tunnels to the Island of Death were the only way out of the barracks for the thousand-odd gladiators there. The stairs up to the city twisted and wound, with iron doors locked from the outside at several points. Even if by some chance all the doors could be broken down or unlocked, ten men could hold the stairs against an army. In fact there were only four armed men on regular duty in the guardhouse at the head of the stairs. That would be enough to call for help from the soldiers' barracks three streets away, then hold the head of the stairs until that help arrived.

There was a good reason for locking up the gladiators of the Games. A fifth of the thousand were usually beginners, too frightened to be rebellious and often too inexperienced to be dangerous. The rest were among the toughest fighting men Blade had ever seen in any Dimension. Most of them could use almost any edged or pointed weapon with either hand, and feared neither guards, soldiers, the Protector, nor Hapanu himself. Left where they had any chance at all of breaking loose, these men would be trying it once a week.

For the same reason that the gladiators were locked below ground, they were left very much on their own. Food, equipment, medical supplies, and prostitutes for their amusement were lowered down a shaft on ropes. Their water came from two springs in the rocks, and their wastes and dead bodies were dropped down another shaft leading to the Great River. They cared for their own sick and wounded, kept their own discipline, punished their own criminals, and generally behaved more like a small town or a ship's crew than a band of cutthroats. Guards seldom entered the barracks, and when they did they came down forty strong.

"Makes sense, the way everybody sees it," said the man who explained the situation to Blade. He was a one-eyed, bald, and horribly scarred veteran called Old Skroga. He'd been the chief of one of the tribes on the far eastern frontier of Kylan, captured in a border skirmish and sent here to Gerhaa because he was too likely to escape from anywhere on the other side of the ocean. He'd won more than two hundred fights, killed twelve opponents, and been wounded fifteen times himself. There was obviously very little he didn't know about the Games of Hapanu or the men who fought in them. Just as obviously, he wasn't telling Blade everything he knew.

"They try to keep soldiers down here, they'd lose five a week at least," he went on. "We'd lose more, so many we'd give them no fun upstairs before long. So they leave us be and we give them no reason not to."

"What about matching men against each other in the Games?" asked Blade. "Can they afford to leave that to you?"

Skroga looked sharply at Blade. "You see enough, but maybe say too much about what you see. But you see true now. We fight how they say and who, but they don't say 'Fight to the death!' much. When they do, they don't see what they want, and then they change. Why you think so many of us still live and fight after ten years?"

Blade returned Skroga's look. "That's exactly why I thought there must be some agreement about how you fight. I do see enough, most of the time. That's why *I'm* still alive and fighting." He didn't make his tone an open challenge to Skroga, only a firm reminder that he should be taken seriously.

In fact, Blade didn't have much trouble being taken seriously from the first, and even treated with some respect. His size, build, and scars hinted that he was a fighting man. His first few practice bouts with the gladiators chosen to break in new men proved it. They used wooden swords and untipped spears, but in spite of this and in spite of pulling his blows, Blade put two of his four opponents out of action with broken bones.

That attracted a good deal of notice. His fight with Skroga attracted even more. The old man was slowing down a bit, but his experience more than made up for it. Blade found himself having to use all his strength, speed, and skill to hold his own against Skroga. The fight lasted more than half an hour, without either man collecting more than a few bruises, and eventually it was Skroga who called a halt to it.

That fight was enough to mark Blade among the gladiators as a man to watch. They began to stand him drinks, invite him to join them for meals, advise him on the tricks of possible opponents and how to have his weapons custom-built for him when he could afford it.

They were also intrigued by his story. A man who was neither of Kylan nor of the Forest People, but an *Englishman* from beyond the known world, was hard to understand. It was even harder to understand how he'd come to be such a skilled fighter and so iron-nerved that he faced the prospect of the Games with no visible fear. Some said he must be mad, but Blade used his fists on one or two who said this too loudly or too often. After that, most said he must have been not only a warrior but a chief among the English.

Many of the gladiators from the Forest People had heard of Swebon, and they were particularly ready to think well of Blade. As one man put it:

"In all the Forest and among all the People, Swebon is known as a man who thinks each thought three times before he acts. If this Blade is indeed a sworn friend of Swebon, a good man has come to us."

The speaker was a lean, undersized Banum named Kuka, with the middle finger of his left hand missing and a ghastly scar down his right leg. Blade learned that he came from a village the Fak'si once raided under Swebon's leadership.

"It was then that I lost the finger," he added. "I wish I could say that I lost it to Swebon, but I did not. I was running to join the battle when I tripped over a root and fell. The finger was broken, then began to rot, so the priests cut it off." He seemed more amused at his own clumsiness than anything else.

There was another attitude Blade found among the gladiators after he'd been accepted among them. They were all one band. It did not matter what a fighter had been before he came to Gerhaa, whether Forest People or Kylanan. It didn't matter what tribe of the Forest People he'd belonged to. It didn't even matter what crime he'd committed, if he was a criminal. He was accepted or rejected for what he did as a fighter in the Games of Hapanu, and for nothing else.

To be sure, the Ten Brothers, the informal committee for governing the barracks, had more Kylanans than Forest People on it. That was inevitable, as Kuka himself said.

"Many of those who come to us from the Forest think only that they will die. They do not think how they may live. So they do die, and many of them soon." Kuka gave Blade a sharp, appraising stare. "I think you will live to become one of the Ten Brothers, unless the Forest Spirit is unjust."

"I will rely more on my strength and good steel than on the Forest Spirit," said Blade.

"As you should," said Kuka, and patted Blade's hair.

Once more the notion of the gladiators of Hapanu as the crew of a ship occurred to Blade. They were men apart, cut off from the outside world, able to depend only on each other, living or dying without anyone's caring as long as they put on a good show. They were a *good* crew, proud, skilled, and tough in spite of the inevitable handful of bad apples.

They were also a crew without a captain, apart from the Ten Brothers and Skroga. There was no one who could lead them in one particular direction. If such a leader emerged, what might happen with a thousand tough fighters all ready to march?

Quite a lot, Blade suspected. However, before he could hope to offer himself as that leader, he would have to gain a name for himself. That meant not just surviving but winning in the Games of Hapanu.

Chapter 17

The day of Blade's first appearance in the Games dawned bright, warm, and windy. From his bench in the waiting room at the outer end of the tunnel, Blade could see the steady march of white clouds across a blue sky and feel the breeze on his skin. It carried the sea-smell of the brackish water at the mouth of the Great River.

The sunlight and the sea-smell were things about Gerhaa Blade could enjoy. He hadn't realized until he left the Forest how tired he'd become of the greenish tinge to the sunlight, the windless heat under the trees, the odors of vegetation, decay, and sluggish streams. Gerhaa was a welcome contrast. It would have been positively lovely, if he hadn't been about to fight for his life to amuse its decadent people and worse-than-decadent ruler.

The waiting room was long and low. On benches along either side sat fifty-odd gladiators. All wore open-faced helmets, leather loinguards, ankle-high boots, and leather wrist braces. The weapons were more varied. Blade saw broadswords, short swords, clubs and maces, daggers, throwing and thrusting spears, weighted nets and ropes, things like pitchforks with barbed points and heavy crossbars, and things like golf clubs with oversized heads and spikes on both ends of the shaft. A few of the men carried shields of bronze-sheathed wood, with razor-sharp edges and spikes jutting out of the heavy iron bosses in the middle. Blade had seldom seen such an impressive collection of weaponry in the hands of men who looked so fit and ready to use it.

Down the middle of the room ran a line of well-made litters. By the head of each litter sat two of the men told off by lot to act as litter-bearers and first-aid men in today's Games. Each had a leather pouch slung across his back, holding bandages and medicines. The medical care the fighters in the Games received was definitely on the rough and ready side, as not only the first-aid men but the "doctors" were entirely self-taught. However, they got plenty of practice, and they had to learn fast. If they didn't, they were likely to die in their next fight or even in a "brawl" in the barracks. Blade hadn't seen anything like the Shield of Life in Gerhaa, but he was reasonably confident of receiving decent medical care if he had the bad luck to be wounded.

From beyond the mouth of the tunnel Blade heard the swelling rumble and murmur of the crowd as it gathered in the amphitheater overhead. Women's voices rose high and shrill, vendors praised their fruit, wine, and sweet cakes, pet dogs and monkeys barked and squealed. Just as the din seemed to be getting out of hand, a drum began to roll. Then horns sounded and two huge brass gongs began to boom.

No words were needed. Except for Blade, all the men in the room had gone through the ritual many times, and Blade had heard it described until he could have done it all in his sleep. They marched out of the waiting room, onto a wooden draw-bridge forty feet long and thirty feet above the water. Underneath two boats full of soldiers rowed back and forth, and Blade saw Ho-Marn sitting in the stern of one. The officer recognized him and called out cheerfully, "Good blooding, Englishman."

"As Hapanu wills it," Blade shouted back. It was a ritual response to a ritual good wish, but then Ho-Marn could hardly do or say anything for Blade here that would call attention to himself.

Blade looked over his shoulder at the amphitheater. Not quite a full house—no more than half of the ten thousand seats were filled. A good crowd, though, for a Game where the Protector wasn't attending. The nobles' seats at the front of the great bowl carved into the side of the cliff were almost filled. Blade saw ranks of colored silks and velvets, veils and scarves floating in the breeze, noticed the sun winking from brooches and jeweled rings, could almost smell the heavy perfumes. The only thing the noblemen of Gerhaa spent more money on than their own vices was the vices of their wives and mistresses.

The gladiators carefully avoided keeping in step as they crossed the bridge. This was a point of pride with them, for each man to march at his own pace. It showed they were not the soldiers, let alone the Protector's Pets!

At the other end of the bridge a flight of stone steps led down to the sandy arena covering most of the Island of Death. A low fence of pointed iron stakes surrounded the sand. It did not block the spectators' view of the blood and death on the Island, but it kept gladiators from falling into the water lapping around the Island.

In the water lay a more certain death than any a man could face in the arena. The waters of the Great River around Gerhaa swarmed with hungry life—a variety of Horned One, sea snakes, giant eels, things like sharks and barracuda, dozens of kinds of smaller creatures with large appetites. Anyone who found himself in the water would die quickly if he was lucky.

As the last man reached the arena, the drawbridge rose with a clatter of chains and a creak of timbers. The cheers of the crowd drowned out the drumrolls and horn blasts. Blade looked across the arena as the gladiators spread out along the railing. The trampled yellow sand was beginning to blaze like a pool of molten gold as the sun grew brighter. Out there on the hundred-yard circle lay the only way back across the drawbridge for every man now standing by the railing. Some would return on their feet and others on the litters, to live or die as their wounds and their comrades' skill dictated. Those whose lives ended on the sand would not return at all. They would still be lying on the sand when darkness came. Then the Horned Ones would also come, slithering and snuffling through the gaps left in the fence just for them. When they slipped back into the water, the bodies would be gone.

The whole system of the Games in Gerhaa and the Island of Death was an ugly one, reeking of a sadistic imagination. No doubt it was supposed to fill the gladiators with terror and a degrading sense of being doomed and helpless. In fact, it only gave the gladiators an even stronger sense of being men apart, standing together against that doom, only able to trust one another. Blade wondered how long it would be before someone outside the fighters' barracks discovered what a deadly thing the people of Gerhaa had created in the pursuit of their own amusement.

The Captain of the Games was always an experienced fighter, often one of the Ten Brothers. Today the Captain was Kuka of the Banum. He was assisted by two Lesser Captains and the Crier of the Games. The Crier was always chosen for his loud voice, and was given a large gold-mounted seashell both as a badge of office and a sort of megaphone. He was supposed to be heard in the most distant seats of the amphitheater and usually was.

127

Kuka marched out into the center of the arena while the Crier climbed back up the stairs and announced the first fight. "Three on three, with casting spear, short sword, and shield. Wearing the red—" three names Blade didn't catch. "Wearing the green—" three more names, the last one producing a mixture of cheers and boos. There was a short pause as the six fighters marched out onto the sand. Kuka stepped back, and the last bets were made in the audience. Then Kuka raised his spear of office and the fight began.

After a short time Blade stopped paying much attention to it. The six men were all well-matched, past the beginner stage but none of them real experts. One of the men wearing green seemed to be fond of tricky swordwork. No doubt he was the one who'd been cheered and booed by the crowd. He was spectacular to watch, but Blade suspected the man would soon be crippled or dead if his skill didn't catch up with his desire to show off.

The first fight of the Games was seldom more than a warming-up for later, bloodier events. When it was over, four of the six fighters walked out of the arena on their own feet. Neither of the two who came out on litters was dangerously hurt.

Two more fights went by without any spectacular bloodshed, and Blade began to expect trouble. His fight was the next but one, and he could hear the rumble of the crowd growing behind him. They were beginning to want a little gore and guts on the sand. If they didn't get it before he came on, they might be howling for his.

Blade was lucky, although his good luck was bad luck for one of the men in the fight before him. The unlucky man took a sword cut across the thigh, thought his manhood was gone, and suddenly went berserk. The other three fighters had to turn against him and almost hack him to pieces before he died. The yells of the crowd showed that their taste for blood was satisfied for the moment.

Blade still felt five thousand pairs of eyes riveted on his back as he marched out into the arena to face his first opponent. He'd have more than his share of the attention, too. A new fighter making his debut was always matched in single combat.

Blade's opponent was a Kylanan peasant sold to the Games for debt. He was as strong as an ox and not much smaller than one, but still fast enough on his feet to be a thoroughly dangerous opponent. If Blade hadn't already known this, he would have learned it with the man's first swordcut. It came at him like a flash of lightning, and there were more flashes in front of his eyes as the sword clanged off his helmet.

The other man stepped back to give Blade a chance to recover. This wasn't a fight that had to end in blood. Blade listened to the mixture of cheers and catcalls from the crowd, and tried to interpret it. What kind of show were they expecting from him and the peasant?

Well, whatever they were expecting, he'd give them a surprise they'd remember. He stepped forward again, made a clumsy swing with his own sword, and got his shield up barely in time to block his opponent's weapon. A half-second slower and he'd have lost an arm. The uproar from the crowd was even louder.

Blade followed the same pattern three more times, and listened to the crowd between each exchange. He'd guessed just about right. They thought he was a hopeless amateur, a beginner who'd never live to become experienced. They were waiting for his opponent to get through playing with him, hammer down his guard, and send him out on a litter.

They're going to have to wait a while before they see me on a litter, thought Blade. He let four more blows come dangerously close. The last two jarred him so violently he wasn't sure all his bones were still in one piece. It was time to stop playing, before the other man's luck turned.

Suddenly the frightened amateur desperately defending himself became a smoothly-moving fighting machine. Blade closed in, took a swordcut on top of his shield, thrust the shield's spike at his opponent's face, and at the same time brought his sword around. It crashed into the peasant's helmet with a clang like a great bell, knocking the helmet askew on his head. The man staggered, but strength and stubbornness kept him on his feet. Blade shifted his grip as the man's guard dropped, smashed him across the left elbow with the flat of the sword, and finally hacked the spike off his shield. The man still tried to raise his sword, but Blade parried it, then let his own edge slip down to open a gash in the back of the man's sword hand.

"Yield?" he asked.

"Yield," the man gasped. He'd barely worked up a sweat, but his wits seemed fuddled. Perhaps it was the blow on the head, perhaps it was simply the astounding transformation of Blade.

Blade's opponent wasn't the only man surprised at his

transformation. The crowd gaped at Blade's attack in stunned silence. Then as his opponent threw down his weapons, it seemed everyone started cheering at once. Blade looked back and saw scarves and bunches of flowers waving. He even heard the "Hooa-hooa-hooa!" cry that real experts in the crowd used to hail particularly impressive pieces of work in the arena. His career in the Games seemed to be off to a good start.

Kuka came up to the two fighters and asked Blade's opponent if he wanted a litter. The man shook his head, then raised his wounded hand in salute to Blade and walked off toward the fence. The Captain looked Blade over from head to foot, as though he was counting the pores of Blade's skin. He seemed about to speak, then shook his head slightly and signalled Blade to follow his opponent to the sidelines.

Back in his place by the fence, Blade drank the water and ate the fruit the litter-bearers handed him, then let them sponge him off with scented oil. He was aware that other fighters beside the Captain were looking oddly at him. Two or three muttered to each other behind their hands as they looked at him. Blade ignored them, preferring to watch the more skilled fighters now at work.

The morning round of fights came to an end. A boat put off the mainland and delivered food for the men on the Island of Death—chunks of fried fish, porridge, vegetable stew, fruit, and beer. The guards in the boat were under the command of Ho-Marn. Again he waved, this time without speaking, and Blade waved back.

In the amphitheater those who had servants ate lunch under embroidered silk canopies. The vendors made the rounds for the less well-off. A dozen drummers gave an impromptu concert in the rear of the amphitheater, pounding away until Blade would have cheerfully gone back to them and slit every one of their drum-heads with his sword. At last the horns sounded again, the gongs boomed, Kuka and the Crier stood up, and the fighting was on again.

Blade fought once, about mid-afternoon, in one of two four-man teams matched against each other. He hadn't intended to try putting on a show this time, but he wound up having no choice. One of the four men on his team was a boy at that dangerous point where a fighter thought he knew practically everything and actually knew very little. He tried an impossibly complicated spear pass and wound up with one leg a bloody ruin. That left Blade facing two opponents, both of them considerably more skilled than his first man.

For ten minutes Blade wove a curtain of steel in front of him, taking a couple of minor nicks and giving a few more. He lost all awareness of how the rest of the fight was going, and whether his teammates were alive or dead. He was only aware of the sweat pouring down him, the stinging of his cuts, the flash of his opponents' weapons, and the growing roar of the crowd behind him.

Eventually something else crept into Blade's mind—a growing anger at both his opponents and at the crowd behind him, apparently ready to go on cheering him all day if he would go on sweating, bleeding, and giving them a good show. The anger grew, and as it did so did Blade's strength and speed.

Suddenly one of his opponents was reeling back, cheek and temple gaping open, half-blind with pain, surprise, and the flowing of blood. The other man didn't stop or slow down for a moment, but alone he was no match for Blade. In three passes Blade wounded him three times, lightly in the thigh and shoulder and more seriously in the right arm. Blade didn't need to ask him to yield.

As the roar of the crowd died away, Blade realized that he was the only one of the eight men still on his feet. He pulled off his armband and was applying it as a tourniquet to his opponent's wounded arm when Kuka came up. This time he looked everywhere but at Blade, and his face was so carefully under control that Blade was nearly ready to ask him what was on his mind. This was against the rules of the Games, but Blade usually preferred to be a rule-breaker rather than a corpse.

Instead the Captain dismissed Blade in silence. He drank more water, ate more fruit, had his wounds bound up, and watched the last few scheduled fights. The afternoon wore on, and the air grew heavy with heat, the smell of blood, and the cries of the wounded. At last the scheduled matches came to an end, the three dead men were pulled to one side, and the Crier announced the Challenge Hour.

The Challenge Hour was just what its name implied—a time when any fighter who wanted to challenge another could do so. Most of these bouts were either grudge fights or between expert fighters who wanted to deliberately test each other or show off their skills for the crowd.

Blade was surprised when his name was the first one called

131

out, as the object of a challenge by one Vosgu of Hosh. He'd heard of the man—a thin, dark veteran, so fast that in a fight he seemed to be in three places at once, and with a temper as quick as his steel. He particularly liked to challenge promising beginners and wound them badly enough to take away some of their reputation. Perhaps Vosgu's challenge shouldn't have been such a surprise after all.

They were going to use spear and short sword, without shields. That was going to make things risky, given Vosgu's speed, but not impossible. Blade knew he was about as fast as any fighting man he'd ever met, and he had a good three inches on Vosgu in height and reach.

The two men stepped toward each other, and cheers rose. Blade heard some shouting of "Vosgu!" but he heard even more shouting of "Blade!" Vosgu also heard this, and his dark face turned still darker. As he approached Blade, he already looked ready to kill.

The fighters closed, feinting with their spears, swords held low for a thrust at legs or belly. Slowly they circled each other, eyes never leaving the other man, moving from his eyes to his weapons to his feet and back again. They went on circling until they'd worn a distinct ring in the blood-caked sand. The crowd behind them was silent now, sensing what Blade already knew. This fight might go on for quite a while before the first exchange of blows, but then it would be over very quickly.

The circling and feinting went on, faster now. Blade saw that Vosgu was trying to avoid any predictable pattern of movement. He was doing rather well, and against most beginning fighters in the Games he would have been completely successful. Blade had learned to size up opponents in even rougher places than the Games of Hapanu, so Vosgu was wasting his time.

Suddenly Vosgu whirled, his arm straightened, and he threw his spear without coming up out of his crouch. Blade had the clues he needed, and Vosgu's throwing from a crouch slowed his spear. Blade's own spear lashed out, caught Vosgu's in midair, and sent it flying halfway across the arena. Kuka had to jump aside to avoid being skewered by it.

Vosgu stood, eyes and mouth open, completely stunned and completely vulnerable. Blade ignored the gasps of amazement from the crowd, took his time, and threw his own spear with total precision. As he'd intended, the spear opened a gash along Vosgu's ribs, then flew on to strike the sand and stand

132

there quivering. Before Vosgu could recover from the new shock of not being dead or dying, Blade closed in. He slashed Vosgu's swordarm to the bone, then punched the man in the jaw. As he went over backward, Blade knelt beside him, sword's point at his throat.

"I think the best thing for you is to yield," he said with a grim smile.

Vosgu seemed to agree. He nodded, then Kuka was coming up at a dead run and everybody in the amphitheater was on their feet, cheering, shouting Blade's name over and over again, and throwing flowers, scarves, empty baskets, and everything else that came to hand into the water and onto the sand. Blade rose to his feet, with a sigh of relief and slightly shaky legs. At the moment the audience seemed to have more energy than he did.

This time the Captain of the Games didn't waste any time looking at Blade. "Why didn't you kill Vosgu?" he snapped.

"Why should I?" asked Blade quietly.

That silenced the Captain and left him with his mouth gaping open. Eventually he shut it and did look at Blade, with an open suspicion that bordered on hostility.

"Are you going to—*play* with your opponents?" Kuka finally said. He said the word "play" as if it was an obscenity.

Blade laughed. Now he understood everybody's problem. The other fighters thought he had a sadistic streak in him, and took pleasure in making his opponents look like fools before he waded into them seriously. Blade shook his head.

"No, Kuka. I'm not a fool, and don't treat me like one. I couldn't expect to do that and live for long. Even if my luck didn't run out, my comrades of the Games would turn against me and arrange my death. I want to live as long as I can in the Games. I do have the skill to defeat many of my opponents without killing them. I'm going to use that skill if I can. Do you have anything to say against that?"

"No," said Kuka. "I don't. Neither will most of the other fighters. And the people there—" with a thumb jerked toward the amphitheater, where the cheers were still rising. "What they'll say, I don't know. It won't be against you, I suspect. You may get a mighty name for yourself faster than any man in the history of the Games in Gerhaa." He shook his head. "That's a gift from Hapanu, but like most of his gifts it's a sword with two edges and a life of its own. Don't get cut to pieces by your own good fortune, Blade."

Kuka looked back at the amphitheater. "Now I'd say you

should go over and give those bastards a few words. 'Thank you all' should be enough."

Blade nodded and started off. He was certainly prepared to thank the people in the amphitheater, if their cheers would make it easier for him and Meera to get out of Gerhaa alive.

Chapter 18

Kuka turned out to be right. Within weeks Blade was the most famous gladiator in the Games, except for a few veterans who'd been fighting for up to twenty years. He was certainly the most famous beginner in the history of Gerhaa.

Some of the fighters were jealous, but only a few could be suspected of harboring grudges. Skroga put it bluntly:

"It'd be different, you wanted to cut up men left and right. They know you don't kill much if you don't have to. They also know you're good enough, mostly you don't have to. So your big name won't hurt them."

The only real complaint anyone seemed to have against Blade was that he hadn't killed Vosgu of Hosh while he had the man at his mercy. "The ghosts of a lot of beginners would stand up and cheer louder than the bastards in the stands if they saw Vosgu with steel between his ribs," one man said.

"The bastards in the stands" were a different matter from Blade's comrades. Their favor could raise a gladiator to the heights, but it seldom lasted long enough to keep him there. Blade knew that he was in another race against time, a deadly one, and there was no guarantee he'd win. He didn't even know where Meera was, let alone how to reach her and get her out of Gerhaa.

For the time being, though, he was fairly well off. The crowd seemed to like his style of fighting, even if it led to spectacular displays of skill rather than gruesome piles of bodies for the Horned Ones. The spectacle grew even more brilliant when Blade began to be matched against more experienced fighters. They met him at his own level, and once he and Skroga went at it with sword and shield for a solid hour and a half. By the time they finished, the water between the amphitheater and the Island was practically carpeted with scarves and flowers.

Blade was helped along by a piece of good luck. Three weeks after his first fight was one of the great religious festivals, with more than a hundred fights spread over four days. Blade fought seven times, the last two times as the leader of a team. One team was six men, the other twenty. Only four men in the history of the Games had ever been team leaders their first year, and none the leader of a team of twenty.

That not only helped Blade's reputation among the crowd, it helped him among his fellow gladiators. They now knew he could lead with the same skill he'd showed in fighting. A few still objected to this rapid rise of a beginner, but practically no one didn't trust him or admit his extraordinary abilities.

All this was helpful, but still not enough. What finally opened doors for Blade was gaining a reputation among the noblewomen of Gerhaa.

Blade's first summons to a noblewoman's bed set something of a pattern for the others.

As he marched across the bridge to the Island of Death one morning, he saw something fall to the planks at his feet. It was a lady's golden arm ring, with an embroidered silk scarf trailing from one side and a piece of parchment tied around the other side. He started to step over it, then saw his name written in Kylanan script on the parchment. He picked it up and tied it to his belt, then marched on across the bridge with the rest of the fighters.

He wasn't scheduled to fight until a team event halfway through the afternoon's program, so he had plenty of time to unwrap the parchment and read it. In fact, the message was so short he was easily able to memorize it.

Blade the Englishman

If you are fit after today's battle, show the scarf and ring to the guards at the entrance to the barracks. They will let you pass out. Come to the rear door of the House of Taranda in the Street of the Wheelmakers, between the second and third night hour, and follow he who lets you in.

Blade was folding up the parchment when Skroga came over to him and looked down at the scarf and ring, then at Blade. "It was for you?"

"Yes."

"Not a surprise to me. Don't hope for too much, and guard your back. Some places in Gerhaa can do more hurt to those of the Games than this Island."

136

"I've survived in such places, Skroga. But thank you for your warning."

"Good luck be yours, then." The older man turned away without a further word, but some of the other fighters were now staring at Blade. He stared back until the men found other things more worth their attention.

The fighting went as smoothly as a factory assembly line that afternoon. Blade wound up sweaty and bruised but unhurt. After his bath and a light supper, he pulled the cord that rang the bell in the guardhouse on the surface. As usual when there was only one man coming up, they lowered the sling used to deliver prostitutes and supplies for the fighters. Blade climbed into it, was hauled up to the surface, and presented the scarf and ring to the men waiting there.

All of them laughed coarsely and one of them was bold enough to slap him on the back before their captain called them to heel. The captain frowned at Blade, then nodded and gave him a Slave Pass.

"Very well. Go where you've been called. But if you're not back by dawn, you'll be posted as a runaway. You understand?" Blade understood. Runaway slaves in Gerhaa were tortured to death, painfully and horribly. Slow disembowelment was the current fashion. Right now he was particularly determined to live. This call to the House of Taranda had interesting possibilities, even if it started from nothing more than some lady's unsatisfied lust. Blade thanked the guard captain with elaborate humbleness, then walked out into the evening.

The walk was long and several times he was stopped and had to show his pass. By the time he reached the back gate of the House of Taranda, it was completely dark and raining heavily. Blade splashed through ankle-deep water rushing down the streets toward the drains that carried it into the Great River. For at least a few hours tomorrow the twisting, stinking streets of Gerhaa would be almost clean.

Once he'd knocked on the back gate and showed his message, things moved swiftly. A cloaked servant led him up a winding stairway inside the wall of the house. A small door opened at the head of the stairs, and beyond the door lay a richly furnished bedroom. The carpets on the floor were ankle-deep, the bed was richly carved and inlaid with Blood of Hapanu and pearl-shell, tapestries covered the wall, and herbs burning in several brass pots perfumed the air.

On the bed a dark-haired Kylanan woman reclined. She

wore a loose red gown slashed to the waist between her full breasts and to the thigh on either side. A jeweled girdle held her waist in. Her face was too broad for real beauty and was practically caked with makeup, but she was far from unattractive. Blade found his opinion of the noblemen of Gerhaa dropping another notch, if they left women like this seeking the embraces of fighters from the Games.

As Blade stepped into the room the door closed behind him and the woman rose from the bed. She smiled. "You are as magnificent here as when you fight upon the sands," Blade was wearing only his gladiator's outfit. The woman reached out a hand and ran it over his shoulders and down across his chest. "There is all the strength in you anyone could need. Such a night I shall have!" Blade couldn't help noticing the "I." Apparently he wasn't going to be much more than a living tool for the lady's pleasure.

The woman pointed with one hand to her pillows, while the other hand went to the clasp of her girdle. Nestled between the two pillows Blade saw a small ivory-handled riding whip. He looked back to the lady as the girdle fell to the floor. She shrugged her shoulders and the gown followed it. Her breasts were massive, almost too large in proportion to the rest of her body, but firm and solid.

"Well?" she snapped. "Are you all muscle and no sense? I thought you were more, and so did others. If they are disappointed . . . ." She left the threat unfinished. Instead she turned away from Blade and threw herself face down on the bed, her ample buttocks raised.

Blade decided to play the role the lady was giving him. It wasn't much to his taste, but being hauled off to a slow and painful death was even less so. He stepped up to the bed, reached for the whip with one hand, and ran the other lightly down her back. She grunted in annoyance. "Later, later, for that. First the whip."

Blade suppressed a sigh. Then he raised the whip and brought it down across the lady's buttocks with all the strength in his right arm. She screamed and quivered all over, but it was a *happy* scream. For a moment Blade was almost sure he was going to vomit. Then he struck again, and again, and again, throwing himself into the lady's game to shut out of his mind the obscenity of her pleasure.

Suddenly she was no longer screaming, but writhing and sobbing, pressing herself flat on the bed and clawing at the blankets with fingers and toes. Her buttocks were red with a pattern of criss-crossing stripes. Blade hadn't drawn blood, and didn't know whether to be glad or sorry.

Then the woman turned over. Her hair was a tangled bird's nest, her large nipples were now immense and swollen, and the hair between her thighs was drenched. Her mouth was so slack that Blade expected her to start drooling like an idiot. Instead she sat up and reached out with both hands, hooking her fingers over Blade's loinguard and drawing him toward her. "Off with that, you!" she gasped. "Off!"

At the moment Blade would rather have made love to a Horned One. However, he had no choice. He reached down, plucked the woman's hands from his loinguard, and started unhooking it.

The lady with the whip was the first. She wasn't the last. Fortunately most of the others didn't have her peculiar tastes. They were just as demanding, but only demanded what a normal man could give a normal woman. That was just as well. Blade had plenty of stamina for the hungry women of Gerhaa, but he had no stomach for perverts. If he'd had to deal with too many like the lady with the whip, his temper would have snapped sooner or later, with disastrous results.

As it was, going to bed with Richard Blade, super-gladiator, became a fashion among the idle, neglected, curious, or merely lusty ladies of Gerhaa. Not just among the noble-women, either—the wives of respectable merchants some-times found him to their taste. Once four middle-aged matrons gathered together and entertained themselves with Blade. The scene reminded Blade of a bridge party so much that he had to fight back laughter. The only difference was that in-stead of decorously playing cards, the ladies were all naked and practically fighting for the next turn at Blade. That ses-sion nearly wore Blade out, for the ladies not only knew what they wanted but knew how much.

Sometimes Blade was given a handful of copper coins or one or two silver ones. Sometimes he was given odd bits of jewelry or the silk scarves that every lady in Gerhaa seemed to have by the dozens. Most of the time he was given nothing at all. No doubt the chance to get out of the fighters' bar-racks and have dozens of the choicest women in Gerhaa was considered to be enough of a reward.

Blade wouldn't have called most of the women particularly choice, but he was indeed getting rewards far more important than money. He was learning his way around Gerhaa. He carefully memorized streets and alleys, until he could have found his way around some quarters of the city in total darkness. He was also learning a few of the city's secrets—or at least things which had been secret from the Forest People. He didn't have to ask many questions, either. Mostly, it was just a matter of keeping his eyes and ears open and listening to the murmurs of love-drunk women.

The Kylanans were familiar with the *kohkol* tree and its sap. It was the secret of their crossbows and siege engines. They took ropes of woven hair, soaked them in boiled *kohkol* sap, then smoke-dried them. The result was something like an incredibly tough rubber—and extremely powerful weapons. Blade even heard hints that Gerhaa's bows and catapults were better than the ones at home in Kylan. He couldn't help wondering what the Emperor of Kylan might think of that, if it was true.

The other secret was that Gerhaa was not nearly as strong as it seemed. The walls were indeed nearly impregnable, and the ships patrolling the Great River were enough to stand off the canoes of the Forest People. The garrison was not nearly as formidable. It numbered barely three thousand armed men permanently on duty, half regular Kylanan soldiers and half the Protector's Pets.

These weren't supposed to be all the city's defenders in wartime, of course. There were the nobles and their household retainers, most of them armed and trained. They might be formidable and they would almost certainly be loyal to the Protector. Too many of them owed him too much to do anything else.

Free citizens with a certain amount of wealth were also supposed to keep weapons and be ready to turn out with them. From what Blade could see, most of these weapons were useless and most of the people didn't know how to use them. Even if they turned out, how much could they do?

What was there to bring against these defenders? There were the fighters of the Games. There were the poor, who would almost certainly fight against the Protector, whose Guard abused them for sport. There were the household slaves, who would fight almost anybody for a chance at freedom. They might not fight very well, for most of them were women, boys, or old men, but they would fight without caring about the cost to themselves. Finally there were the Forest People, however many of them could make their way down the Great River to the city.

It might be impossible to gather all these enemies and hurl them at Gerhaa, but "impossible" wasn't one of Richard Blade's favorite words. *Gerhaa could be taken.* Blade was as sure of that as if he'd seen the words carved on a block of the city's walls. When it was taken, the danger to the Forest People would be gone, perhaps forever and certainly for generations.

Now all he had to do was create that impossible alliance and unleash its armies against the Stone Village.

Chapter 19

Blade had been fighting on the Island of Death by day and in the bedrooms of Gerhaa by night for several weeks when one morning Skroga approached him.

"Blade, I will speak with you."

"I am willing."

"Where no other can hear us, please."

Blade nodded and rose without another word. He followed Skroga past the mouth of the shaft to the surface, and on into the tunnels beyond. These were seldom visited, and the smell of mold, dampness, and decay was overpowering. Soon they were even beyond the lighted area. Skroga took a candle from his belt, lit it, and led the way on through the darkness.

Blade began to wonder why Skroga was leading him out here, alone and nearly unarmed. He had nothing but his eating knife, while the older man wore a broadsword and fighting dagger. Perhaps Blade would have the edge if he got the fight down to bare hands, but even that wasn't certain. Skroga's tribe had a system of unarmed combat similar to karate. As a young man, Skroga had been an adept, and what he'd lost since then in speed he'd gained in experience.

Finally they stopped at a place where Blade could hear water dripping and see a dark pool at the edge of the light cast by Skroga's candle. He could also see something else that made him rather wish Skroga had chosen another place to stop. At the very edge of the pool lay a white skeleton, the skull detached and crushed in by a terrible blow. Blade slowly shifted position, trying to face Skroga and at the same time keep his back to the solid rock wall.

Almost conversationally, the old gladiator said, "There are tales. Beyond this pool you find caves. Caves to give a way out to the world and freedom."

"Do you believe that?"

Skroga shook his head. "I wish it, but no. We go out of

142

here on the bridge to the Island, or down the dead men's holes."

Now Blade could guess what Skroga might be suggesting. He decided to gamble on that guess being right. "There is also the tunnel between the barracks and the guardhouse. Such a tunnel goes two ways."

"Yes, it does. But there is the guardhouse."

Blade smiled. "And if there are no guards in the guardhouse?"

"How is this to be?"

"There are ways. I do not know any of them now, but I can look and listen for them."

"You know you can do this?"

"Yes. I have already done it." Blade laughed, sending harsh echoes rolling around the tunnel in the darkness. For a moment it sounded as if the earth itself was laughing. Skroga stiffened at the sound. Before the older man could recover, Blade went on in a businesslike tone.

"Skroga, I think it is time to stop playing with our words and speak like wise men. At least I know you are wise, and I hope you think I am. You want me to use my ability to move about in Gerhaa to help the fighters of the Games break out to freedom. You brought me here to ask me that, and to kill me if I refused.

"You will not have to kill me. There is *nothing* closer to my heart than freeing the men of the Games. I must add one thing, however. Without freeing all of Gerhaa from the Protector, the fighters cannot hope to stay free long. Once they are free of the barracks, will they go on fighting until the Protector is cast down?"

Skroga pulled at his beard with both hands, until Blade expected it to come away in handfuls. Finally he nodded. "Yes. Swine like the Protector are cursed by all the gods the fighters honor. I think the Ten Brothers will say—go on fighting. When they say this, most fighters will obey."

"Good." Blade suspected that in the simple process of breaking out of the barracks the gladiators might do so much damage the Protector would be finished. He was still glad that Skroga was willing to continue the fight until Gerhaa was free. Without his influence, it might be hard to persuade the gladiators to go on fighting for the benefit of the Forest People, let alone the people of Gerhaa who'd cheered their dying in the arena.

Blade saw that Skroga seemed to be expecting him to go

on. "Obviously the best way to escape is to take the guard-house by surprise, then open the doors in the tunnel. We can all get out quickly that way, faster than they can bring up soldiers to stop us."

In answer to the implied question on the other's face, Blade shook his head. "No, I don't yet have a sure way to do this. I want a sure one, because we'll only get one chance. But I'll start looking harder now that I know I have the fighters behind me. I would have spoken of this before, but I could not be sure what would happen to me if I did." Blade stopped as he realized Skroga was weeping silently out of sheer joy and sudden hope.

Blade waited for the old man to calm himself, then asked, "Skroga, you brought me out here to kill me if I didn't give the right answers. Have you had trouble with men like me before?"

Skroga nodded and spat savagely into the pool. "Yes. Before the Protector, there was one like you—had fun with the ladies. One of the Ten Brothers asked him the same as I asked you. He told soldiers that night. Fifteen fighters were taken and tortured to death.

"Then there was a second, three years ago. He loved men, not women. Soon he spent nights with the Protector. We are not fools, so we asked him nothing."

"What happened to him?"

Skroga shrugged. "Only tales, nothing sure. They say he got into fight with Protector. The Protector hit him with the big staff. That was his end." That was also a tale Blade could believe. The jeweled staff looked heavy enough to crush a man's skull like an eggshell.

"So I'm the third man to offer the fighters a way out?"

"Yes."

"Let's hope it will be a case of 'Third time lucky'."

Skroga seemed to recognize the saying. "Yes."

They shook hands and turned back the way they'd come.

Blade was determined to do everything he could to break the fighters loose as soon as possible. Unfortunately, for a while it looked as if all his determination wasn't going to make much difference.

The best way to surprise the guardhouse and open the tunnel was easy to find. Directly above the mouth of the tunnel leading to the drawbridge and the island of Death was thirty feet of sheer cliff. At the top of that cliff was the end of a dark, twisting alley, closed only by a rough wooden railing. From the end of the alley, somebody could throw a rope down to the mouth of the tunnel. A few agile men could climb up that rope. After that they could slip through the back streets and alleys to the weakly-held guardhouse, surprise and kill the guards, hold the guardhouse, and unlock the doors in the tunnel. Then all hell, not to mention a thousand savage fighting men, would break loose in Gerhaa.

Given a dark night, a little luck, speed, and secrecy, it was a sound plan. The only problem was finding someone to stand at the end of the alley and throw the rope down!

Blade set out to find that someone, and took blood-chilling risks in his search. If there'd been anybody recording Blade's questions over the next few weeks, he would have been dead several times over. Fortunately, in this Dimension the age of electronic eavesdropping and scientific secret police was centuries away. So Blade survived, but he didn't succeed until one night when he found Ho-Marn in charge of the guardhouse.

The captain didn't speak as he gave Blade the Slave Pass, but he squeezed Blade's hand in a peculiar manner as he handed it over. As soon as Blade was out of sight of the guardhouse, he stopped and examined the pass. It looked like the usual sheet of leather, but on close examination Blade saw it was two pieces pasted together. Blade pried them apart and by the light of a street torch read the paper that fell out:

Blade,
    You will soon go to the House of Chorma. The lady there likes women in her bed as well as men. When she asks where to find women, tell her that there are many fine women for her at the Twelve Serpents in the Street of the Happy Houses. Do as you think best after you have brought the lady to the house.

Blade wasn't surprised at the message. In fact, he was no longer surprised at anything Ho-Marn did. He was beginning to suspect that Ho-Marn was playing a deep game of his own, and didn't like not knowing what that game might be.

Blade was still surprised when he reached the House of the Twelve Serpents, asked for a woman of his own while Lady Chorma amused herself, and found himself facing Meera.

Like the other girls of the Happy Houses, Meera was naked except for wisps of silk around her neck and waist, a

145

silver arm ring, and makeup applied with more enthusiasm than good taste. In spite of this, she seemed to have developed a certain dignity, and wore her nudity with the same grace she might have shown with the most elaborate gown. The wound in her leg had healed, leaving only a faint scar.

She wasn't particularly happy in the House of the Twelve Serpents, but she was sane, alert, and determined. "It could be much worse," she told Blade. "This is not one of the Houses where for a price a man can hurt a girl until she's dead or crippled for life. The mistress of the house is of the Forest People, and her steward and lover is a freedman with Forest People blood in him. They try to make it as easy as possible for new girls from the Forest."

"Did Ho-Marn—the soldier who captured us—have anything to do with your coming here?"

Meera frowned. "He could have. I saw him in the crowd when I was sold, talking to the steward. He has also been here a few times since, though he has never taken me." So Ho-Marn might have kept his promise to see that Meera went to a good house.

Meera smiled. "Blade, if we are going to talk of such matters—it is better if you do with me what men come here for." She pointed to the walls and then to her ears. Blade understood—there might be eavesdroppers. He stood up, held out his arms, and drew Meera to him.

Very quickly he discovered that her months in a Happy House hadn't destroyed Meera's ability to respond to him. He also discovered that in spite of all the other women he'd had in Gerhaa she was still something special. It was a long time before they remembered or cared that they had more serious things to talk about. Then they talked with Meera lying in Blade's arms, their heads so close together that any eavesdropper would have needed a microphone to make out what they were saying.

Meera quickly understood what Blade was planning and what he needed. She wasn't completely sure she could provide it, but she was willing to try.

"The first man I must talk to is the steward. He had a tavern of his own when the Protector came. There was a fight and some of the Pets were hurt. The Protector took the tavern and wanted to send the steward to the galleys. He would have gone, if our mistress had not brought him here. He does not love the Protector."

"Can he be trusted to keep his mouth shut?"

"If it will help bring down the Protector, yes."

"The job will need more than one man, you know. Does he have friends who can be trusted?"

"He does. But—what happens after the Protector falls? We of the Forest can go home, but what of those with homes in Gerhaa?"

"I want to see Gerhaa free, a home for all who fought the Protector. So do my friends among the fighters of the Games."

"Can *they* be trusted?"

"Some of them can. As for the rest—well, I will see that anyone who helps bring down the Protector ends his days in freedom, or die. I wish I could promise more, but I can't."

"That should be enough for many, I think. They do not want to lie in the sun and drink honey the rest of their days, only to live without fear of the Protector."

"I'll trust anyone who wants that, if they'll trust me."

After this Blade and Meera made love again. Then Lady Chorma called for Blade to escort her home, so that was all Blade was able to do on his first visit.

By the time he came to the Twelve Serpents a second time, Meera had done her work and the steward was starting his. He and Blade talked, and the steward promised to try finding at least six reliable men.

The third time, the steward had five of the men and Blade met two of them. "They are none of them strong fighting men," the steward said. "The swords must be in the hands of you fighters of the Games. For all else, you can trust me and mine." He sighed and shook his head. "I think of what we hope to do, and sometimes I think I dream."

"It won't be a dream much longer," said Blade, mentally crossing his fingers as he spoke. They were now very nearly committed past all hope of survival if someone did turn traitor. He and Meera and all their allies would die horribly, the guardhouse watch would be reinforced, and possibly no fighter of the Games would ever be allowed out of the barracks again. Even worse, the Protector's power would be safe for many years to come, and his attack on the Forest People would continue. Then the Forest People might be doomed, unless Swebon could develop the laminated bows by himself. The gladiators' escape and the capture of Gerhaa would have to take place within a month or two at most.

Then on the fourth visit to Meera, Blade learned they would have to move even sooner than that.

Chapter 20

"Ho-Marn actually came to me," said Meera. "He told me—" she looked away "—the same way you and I talked." She laughed. "For a man that old, he has much strength, and he was very kind."

"Yes," said Blade. "I think he is our friend, although I wish I knew why. But what did he say?"

Ho-Marn brought warning that a fleet was coming to Gerhaa from Mashom-Gad. There were rumors that it was being sent by the Protector's friends among the nobles and merchants of the mother city. It was known for certain that the fleet had more than forty ships, and it carried three thousand armed men for the Protector's Guard.

With more than six thousand men at his command, the Protector would be nearly impossible to overthrow. Even if the Guardsmen weren't particularly good fighters, there would simply be too many of them. The fighters of the Games would only escape to a quicker death than they'd find on the Island of Death. Anyone who helped them would die horribly without even a chance to strike back.

"So we have to fight now," said Blade. "And I do mean *now*. If we could do it tomorrow night—"

"I'll ask the steward," said Meera. She gripped him more tightly than ever. "Blade, I'm frightened. This fighting isn't like what we knew in the Forest. It seems to go on and on, with no end until the whole world is running blood."

He stroked her hair and ran his fingers down her back. "You're right. But we have no choice. Or rather, we have two choices—let the Protector win or at least try to put an end to him."

"That's not much of a choice."

"I know. But that's all we have."

Blade dreamed of running across an endless plain of short green grass. Behind him ran the Protector, screaming obscenities and waving his great staff. Sunlight blazed from the Blood of Hapanu, so that the Protector seemed to be waving a great red flame. Behind the Protector ran his Guardsmen, transformed into monsters with long green fangs and yellow scales, led by a Cha-Chern with a long forked tail. Overhead was a silvery sky, and a hot wind blew against Blade's skin.

Then the silvery sky started turning dark, the Guardsmen faded away, and Skroga stood where the Protector had been. He reached out a hand to Blade and spoke softly.

"Wake up, Blade. It's time."

Blade took a deep breath to drive away the last shreds of his dream, then sat up on his cot. A few more deep breaths and he was awake and ready for action. He stood up and felt the familiar sensations of his mind and body preparing for battle. All his senses seemed abnormally acute, so that the dripping of water sounded like drumbeats and the breathing of the men on the cots nearby sounded like a laboring steam engine. His mind was working with unnatural speed and clarity, and familiar thoughts raced through it.

This is the moment when turning back becomes impossible. The fight has started, and we have to go forward, to win or die. It was usually a relief to Blade when things reached this point. He hated waiting more than anything else.

Skroga led him past one roomful of sleeping men after another, until they reached the entrance to the tunnel out to the drawbridge. Four other men were waiting there. Blade knew all four of them, and he'd led two of them in team fights. They were all young, tough, and wiry. All four wore rough garments of blankets and sheets, patched together into something like a citizen's clothing. In the darkness of the back streets, they'd probably pass. All four had swords and daggers belted on over their garments and wore broad grins.

"Let's go," Blade said. Skroga gripped him by the shoulders and stepped back. The older man simply wasn't agile enough to climb ropes in the darkness. He'd be doing his share tonight, though, leading the men up the tunnel once Blade's party had the door opened.

All five men had rags tied around their feet, so they padded down the tunnel as softly as mice. At the end of the tunnel Blade peered around the side of the drawbridge. The night was clear, but the dampness in the breeze hinted there might be rain on the way. tI would help them if it came, but they couldn't wait for it. Blade leaned out as far as he could and whistled softly three times.

From above the signal was repeated. Then there was a faint hiss, and a stout rope was dangling in front of Blade. It was knotted at two-foot intervals, and on the end dangled Meera's silver arm ring. Blade stepped back and nodded to the others.

"The rope's down. Remember—only one man at a time. If you feel yourself slipping, freeze until you've got a grip again."

Blade stepped back to the opening, made sure his sword and dagger were secure, gripped the rope, and pulled himself out into space. For a moment he felt the rope slipping, lowering him toward the dark water and whatever might wait there. Then the rope jerked and held steady. Blade started to climb.

The rope was as rough as sandpaper, but the roughness helped him grip it. He went up as fast as he could, not looking down or out. There could be nothing on the Island of Death except Horned Ones, but sometimes boats swung close by the amphitheater at night.

Then he was climbing past the last knot, reaching up for the wooden railing, and meeting several pairs of hands reaching down for him. He was hauled over the edge, scraping his nose on the filthy stone of the pavement, then pulled to his feet. The first face he saw was Meera's.

"What are you doing here?" he hissed.

"The mistress closed the Twelve Serpents tonight," said the steward's voice behind him. "She will tell anyone who asks that two of the girls are sick. Hapanu alone knows what it may be! She will hide us, if we cannot do our work tonight."

If they didn't take the guardhouse and release the fighters, no hiding place would save them from the Protector, but Blade didn't see any point in mentioning this.

Blade leaned over the edge and whistled the signal to the men below. A moment later the rope started quivering as the first man started climbing. Blade had picked them for agility, and in five minutes they were all standing beside him. The steward and one other man came with Blade and the four fighters as guides, while the other four men and Meera got ready to return to the Twelve Serpents. Blade drew Meera aside.

"Pack food and clothes for a journey upriver. "I'm sending you back to Swebon."

"Blade, don't you—?"

"I'm not doing it just to save pour life, you silly woman. *Think!* Somebody has to get back to Swebon, tell him about what's happened, give him the secret of the strong bow. Who else does he know well enough to trust?"

"Ah. I understand."

"Yes. You and the men I'm sending with you have to leave tonight. Even if we take the city, the Protector may still have it surrounded by dawn."

Meera kissed him and went off with the others from the Twelve Serpents. Blade waited until they were out of sight, then led his own men off toward the guardhouse. They tried to move as silently as ghosts, eyes and ears probing the darkness and hands never far from sword hilts. They kept to the darkest alleys and the narrowest side streets, and more than once Blade had to stop and reorient himself to keep from getting lost.

They weren't seen, let alone challenged, but the journey took so long Blade was half-expecting dawn to break in the east by the time they were in sight of the guardhouse. Blade crept up to the nearest of the bronze-barred windows and peered in. There were five men inside, including a Guard officer with his back to the window. As Blade tried to see what weapons the men had ready, he heard footsteps behind him and rose from his crouch.

A fat soldier was hurrying across the cobblestones, sweating, red-faced, and breathless. The Guard officer stepped toward the door to meet the man. Blade saw he was Cha-Chern. Then the fat soldier saw Blade lurking in the shadow of the guardhouse. He let out a scream that raised echoes, whirled, and ran.

Blade's men leaped out of their hiding places as the soldier dashed away, but he was out of sight before they could move to cut him off. Blade covered ten feet in a single leap and met Cha-Chern at the door. The officer recognized Blade and his face went pale, but his sword was out and flickering toward Blade like a poisonous snake. Blade parried Cha-Chern's first thrust with his dagger, then chopped down with his own sword. It was a brutal blow, like a butcher chopping meat, but there was no time or room for anything else. It caught Cha-Chern in the side of the neck and sent blood spraying. The Guardsman had the strength to thrust once more, his point nicking Blade's ribs. Then he reeled forward, giving Blade a chance to swing from the side. Cha-Chern's head lolled on his neck, he went down, and Blade leaped over the fallen man into the guardhouse. His men came boiling in after him.

It wasn't a fight in the guardhouse, it was a massacre. The exchange of blows lasted more than thirty seconds only because Blade's men didn't have enough room to work faster. When the last scream died away, all four guards were dead and so was one of Blade's men. Blade picked up a bloody ring of keys from the table by one window and handed it to a man.

"Start getting the doors open."

"How much time do we have?"

"I don't know. That messenger who ran off will be bringing more soldiers, I'm sure of that. Assume you won't have any time at all."

The man nodded and started trying keys in the lock on the first door. Blade and the two remaining survivors of his party started blocking off the two windows of the guardhouse. The building was built of stone with a slate roof, so there was no way it could be burned. Three men could easily hold the door against a strong force of attackers. The only thing Blade feared was crossbowmen firing through the windows.

They had one window blocked with the table and were lifting a bench into the other when Blade heard the tramp of feet and shouted orders. As they wedged the bench into place, three crossbow bolts slammed into it, nearly knocking it loose again. A moment later fists, swords, and spears started thumping and clanging on the locked and barred door. The solid planks hardly quivered. Against anything but a battering ram, the door could hold for quite a while.

Somebody out there must have had the same idea. Blade heard a voice giving orders to break into nearby houses and look for logs or heavy pieces of furniture. Several sets of feet hurried off, and several more arrived. Blade and his two comrades cleaned up the guardroom by dropping all the bodies down the freight shaft.

As the last body vanished, they heard a rumbling of wheels on the pavement outside. A moment later something started crackling below one window, and Blade smelled sharp, pungent smoke. He stiffened. Those wheels sounded like the soldiers had brought up a cart or wagon, either to batter down the door or block it from the outside. As for the fire—the guardhouse might not burn, but it could be filled with smoke until no one could breathe inside it. Blade realized that he

152

hadn't thought of everything the enemy might do against the guardhouse.

The crackling grew louder, and Blade began to see an orange glow through the cracks in the bench. Gray smoke began curling in through the window and flowing down toward the floor. Blade felt his eyes beginning to water, and one of the other men started coughing violently. The soldiers must be putting something on the fire to make the smoke poisonous.

Blade pushed open the tunnel door and shouted, "How far are you?" There was no answer, and as Blade caught his breath he felt as if he'd inhaled a lungful of paper. By the time he stopped coughing he realized that there was only one thing to do—open the door to let the smoke out, and rely on hand-to-hand fighting to keep the soldiers out until the fighters came up from below. That would be running a close and deadly race with time, but all the alternatives were even worse. Blade had a moment's ghastly vision of the Protector sealing off the barracks, then flooding it with the poisonous smoke to slaughter the gladiators like an exterminator slaughtering rats in a cellar.

Blade motioned toward the door—he could barely speak —and the other men nodded. They understood. Together all three of them lifted the bar. Then Blade motioned the others to stand aside while he threw the bolt and heaved the door open. Fresh air poured in and the smoke swirled out, so thick that it was a moment before the soldiers outside realized the door was open. By that time Blade and his comrades were ready and waiting.

The first two soldiers to come through the door died before they realized the door was open. Blade nearly beheaded one. The other was stabbed in the thigh, then had his throat cut as he lay on the floor. The next two men who came in were more alert, but didn't last much longer. One slipped on the blood of his dead comrades, and Blade split his head as he crashed to the floor. The other got all the way inside the guardhouse before one of Blade's comrades caught him and pushed him down the shaft.

The echoes of the falling man's screams were dying away before Blade heard two new sounds. One was the rumble of the cart being pulled away from the door. The other was a swelling pound of feet and clatter of weapons from deep inside the tunnel. The soldiers ready to enter the guardhouse also heard the noise from the tunnel and backed away from the door. Then the door to the tunnel flew open and the man who'd gone down to unlock the doors burst out. His eyes were wide and he waved a spear so furiously that he nearly skewered Blade. Hard on the man's heels came Skroga and Kuka, and after them all the fighters of the Games of Hapanu, the doomed men of the Island of Death, on their way to freedom and vengeance.

They came up the tunnel like water out of a high-pressure hose, shrieking warcries, curses, and prayers to all their gods, waving every sort of weapon Blade had ever seen in the Games. They came on so fast and so furiously that any soldiers in the guardhouse would have been trampled to death before a weapon touched them. Blade had to fight with knees and elbows and curses to keep from being pushed down the shaft.

Eventually he was caught up in the mob and propelled through the door like the cork out of a champagne bottle, into the open street. By then half the soldiers who'd been attacking the guardhouse were dead or dying, and the other half were sprinting off in all directions, gladiators hard on their heels. As Blade expected, the gladiators weren't taking prisoners.

By the time most of the fighters reached the open, reports were coming back of soldiers and Guardsmen also out in force. It was impossible to tell from these reports exactly what was happening, and for the moment Blade wasn't particularly worried. The Protector would certainly know what was happening by now, but it would still take time to gather his men. It might take even more time to persuade them to advance against the fighters of the Games, armed, desperate, and ready to fight to the death.

There was still no time to lose. Some of the gladiators apparently expected Blade to make a long speech, but he flatly refused to do anything of the kind. Others wanted to go to the waterfront at once, take ships, and sail off at once, never mind where. Blade sent these to Skroga. He himself started choosing men for various special jobs.

Some were to go to the quays, hold them, capture as many ships as they could, and burn the rest. Others were to go to the House of the Twelve Serpents. Meera was to be brought directly to Blade, while the steward and his men would act as guides for the streets of Gerhaa. Still others would start searching all the houses in the areas they'd already cleared of soldiers. Anyone who resisted should be killed, anyone who did nothing should be left alone, anyone who wanted to join should be armed and enlisted.

When Blade finished giving all his orders, he called for parchment and ink, then sat down and wrote out a letter he'd long since worked out in his mind.

Swebon

Meera brings this letter, to tell you that the Free Fighters and their allies now rule in Gerhaa the Stone Village. The power of the Protector, the great enemy of all the Forest People, is dying, but it is not dead. To finish the victory, the Forest people must unite and come to Gerhaa.

Meera also brings the secret of the strong bow, which I have discovered. This bow will drive arrows into the hearts of Treemen and through the armor of the Sons of Hapanu. It is a weapon the Forest People can use to destroy all their enemies, or to destroy each other.

So that they may destroy their enemies, I ask that you take oaths from all the chiefs, to end the warfare among the People. Only those chiefs who swear this oath should be given the secret of the strong bow. This is my wish, and my curse is upon any who do not heed it.

I also ask that you take care of Meera. I have had another vision during my time in Gerhaa. It tells me that when Gerhaa has fallen forever and the Forest People are safe, I must return to England. Meera will need protection, and you are a man she will accept and honor. I have not told her of this vision and I ask you not to, for it would only cause her grief now.

May the Forest Spirit be with you, and bring you and the People swiftly to Gerhaa and victory.

Richard Blade of England

Then he rolled up the letter and coated it with wax. He picked up the other parchments he'd prepared for Swebon and along with the letter sealed them in a bronze drinking horn looted from a nearby house.

As Blade was finishing this job, Meera and the other people from the House of the Twelve Serpents arrived. Right after them came the twenty-five men chosen to escort Meera and Blade's message upriver to Swebon. Skroga was with them. Blade and Meera embraced, then the steward led her toward the waterfront. Blade had to stay at his improvised command post, but Skroga went to see them off. He returned an hour later, to report that they were safely on their way.

"On their way" didn't mean safely home, but it certainly meant they were past the biggest obstacle, the enemies around Gerhaa. There would still be raiding parties and the garrison of the camp at the river junction to be avoided, but these would soon be hearing the news from Gerhaa. When they did they'd have other things on their minds than looking for three canoes. At least Blade hoped so—and for the moment, hoping was all he could do to help Meera and her party. He turned his attention back to sorting out the situation in Gerhaa.

This situation proved remarkably hard to sort out, because the garrison put up a stubborn resistance. Some of the regular soldiers deserted, frightened or unwilling to fight beside the Protector's Pets. Very few of these joined the rebels. Most of them ran off into the countryside to hide among the farmers and hunters, or boarded sailing ships and headed out into the ocean, bound home for Kylan.

The regulars who didn't desert fought well, with a grim, sullen determination that no rabble of gladiators and the sweepings of Gerhaa's streets was going to beat them. The Protector's Pets also fought fairly well, once a few of their more useless officers managed to get themselves killed in action. One dying prisoner gave Blade a hint why.

"Emperor—thinks Protector—ambitious. He don't hold—city—Emperor has chance to—" A rattle, a gurgle, then the man coughed blood and died. Blade rose from beside the body, wishing very much he had Ho-Marn here to question. More and more he suspected that the gray-haired officer knew most of whatever political secrets lurked in the shadows of Gerhaa. More and more he was certain that knowing those secrets would increase the chances of victory for himself and the people he was leading. Unfortunately Ho-Marn was nowhere to be found alive or dead.

The Protector himself was hard at work, leading his Guardsmen and organizing the defenses of the part of Gerhaa still not in rebel hands. In his bright red leather suit and black-enameled mail shirt, he was a conspicuous object wherever he appeared. Dozens of arrows and spears were hurled at him, killing men all around him, but the Protector himself seemed to bear a charmed life.

156

Blade had to admit that he'd underestimated the Protector. The man might have every imaginable vice and a few better not imagined, but that didn't make him a fool. With his back to the wall, the Protector was fighting with skill and courage worthy of a far better man.

The Protector's leadership, the fighting of the men under him, and the tangled streets of Gerhaa kept the rebels from sweeping their enemies completely out of the city. By the afternoon of the second day, a solid line of barricades rose across the city, dividing the two sides as rigidly as if they'd been on separate islands. A few bold spirits on either side tried to leap from roof to roof, or slip through the cellars. They were too few to make any difference, and most of them were quickly hunted down and killed.

To balance not being able to take the whole city, the rebels did take the wall on the river side. On top of each tower along the wall was a large catapult. In the cellars of the towers were hundreds of crossbows, swords, and suits of armor, along with stones, arrows, and barrels of oil for making firepots.

Blade promptly had the weapon and armor distributed to the men the rebels had recruited in the city. The catapults were manned, and after a good deal of trial and error and a few bloody accidents, they opened fire on the ships in the harbor. Some of the tougher captains tried to brave the shower of stones and arrows, then Blade's catapult crews brought up the oil and started shooting firepots. Atfer three ships went up in flames, the surviving captains decided discretion was the better part of valor. By nightfall all the Kylanan ships were anchored several miles from the walls of Gerhaa, and the rebels were temporarily safe from attack by either land or sea.

As this fact dawned on the gladiators, Blade began to hear the sort of mutterings he'd been afraid of from the very beginning.

"How many ships we got, down at waterfront?"

"Thirty, maybe."

"We could all get ourselfs into 'em, then."

"To go where?"

"Upriver, mebbe."

"The Forest People—what they say?"

"Half o' the fighters are Forest People. Other half—well, we fight good against Kylan. Mebbe they won't mind havin' us up there with 'em."

"I'll be thinkin' about it."

By the time he heard basically this same conversation three or four times, Blade decided he'd better find Skroga. A crisis seemed to be in the making, and it was going to be all the worse because of the number of armed city people who'd joined the gladiators. Most of them were armed now, none of them had any place to go, and they would be furious if the gladiators started abandoning them. If the two factions of the rebels started fighting each other, they would be handing victory to the Protector on a silver platter.

Skroga was nowhere to be found, so toward midnight Blade grabbed some bread and sausage, then wrapped himself in a looted blanket and lay down in a corner of the guardhouse. He felt as if he hadn't slept at all when he awoke, to find the sky gray with dawn and someone shaking him furiously.

"Blade, Blade, wake up. Vosgu of Hosh is calling on the fighters to leave Gerhaa and go into the Forest. He is speaking in the Street of the Silversmiths. You must come!"

Blade jumped up so fast he tripped over the blanket. He untangled himself and recognized the man who'd awakened him—the son of a barrel-maker who'd joined the rebels almost at once and been mortally wounded within a few hours. The young man was sweating, but his hands and gaze were very steady.

Blade had slept in his clothes and shoes. He snatched up his sword and dagger, sheathed them, then grabbed a spear from a cluster leaning in one corner.

"All right. Let's go."

Blade and his guide covered the mile of mud and cobblestones to the Street of the Silversmiths at a steady trot. They were still too late. By the time they arrived, Vosgu was shouting to a crowd of more than five hundred armed men. Twothirds of them were gladiators of the Games, but around the fringes were solid clusters of men from the city. Their faces were grim, they were fingering their weapons, and a few of the bolder spirits were shouting obscenities every time the gladiators cheered.

"So what do we owe those of Gerhaa, in truth?" Vosgu was saying. "They fight beside us now, or so they say. But for years they sat and cheered our dying. Shall we forgive them all these years for two days' aid?"

"No!" one of the gladiators shouted, and his angry cry was echoed by others.

"A wise man has spoken the truth," cried Vosgu. "Listen

158

to him, brothers of the Games. Listen to him, then march to our ships and—"

"*No!*" thundered a familiar voice from a dark alley. "I say *no,* Vosgu of Hosh, fool and coward! Brothers, listen to me." Skroga stepped out of the alley and shouldered his way through the crowd to the upturned barrel Vosgu was using as a platform.

"Listen to me!" he shouted again. "Do not heed this man. He would curse you all. What god will aid men who abandon their friends? What god will not curse them? Answer that, any of you!"

"Are the city people our friends?" someone shouted. He sounded uncertain rather than angry.

"Who else?" replied Skroga. "Do you expect mercy from the Protector." That drew laughter.

"The Forest People—" began someone else. Skroga snorted in derision.

"The Forest People! Many of you were once of the Forest. What do you say to a man who asks you for help, if he deserts friends on a battlefield? What do you think wise chiefs like Swebon will say if you come now?" There were mutterings, and Blade heard at least one man say, "Mebbe he's right. Don't much like city people, but if we have to stay. . . ."

Skroga sensed he had the audience shifting toward him. He stepped forward, turning his back to Vosgu as he did so. The man on the barrel acted so swiftly that Blade couldn't even shout. His sword slashed down, easily cutting through Skroga's leather cap and into his skull.

I should have killed that bastard when I had the chance, thought Blade. Then he let out a roar that turned every head in the crowd toward him. His arm came up and then his spear was standing out from Vosgu's chest. The man dropped his sword, looked wildly around him as if he couldn't believe what had happened, then toppled off the barrel.

Before Vosgu stopped twitching, Blade pushed his way through the stunned crowd and sprang up on top of the barrel. He pointed to Skroga and then to Vosgu's body. Those gestures were enough to keep the crowd silent as he spoke.

"Skroga, the man we all honored, has been murdered. His murderer is also dead. That murderer was once one of us before he became a traitor and a fool, but Skroga still died fighting for our freedom. For *all* our freedoms—fighters of the Games, city men, and Forest People. Skroga made no difference among them. Certainly the Protector will not. Can we do less?"

By then Blade knew he had his audience. In only a few more minutes, Blade knew the fighters of the Games would stand by Gerhaa to live or die with the city in battle against the Protector.

Chapter 21

There was plenty of dying before the battle was over, but not immediately. In fact, the two sides settled down to what seemed more like an armed truce than a war.

The Protector's forces held about a third of the city itself, and all the settled countryside beyond it. The rebels held about two-thirds of the city, including the riverside. The rebels couldn't break out, but the Protector's troops couldn't get in. The rebels' barricades were as strong as the Protector's, and while the armed city people weren't particularly good soldiers, they were desperate. Behind barricades they could fight well enough to delay any attack until the fighters of the Games came up. Then the balance shifted, because one trained fighter of the Games was worth two regular soldiers or three of the Protector's Pets.

So the Protector couldn't get at the rebels and the rebels couldn't get out of Gerhaa. The catapults on the towers along the waterfront kept the Protector's fleet from closing in and launching an attack on the cliff. At the same time, the catapults of the fleet sank many of the rebel ships tied up along the quays. Blade was very glad he'd sent off Meera and her escort in the first few hours of the rebellion.

Holding the countryside meant the Protector's men wouldn't run short of food or water. Fortunately for the rebels, Gerhaa was normally stocked with several months' worth of food, and they'd captured most of the warehouses and wells. Blade worked out a system of rationing, and he expected it would be at least two months before any of the rebels really started getting hungry.

Unfortunately, hunger wasn't the greatest enemy. At the moment the Protector was short of reliable men. He had the survivors of the original garrison, both Guard and regular, plus the nobles and wealthy merchants who'd armed themselves. He was keeping most of the latter out patrolling the countryside, since most of them had horses but few of them could face the fighters of the Games in battle. The Protector couldn't afford to lose men, so he couldn't afford to take many chances.

All this would change when the fleet from Mashom-Gad arrived with the Protector's reinforcements. Then he'd have enough ships and men to launch attacks on the rebels in two or three places at once, and enough trained soldiers to match the fighters of the Games. He'd even have enough siege equipment to hammer away at the rebel-held parts of the city for days before he launched the attacks. Blade wasn't sure the rebels' courage would survive such a bombardment.

When the fleet from Mashom-Gad finally did arrive, it was closer to fifty ships than forty, and some of them were huge vessels flying the Imperial banner of Kylan. Two days later the rebels captured their first prisoner from the reinforcements, and the situation began to look even more complicated. At least a thousand of the reinforcements were regular soldiers of the Imperial army of Kylan, under one of the Emperor's toughest generals. They kept very much to themselves, and the regular soldiers of the garrison of Gerhaa were beginning to look to the general rather than the Protector for leadership.

At least the prisoner said so, although Blade wasn't ready to believe all of it. Prisoners in every war in every Dimension tended to say what they thought their captors would like to hear. On the other hand, the bad blood between the regulars and the Protector's men was certainly a fact. The arrival of Imperial reinforcements *could* have made it worse, and if it had—

Unfortunately, there was a catch to this. Fear that matters were slipping out of his control could drive the Protector to drastic action. So could a desire to retrieve his rather battered reputation by leading a successful attack on the city.

The race against time was still on. If anything, it was getting tighter. Would Swebon lead the tribes of the Forest People down the Great River before the Protector led his reinforced army against the rebels of Gerhaa?

Swebon heard the drums begin to beat before he stepped out of his hut. As he walked toward the riverbank, they grew louder. He'd never heard so many drums beating all together, and that was no surprise. Never in all the years men had lived in the Forest had so many warriors been gathered together in one place. Never had warriors of all the Great Trbes and many of the small ones gathered together in peace. Never had any warriors gathered to sail upon the Great River and make war against Gerhaa the Stone Village. The night was warm, but Swebon shivered at the thought of what was happening in the Forest.

It did not all begin with Blade, as some of the chiefs and priests and many of the warriors thought. No one saw it at the time, but it really began when the Protectors of the Stone Village began to strike hard blows at the Forest People. Yet Swebon knew that he hadn't seen that himself before Blade came to tell him, so perhaps everything did begin with Blade after all.

Certainly without Blade, this gathering of the warriors of the tribes of the Forest would not be as it was. They could not hope to travel by night, if he hadn't taught them to make the sticks against the Horned Ones. There were many of those sticks in each of the five hundred canoes drawn up along the river's bank tonight.

They wouldn't have the strong bows, if Blade hadn't gone into the Forest and found the woods and boiled the *kohkol* sap. It was unfortunate that there weren't enough of these bows to give one to every warrior sailing against the Stone Village. The bows were not hard to make once a man knew how. Swebon himself was a warrior, not a carpenter, yet he'd made three. Meera had made two. But with everything else that had to be done, there was only time to make strong bows for one man in four. That might still be enough, because only the best archers of each tribe carried the strong bows.

There would not be warriors of all the tribes gathered here tonight without all that Blade had done. The strong bow was only part of it. More important was his leading the men of the Games of Hapanu against the soldiers of the Protector. He showed to all the Forest that the Stone Village could fall, if the Forest People brought all their strength against it. If there had not been a Blade to show this, Swebon knew that no chief or priest in the Forest would have thought of it.

Indeed, some of the priests were against all this, even after Blade had shown how it could be done. How many, Swebon did not know. None of the priests of Four Springs village had done anything suspicious since the day Meera returned and he spoke to them. Perhaps this was because of the way he spoke to them.

"One of you has worked with my brother Guno to kill

Blade the Englishman, then to kill me," he began. "In doing this he has worked against the Forest People and for the Sons of Hapanu. He has worked as if he wanted to sell his brothers and sisters into slavery in the Stone Village.

"He is evil.

"But I do not know who this evil priest is. Also, I do not want to punish good men for what evil men have done. So I will do nothing to anyone. But from this moment until I say otherwise, two warriors will be with each of you every moment of the night and day. They will go where you go, see what you see, and tell me everything you do and say. If I learn from them who is the evil priest, he will be thrown to the Horned Ones."

After that, the priests were silent and most of them worked hard. That was enough for Swebon. Any man who worked hard now was helping to save the Forest People, whatever he did before. Much hard work was needed before the men of the tribes came together at Four Springs village to sail against Gerhaa.

Four thousand warriors were gathered here tonight. Swebon was the high chief over all of them until the Stone Village fell, although he did not lead the greatest number of warriors. But one chief spoke for all when he said:

"We must all follow one man to destroy the Sons of Hapanu, who do the same. Swebon should be that man. He is as wise as any of us. Also, Blade trusts him and he trusts Blade and knows how the man from England thinks in war. This is the War of Blade, so how can we find a better chief than Swebon, the friend of Blade?" No one could answer that question.

With the other chiefs, Swebon spent much time looking at the map Blade sent them. Meera helped them to understand how Blade had drawn it. In fact, at first she understood the map much better than Swebon or any other chief. No doubt Blade told her much, but certainly Meera was a very wise woman.

The Protector would have some of his men on land by the walls of the city, and others in ships on the Great River. How many would be in each place, Blade did not know. He did want the Forest People to send most of their men against the ships. Swebon did not need Meera to tell him why Blade wanted this.

To destroy the ships of the Sons of Hapanu would cut them off from their homeland. The homeland could send them no more men or weapons. The Protector would be at the mercy of the Forest People and the men in Gerhaa. Even if he did not give up the fight at once, the Forest People could go into Gerhaa any time they wanted, with warriors, weapons, and food. The Protector's enemies would get stronger and stronger, and he would have to give up or die sooner or later.

Before that happened, Swebon knew there would be much terrible fighting. He could not avoid this, and neither could Blade. Both of them could only hope not to lead too many of their people to their deaths. Swebon had a plan he thought would help, and the other chiefs agreed that it was a good one.

Trees stretched close to Gerhaa on the west—not the true High Forest, but thick enough so that the Forest People would be at home there. Some of the best warriors would go into these trees, creep close to Gerhaa, and do as much harm as they could to all the Sons of Hapanu they could find. They would not fight large bands of the enemy, but they would fight with the strong bows, so when they struck they would strike hard. Blade said the Sons of Hapanu did not know of the strong bow, so many would die and others would lose their courage when they faced it.

The Protector would not know how many men were coming from the Forest against him. He might think there was a mighty army. Then he would take men from the ships. When he did this, all the Forest People on the Great River in their canoes would come to attack the ships. Three thousand warriors would strike all together. Swebon did not see how the ships could stand such an attack.

So it would be, if the Forest Spirit allowed it. The Forest Spirit would certainly take many brave men as the price of the victory, and Swebon knew that he himself might be among them. But if they won, and he survived—

If he survived, he would do what Blade asked of him—take Meera as his woman. She was wise and strong and beautiful, and their sons and daughters would be chiefs or the wives of chiefs.

As if his thoughts were calling her, Meera stepped out of the darkness. She wore a man's clothing, with a patch of the skin of a Horned One tied across her breasts. A strong bow and a quiver of arrows were slung across her back. In the dim torchlight she looked like something neither man nor woman nor indeed quite made out of flesh and blood, but something sent from elsewhere by the Forest Spirit.

Swebon knew that she was flesh and blood. He looked forward to the pleasures he would get and give when he took her to his bed. That was one reason why he was glad Blade was going to be returning to England soon.

Meera was the most selfish reason he had for wishing Blade to be gone, but she was not the only one. Swebon meant everything he'd said to Blade about the man from England being a chief warriors would follow. So many would follow him, perhaps, that Blade might begin to think of ruling not only in Gerhaa but in the Forest itself. It would take a fool not to see that this might be, and Blade was not a fool.

Only a fool would also yield without a fight, and Swebon was not a fool either. Without either man truly wishing to be the enemy of the other, he and Blade would sooner or later be at war. Then one or both of them might die, and certainly many men of Gerhaa and the Forest. Nothing would come of all this dying, except to undo the victory they had won over the Protector. That must not be, and perhaps whoever sent Blade his vision knew this.

Swebon laughed and beckoned Meera to follow him toward the waiting canoes. The Forest was large, and it would be larger still when the Protector was thrown down. It would never be large enough to hold two such men as Richard Blade of England and Swebon of the Fak'si.

Chapter 22

Blade was standing by the railing of the balcony at the top of the central tower of the Protector's palace when the messenger came from Swebon. From the balcony he had an excellent view of Gerhaa in all directions, out to the farmlands to the north and the Great River to the south.

To the north the campfires of the besieging army were beginning to glow in the twilight. They were divided into two groups, a good mile apart. The one on the left held the Protector's men, the one to the right the regular Kylanan soldiers. He'd heard reports that men had been seen going into the Protector's camp all day. Certainly there seemed to be more campfires in it tonight than there'd been before.

To the south the Great River shone like dark bronze as the light faded. Lanterns twinkled in the rigging of the ships anchored in the harbor, some almost at the base of the cliff. As Blade watched, he saw something black rise into the air from between the masts of one large ship. It flew high over the riverside wall, then plunged down into the city. Blade heard the crash and could imagine the screams, the clouds of dust and splinters, and the soldiers running to help the victims.

The noose was tightening around Gerhaa, as it had been tightening for ten days. Everyone in the city felt as if the noose was around his own neck. Tempers were getting shorter as the last desperate battle seemed to be coming closer. It was almost impossible to get the men on the barricades to take prisoners now. Blade hadn't heard what was happening in the enemy's camp since four days ago.

Another stone flew from the anchored fleet and crashed into the city. Blade winced. In the first few days after the fleet's arrival, their siege engines knocked down many of the towers on the city's riverside wall and drove the defenders off the rest. The catapults no longer kept the Protector's ships at a distance. Even in the fading light Blade could recognize the four ships where wooden siege towers were rising on the decks. When those towers were finished and the ships filled with soldiers, they would be towed close under the cliffs. Then Gerhaa would be attacked from two directions at once.

What then? Blade was far from certain that the rebels could hold against a double attack. Even if they did hold, the battle would be savage and bloody. It might not leave enough people alive on either side to give anyone an advantage. That would be a victory of sorts, at least for the Forest People. But what about the people of Gerhaa, who deserved better after all they'd endured from the Protector and now from their struggle to overthrow him.

Crash, crunch, thud! Three more stones in rapid succession. This time Blade didn't have to imagine the clouds of dust rising. Something large must have collapsed. At least the rubble would make good barricades, and the besiegers hadn't used firepots yet. They probably wouldn't, either. The Protector's wealth and that of most of his supporters was still inside Gerhaa. The last thing he'd want to do was risk burning it.

Behind Blade someone coughed, to get his attention. He turned and saw Kuka. The man was red-eyed and even thinner than usual. One arm was crudely bandaged, and Blade knew that arm would become infected if Kuka wouldn't take time to have a doctor look at it. If there could only be the Shield of Life in Gerhaa. But there wasn't, so Kuka might very well lose his arm.

Then Blade noticed the man standing beside Kuka, and stared. It was one of the men he'd sent upriver with Meera. In fact, he had Meera's silver arm ring tied to his belt. He wore a crude shirt and trousers of soaking-wet rawhide, and all his exposed skin was caked and stinking with some sort of grease. Somehow Blade had the feeling the man's appearance meant good news. He smiled.

"Welcome back, my friend. What does Swebon say?"

Blade and Kuka both listened intently as the man described the army Swebon was bringing down the Great River and his plans for using it. As Blade expected, the plans were sound. Swebon did not have very much to learn about war in general or even about the use of the new bows. No doubt the men he'd sent ashore to make a diversion behind the Protector were the reason troops were going ashore from the ships.

When the man was finished, Blade asked him a question. "How did you get here, and what are you wearing?"

"I swam."

"You swam in the Great River?" Blade couldn't hide his surprise.

"Yes. The idea came from a priest of the Kabi. He said that only the Horned Ones in the Great River touch dead meat, and they do not come out by day. So if I swam by day and smelled like a dead thing, I would be safe."

That explained the skins and the smelly grease—no doubt hides and fat from well-decayed carcases. "Is Swebon going to use this priest's trick with other men?"

"He did not tell me, and I did not ask."

"Swebon is wise," said Blade.

"Not as wise as you are, Blade," said the man.

Blade shook his head. "That is for the Forest Spirit to decide, not us." He turned to Kuka. "I think we'd better start getting ready to help Swebon when he comes." He listed the things they'd need, including three hundred picked fighters with the best weapons and armor to climb down the cliffs and join in the attack on the ships. Blade would lead that force himself.

"Blade, you cannot risk—" began Kuka.

Blade shook his head. "I won't ask someone else to risk himself in this. Besides, the men of the city have a good leader in you."

"Me?" Kuka seemed stunned.

"Yes, you. And that's why if you don't have the doctors look at that arm, I'll knock you down and drag you to them myself. You will be needed."

Kuka laughed. "All right, Blade, I'll go, I'll go."

The last of the light faded. Kuka went off to see the doctors and several messengers went off with Blade's orders. Blade ate stale bread and cheese with the mold scraped off, then settled down to spend the night up on the palace tower.

At the second hour of the night, a messenger returned. He reported that men were leaving the Protector's camp. Some appeared to be marching back toward the river. Others were marching inland.

At the third hour, another messenger came. The rope ladders for going down the cliff to the river were all ready. So were the new barricades built behind the old ones on the landward side of the city. Many women were asking to help man these barricades, or at least stand in the windows and throw stones and roof tiles down on the Protector's men.

Blade gave his permission. Fighting from behind solid barricades, fifty men could hold off five hundred, but a second line of defense never hurt. Even a handful of the Protector's men loose in the rebel rear could do a great deal of damage.

Shortly before the fifth hour, Blade saw movement among the ships in the harbor. One by one, about a dozen crept out from the eastern end of the harbor into the open river. There they stopped, apparently anchoring again. In the darkness Blade didn't know what ships they were. He did recall vaguely that most of the ships flying the Emperor's banner were at the southern end of the harbor, but he couldn't be sure. He decided he was getting too tired to think clearly. He'd have to get some sleep, or he'd be no good when and if things did start to happen.

When Kuka returned, he found Blade sound asleep on the floor of the balcony, wrapped up in his cloak and snoring like a small thunderstorm.

Swebon saw a hint of dawn in the darkness as he looked downriver. He could also begin to see the looming mass of the Stone Village and the ships near it. He didn't think the men on the ships could yet see him or all the canoes behind him. A faint mist lay over the river, and Swebon himself couldn't see most of the canoes when he looked astern.

He knew they were all there. No man would violate the oath he'd sworn, even if he could resist the idea of helping to bring down the Stone Village and the Sons of Hapanu. The courage of the warriors following him had survived even the knowledge that there would not be much of the Shield of Life. Only the worst wounds would have it at once. The others must wait until the People went upriver again. Perhaps Blade or the fighters of the Games had some knowledge that could help the wounded.

There were not as many men in the canoes now as when they started the journey. The Great River was still a dangerous place for the Forest People, even if they no longer needed to fear the Horned Ones so much. Too many warriors and weapons now lay at the bottom of the Great River.

Now the mist was beginning to lift. Soon the men on the enemy ships would be able to see the canoes. It was time to launch the attack. Swebon motioned to the man behind him to pass up the great horn. He raised it to his lips, took a deep breath, then blew. Behind him other horns replied, and so did the beat of drums. Paddles plunged into the water with splashes, and suddenly there was foam at the bow of the canoe.

170

Swebon blew the horn three more times, then sat down and picked up his own paddle.

Someone was shaking Blade. He grunted, sat up by sheer reflex, then came fully awake to see Kuka squatting beside him. The man's wounded arm showed a brand-new bandage.

"Swebon's canoes are coming down the river toward the ships," Kuka said. He grinned, showing all the gaps in his teeth.

If Blade hadn't already been fully awake, he would have come alert now. He leaped up with a shout. Kuka started and the sentry at the head of the balcony stairs dropped his spear with a clatter.

Blade armed himself and followed Kuka, down the stairs and through the gray streets of Gerhaa. The darkness hid most of the piled filth and the damaged buildings. It didn't hide the fear on the faces of the few people abroad at this hour. The battle they were facing today not only had to be won, it had to be won decisively enough to smash the Protector and end the siege. The people of Gerhaa had endured too much already. They might not be able to endure much more, and it would be no disgrace to them if they couldn't—merely a disaster.

As Blade and Kuka approached the riverside wall, the streets became so littered with wreckage that it was hard to get through. Some of the stones and timbers were being piled into barricades. In the shadows of these barricades the men of Blade's assault party were already waiting. As they saw their leader approaching, some cheered and were immediately cuffed or cursed into silence by Kuka. They fell in behind their leaders and headed for the wall.

Blade scrambled up the half-ruined stairs inside the Blue Bird's Tower and came out on the roof. Keeping low, he peered through a hole in the battlements that gave him a good view of the river.

At the west end of the harbor, the water seemed to be solid with the canoes of the Forest People. The small patches of open water were white with foam from prows and paddles. As Blade watched, one cluster of canoes swarmed around the western fort on the island, concentrating on the side closest to the water. The rest of the canoes came on steadily, like ants scenting something sweet. One ship was already surrounded, men were falling in the canoes around it, and other men were falling on the ship's deck. Blade strained his eyes and made out Swebon standing up in the bow of one canoe, with what could only be one of the new bows in his hands.

Some of the ships were beginning to move now. The smaller ones had sweeps out and looked like spiders crawling across the water. On the decks of the larger ships Blade saw men frantically swinging axes to cut anchor cables. Enough of the current of the Great River ran through the harbor so that a drifting ship would slowly creep down toward the eastern end. There they might find help—from the Protector's galleys, the Emperor's sailing ships, or simply through being able to flee downriver if the wind rose. At the moment there wasn't a breath of air stirring.

Blade looked back down the inner side of the wall at the men waiting there. The grappling hooks and rope ladders were all ready. Kuka looked up inquiringly. Blade shook his head and gave a thumbs-down signal. It wasn't time yet. Sooner or later the canoes would break through to the cliff and the assault party could climb down and join the fight. Even if the canoes didn't come, the current might push one of the drifting ships within range of the wall.

As Swebon's canoe passed the first of the stone houses on the island, he saw the attack on it begin. Men stood up in the bows of canoes, whirling ropes with iron hooks on the ends around their heads. Then they let go and the hooks shot up like arrows from bows, to grip the top of the stone house. As they gripped and held, men started to climb up the ropes.

The Sons of Hapanu had archers on top of the stone house, shooting down at the climbing men and the canoes. Swebon saw several men fall into the river. A canoe suddenly shook and broke in two as a stone landed in it.

Now the first man to reach the top of the stone house swung himself up and over the wall there and started fighting the Sons of Hapanu. From the fact that he was using two war clubs and no shield, Swebon knew the man was Tuk's oldest son. Four Sons of Hapanu went down in front of the swinging clubs, but a fifth drove his sword into Tuk's son from behind. The swordsman shouted in triumph and leaped on top of the wall. Swebon raised his bow, put an arrow in place, drew, and shot. The Son of Hapanu went down on his knees, dropping his sword, then bent forward and fell head-first into the river.

Someone was pounding Swebon on the shoulder with one hand, shouting at him to "Look, look, chief!" and pointing with the other hand. Swebon looked, and joined in the shouting.

The current had drifted one of the enemy's ships up against the cliffs below Gerhaa's wall. It was a ship with a strange tall house of wood standing on it. A man was standing on the city's wall, looking toward the top of the wooden house on the ship. Then he leaped into the air like a great fish and came down on top of the wooden house.

The mist was almost gone now and though the day was going to be cloudy, there was plenty of light. Swebon recognized the man who'd made the leap from the wall as Blade.

The leap from the wall to the top of the ship's siege tower was a long one, even for Blade. He nearly went through the railing on the far side of the platform on top, and felt planks groan and creak under him. For a moment he was at a disadvantage if anyone attacked, but the one man on the platform was too surprised. Before the man could recover, Blade whipped out his sword, split the man's unhelmeted head, and pitched his body down on to the deck below.

The first two men to climb the stairs inside the tower died nearly as quickly. Blade knocked the first one on the head with a loose plank, then stabbed the second in the throat as he climbed over his stunned comrade. This gave a third man the chance to get up on to the platform beside Blade. He wore a scale-mail shirt and a helmet.

Blade stepped back, to give himself room to swing his sword hard against the man's armor. The moment he'd opened the gap, there was a *wsssht-thuk* and the man staggered to the railing, a crossbow bolt in his chest. He slumped to the platform, face showing a mixture of outraged indignation and pain, then died. Blade turned to see Kuka and half a dozen archers standing on top of the Blue Bird's Tower. All along the wall to either side of it, men were throwing rope ladders over the walls and grappling hooks into the rigging of the ship.

The archers on the ship's deck picked off a few of the assault party as they climbed down. A few more died in the fighting on the ship's deck. But the ship's defenders couldn't do a thing to cut the ladders or the grappling lines, so they were quickly overwhelmed by sheer weight of numbers. Blade stayed on top of the siege tower until he'd seen everything he needed to see, then came down. By that time the ship was firmly in rebel hands.

By that time also Swebon's canoe was alongside. The chief came up the side of the ship with a broad grin on his face and blood all over chest and one arm. "It is not mine," he said in reply to Blade's look.

"Good. There is much more work for you before this day is over."

"I hope so. I do not care to let the Sons of Hapanu go easily, now that we have them in our grip."

Blade nodded. "We shall not let the Protector's men go, but I do not know about the Emperor's."

Swebon looked skeptical. "I know they are all our enemies, and that is enough for me."

"I do not know that, Swebon, and I have seen more of what is happening in Gerhaa than you have." Blade lowered his voice as he said this, not wanting to anger Swebon into a quarrel but desperately needing to make his point.

"What is happening in Gerhaa, then?" asked the chief.

I think I'm guessing right, but I'm still guessing, Blade reminded himself. *'If I'm wrong . . . If I'm wrong, I'm not likely to live long enough to feel guilty over it!*

"The Emperor's men have kept themselves apart from the Protector's ever since the fleet came," he said. "Last night the Emperor's ships dropped downriver, and they are now several miles away. What is more, they're staying there. They aren't joining the fight. If we leave them in peace, perhaps they won't."

Swebon looked confused. "The Emperor is also a Son of Hapanu, Blade. Can any of them be our friends?"

Blade shrugged. "Friends? I don't know. But I'm almost sure that the Emperor is the enemy of our great enemy, the Protector of Gerhaa. We should do what we can to keep things that way."

At last Swebon nodded, with a smile that turned into a grin. "Yes. It is said that a wise man does not make water in the cooking pot of the enemy of an enemy or the friend of a friend. So we will not make water in the Emperor's cooking pot." The smile faded. "How shall we tell one cooking pot from another, Blade?"

Blade described the different banners of the two factions. "All ships flying the Protector's banner are fair game. The Emperor's ships are not to be attacked unless they attack us."

Swebon sent messengers off in canoes with the new orders. Kuka climbed down from the walls to speak briefly with Blade, reporting that there was no sign of an attack in the city. Blade told him to get back and make sure there wouldn't be any, and Kuka reluctantly returned to the city. The rest of Blade's assault party climbed into the canoes of the Forest People and paddled off to take more of the Protector's ships. There was no sign of Meera, and Blade could only console himself with Swebon's word that she'd been all right the last time he saw her.

The last two canoes of Blade's assault party were getting ready to leave. Blade said farewell to Swebon, then scrambled up to the ship's maintop to take a final look at the battle.

He'd barely reached the top when he saw that the Protector's counterattack was starting.

There were five heavily-manned galleys in the counterattack. Two of them had catapults at bow and stern, and all of them had their decks crammed with crossbowmen. They crept up the harbor from the east, passing insolently close to the Emperor's quietly waiting sailing ships. Then the oars settled to a steady stroke and the galleys began to move.

As they moved, the canoes of the Forest People swarmed toward them. The galleys held their fire until the canoes were within crossbow range. Then they let fly with everything they had, eighty and a hundred bolts at a time.

The canoes might as well have run into machine-gun fire. In some every man was killed within a few seconds. In others the survivors leaped overboard, preferring to risk the creatures in the river to dying under the hail of archery. Dozens of canoes drifted empty except for bodies, in water rapidly turning red with blood and still lashed with crossbow bolts.

Then the catapults on the two lead galleys opened fire, hurling their six-foot spears as fast as their crews could reload and recock them. One of these spears could skewer three or four men at once, like barbecued chickens on a spit. It could split a canoe in two, capsize it, or drill a hole large enough to sink it within minutes. More bodies joined the ones already floating in the red water, and more warriors thrashed frantically toward the surviving canoes. Some of them reached safety. The Forest People with the new bows shot back and kept the battle from being completely one-sided, but not from being a disaster for the canoes.

Blade didn't know how many canoes and warriors were lost. He only knew that after a while the survivors were paddling away from the Protector's deadly galleys. They weren't fleeing in blind panic, however. They crossed the sand bars into the open river. Then they turned and paddled along parallel to the galleys, just out of crossbow range. The galleys picked off a few more canoes with their catapults, then ceased fire.

It was obvious that the canoe-borne warriors of the Forest People couldn't hope to engage the Protector's galleys when the galleys had room to maneuver. It was just as obvious to Blade that the galleys weren't going to have that room much longer. The harbor narrowed toward its western end, and Blade was at almost the narrowest point. If the galleys had to turn around here, they would be nearly immobile while they were doing it, and if they had a few other things on their minds as well—

Blade leaped into the rigging and slid down the shrouds to the deck. He was issuing orders as his feet hit the deck. Fortunately a good many of the river assault party were ex-sailors or at least boatmen, and the Forest People were at home on the water. His plan was going to need a lot of men who at least knew one end of a ship or boat from the other.

Messengers scrambled up ladders and paddled off in canoes. Kuka was to send every archer and every bolt or arrow in Gerhaa to the Blue Bird's Tower. They should climb onto the wall but stay down and hold their fire until Blade gave them the signal. As many of the assault party as Blade could reach were called back to his ship. Men climbed into canoes and paddled off to the other two ships lying closest to Blade's. Blade himself led a few men in cutting the shrouds of their own ship's mainmast. A lookout climbed into the foretop and called down the progress of the Protector's galleys.

The galleys were now coming on more slowly, stopping to send boarding parties aboard ships captured by the rebels and the Forest People. Some of the men caught aboard those ships fought with foolish courage and died for it. Others managed to scramble into their canoes and get clear. Most of these rallied at Blade's ship, Swebon among them. As the galleys slowly came on, Blade's strength grew, until he had more than four hundred men and sixty canoes within easy reach. More than two hundred of the men were archers with either crossbows or the new laminated bows of the People.

As the galleys came within catapult range, Blade and Swebon climbed to the top of the siege tower to make sure they could see everything. Blade saw the glint of metal on helmets on the wall and knew that Kuka's archers were getting into position. The decks of the three ships he was planning to use were nearly deserted—or at least they'd look that way from the galleys. Behind the three ships lay fifty canoes, in clear sight of the galleys but safely out of bowshot until the galleys had passed Blade's ships.

The galleys now seemed to be stopping and lying on their oars. Blade knew that someone aboard was sure to be considering the possibilities of a trap. After all, three ships lying across the harbor so that they'd force the galleys to pass through in single file and at a crawl?

Blade also doubted that common sense would prevail. Just beyond the three ships lay a solid mass of canoes, the last resistance in the harbor. If the galleys sank those, then they could break out into the open river, to engage the remaining canoes with all the maneuvering room they needed. The temptation to go on would be enormous, trap or not.

The risks of retreating would be even greater. The Emperor's general had to be watching by now. The last thing the Protector could afford was to appear cautious or even cowardly under the general's eyes. He'd already lost far too much; he had to gamble if he wanted to be allowed to keep what he had, let alone have any chance to win back what he'd lost.

The galleys rested on their oars so long that Blade was almost ready to signal the archers on the wall to open fire. If the galleys weren't coming on through, he'd have to hit them as hard as he could where they were. Some of them were within bowshot now, and—

The galley flying the Protector's personal standard was on the move again, foam curling away from her oars. She'd been third in line; now she was coming up to take the lead. One by one the other galleys started to move, falling in behind the flagship.

Blade slapped Swebon on the back and pointed. He felt like holding his breath, as if that could draw the galleys on faster. He didn't feel like cheering yet. Too many things could still go wrong.

The galleys came on as if they were running on rails. They were bearing off to port, toward the smallest of Blade's three ships, the one closest to the island and sand bars. When the Protector's galley was a hundred yards from that ship, Blade leaned over the railing of the siege tower and waved a red scarf on a long stick. He went on waving it until another red scarf waved from the bow of the third ship. A moment later red flames spurted up from her amidships.

Half the ship's hold was filled with barrels of oil for cooking and making firepots, so her catching fire was almost an explosion. Before the canoe carrying the fire party was safely away, flames were towering as high as the ship's mastheads. Sails vanished like dew in the morning, balls of fire danced up and down the tarred rigging, flames gushed out of every port and began to creep out from gaping seams.

The Protector's galley swung to starboard, away from the blazing ship, backing the oars on one side to turn faster than Blade had expected. She did turn, though. She had to. Between the burning ship and the next one, there wasn't enough room for the galley to pass. The only clear water now lay between the other two ships. The Protector's galley stopped turning and backed off another hundred yards. Then the drums started pounding out a fast stroke and the galley surged forward, straight at the gap between the two ships.

Blade let out a sigh of relief. Very little could go wrong now that could defeat his plan. The Protector's galley came on, the other four turning now to follow in her wake. Blade leaned over the railing and shouted to the men below, then axes cut the last shrouds of the mainmast. Wood cracked like gunshots and ropes flailed about wildly. A flying block clipped a bone ornament from Swebon's hair without making him blink. Then the ship's mainmast went over like a toppling pine, plunging into the water just ahead of the Protector's galley.

Blade would have liked to time the mast's fall to bring it right down on the galley's deck. But you couldn't always have everything so neat in a battle. The galley was still too close to the falling mast to stop, and plowed into it with a cracking of timbers and oars and a chorus of screams from the galley slaves below. A good many of the soldiers on the galley's deck were knocked off their feet, and the four galleys astern of the flagship had to back oars frantically to keep from ramming her or each other.

For the moment, the Protector's whole squadron was as immobilized as if it was aground, well within bowshot of all the waiting archers. Blade jumped up and waved a yellow scarf back and forth, as furiously as if the world would end the moment he stopped. Helmets sprouted all along the wall, and the men lying on the decks of Blade's two ships sprang to their feet. Then arrows and bolts poured down onto the decks of all five galleys.

Now it was the turn of the Sons of Hapanu to go down as if they were being machine-gunned. The crossbows could drill through any armor they wore, while the laminated bows could fire three times as fast as anything the Protector's men had ever faced. Before Blade scrambled down to the deck of his own ship, the decks of all five galleys were carpeted with dead and dying Guardsmen, Where the planks weren't covered with bodies, they shone a gruesome red. Blade leaped down into the first canoe to come alongside and ordered the paddlers to take him to the Protector's galley. He climbed up onto the deck just as the Protector himself burst out of the cabin under the fo'csle.

Before he saw the Protector coming at him, Blade hadn't felt the slightest interest in being chivalrous toward the man. He wouldn't have cared if the man died filled with arrows or fell overboard and was eaten by the Horned Ones. Now he saw the Protector advancing toward him, a sword in one hand, the great jeweled staff of office in the other, and tears streaming down his face. Blade wasn't sure what the Protector was weeping for—friends and comrades, lovers, or merely the disastrous end of both his power and his life. He did know that the Protector deserved a fighting man's death.

Blade was carrying a gladiator's shield and a broadsword, and wore only a gladiator's fighting outfit. The Protector came in so fast that his shorter sword left a red line across Blade's ribs and another on his shoulder before Blade could get his shield into position. That was almost the last time the Protector hit Blade, but Blade found he couldn't get through to the Protector either. In spite of his grief and the slippery deck underfoot, the man was as fast and deadly as a hungry leopard.

The two men went around and around, treading on the bodies and the bloody planks, so close together that Blade's archers couldn't risk shooting at the Protector. Blade began to wonder how long this fight could go on, knew that he could eventually wear the Protector down, but also knew that the man might get lucky before then. It wouldn't take much of an edge to let him put his sword into Blade, and he was desperate enough to take almost any risk. Blade decided that he'd better draw the Protector into taking that risk at a time of Blade's own choosing.

Suddenly Blade wheeled to the right, opening his normally shielded side to the Protector. The Protector thrust, Blade wheeled back, and the sharp edge of his shield caught the Protector's sword arm. The sword's point pricked Blade's ribs again, then it clattered to the deck as the Protector's arm dangled limp and streaming blood.

With incredible speed the Protector raised the staff and swung it, knocking Blade's sword out of his hand. Blade blocked the Protector's next swing with his shield, then closed and grabbed the staff. The Protector struggled to tear it loose, then tried to kick Blade in the groin. Blade brought his shield edge down on the Protector's leg and the man went down. Blade dropped the shield and hammered away with the staff until Swebon came up and pulled him to his feet. The great staff could indeed crack a man's skull.

Blade went over to the side and held onto the railing until he felt completely firm on his legs. The thought of the size of the gamble he'd taken chilled him. Yet there could be no doubt—he'd won. The five galleys drifted under an umbrella of smoke from the burning ship. All of them were surrounded by the canoes of the Forest People, and their decks swarmed with warriors and men of Gerhaa. On one, the surviving galley slaves were already being released and led up on deck.

Much more interesting to Blade was a small ship heading up the harbor as fast as her sweeps would take her. From her foremast flew the Emperor's standard, and above it a white flag.

Blade found his voice. He pointed to the ship with two flags. "Swebon, I'll kill any man who fires on that ship with my bare hands."

"I see it comes from the Emperor."

"Yes, and I think it brings some words we'd better hear."

By the time the dead aboard the flagships were separated from the living and laid out on deck, the truce ship was closing in. As the burning ship sank in a cloud of steam, the truce ship came alongside the flagship. Somehow Blade wasn't at all surprised to see Ho-Marn standing at the ship's railing, with an embroidered blue robe over his armor.

"Greetings, Ho-Marn!" called Blade.

"Greetings, Blade," replied the soldier.

Blade took a deep breath. "Ho-Marn, I think the time has come to ask you a few questions."

Ho-Marn laughed. "Blade, I think the time has come to answer them. You have done all I hoped you would do and more."

"And—if I hadn't done what you hoped?"

"Another tool, another time."

"I understand. Come aboard, Ho-Marn."

Chapter 23

Five men sat on the balcony to the main room of what had been the Protector's palace. There was Richard Blade, sitting in the Protector's whitewashed chair with the Protector's staff leaning against it. There was Kuka, Swebon, and Ho-Marn, all still in fighting gear. Finally there was a short, sturdy dark man with gray hair, the general of the Emperor of Kylan. Swebon couldn't begin to pronounce his name or titles, but was willing to call him "Prince," as Blade did.

They were sitting on the balcony because Blade guessed right when he said the Emperor was the enemy of the Protector, even if he might not be the friend of the Forest People. Swebon remembered Blade's describing what the Emperor thought, and was glad that Blade was there to describe it for him. It was good that Blade hadn't gone back to England at once. Swebon would need him for a little while more at least, to teach the Forest People how to understand all the new things which were still coming to them.

He remembered Blade's words:

"The Emperor wanted to bring down the city of Mashom-Gad. It was growing too wealthy and too powerful from selling the Blood of Hapanu. Its nobles and merchants were becoming ambitious, and the Emperor feared these ambitions.

"About five hundred years ago, Mashom-Gad was a powerful independent city. When the Empire of Kylan was founded, the city came under its rule, but was never happy about this. The people of Mashom-Gad sent their ships across the ocean and founded Gerhaa to get back some of their old power. They got back even more when they discovered the Blood of Hapanu and became wealthy through it.

"A few years ago the nobles of Mashom-Gad and other nobles who also hated the Emperor sent the Protector here to Gerhaa. With the soldiers of his Guard, he was to conquer the Forest People. Then there would be a second empire here in the Forest, under the rule of Mashom-Gad instead of the Emperor of Kylan. In time, perhaps the second empire would make Mashom-Gad strong enough to overthrow the Emperor himself."

"They look far ahead in Mashom-Gad."

"Either that, or perhaps far into the past," said Blade. "But you can see why the Emperor became the Protector's enemy as soon as he knew what the Protector was doing in Gerhaa."

"I do. And—the Emperor sent Ho-Marn to Gerhaa to watch the Protector?"

"Exactly. He was also to watch for any weapon for striking at the Protector. He found me."

Swebon pulled his mind back to the present. The Prince had just finished speaking, and now Ho-Marn was translating what his chief said into the tongue of the Forest People.

"—a small garrison of the Emperor's troops, to protect those of his people who wish to do business here in Gerhaa."

"How many?" asked Kuka.

"We can talk of that later."

"How many?" asked Blade, in a somewhat harsher voice. Ho-Marn saw that Blade would not be put off.

"Not more than a thousand will be needed," said Ho-Marn.

Blade and Kuka exchanged glances, then both looked at Swebon. The chief nodded. One thousand of the Sons of Hapanu could not do much against the Forest People, not if they were all busy in Gerhaa. Perhaps they could be dangerous with the help of the people of Gerhaa, but Swebon did not think they would have that help. In Gerhaa, the people were not of the Forest or of Kylan. They were of Gerhaa and only of Gerhaa. They would not be the enemies of the Forest People unless they had reason to fear the Forest People—and Swebon would do his best to make sure that Gerhaa would have no reason to fear the Forest People.

Ho-Marn was still speaking. "A small amount in taxes will be paid in the Blood of Hapanu. This will satisfy the temples of Hapanu in Kylan. Otherwise, the Emperor wishes that the trade in the Blood of Hapanu be open to all free subjects of the Empire. You may sell or not sell to anyone, as you wish."

Swebon was delighted. If the Blood of Hapanu could now be sold to the Sons of Hapanu, the Forest People would never need to fear an enemy again. They could buy all the weapons they could not learn to make themselves. He did not think here was the time or place to say this, however. He would first speak to all the other chiefs and hear their wisdom on the question. He was now Swebon, First Chief of the People, but he was not the only chief and never would be.

Blade nodded. "Is the Prince ready to sign an agreement covering all these terms?"

"I do not think—" began Ho-Marn.

"I do think it would be wise. The sooner we put our agreement in writing, the less chance of any trouble later on. I trust the Emperor, but I do not trust the Emperor's enemies to be silent forever. Mashom-Gad has lost a battle, but that does not mean that it has lost the war. Even if we think they have, they may think otherwise."

Ho-Marn spoke to the Prince in the tongue of the Sons of Hapanu. The Prince laughed and nodded, then replied to Ho-Marn. "He thinks Blade is wise," said the captain. "We will sign for the Emperor, if Blade and Kuka will sign for Free Gerhaa and Swebon for the Forest People."

"I will," said Swebon, and then noticed Meera coming up the stairs to the balcony. She still wore men's clothing, but instead of a bow and quiver carried two gourds filled with the Shield of Life. Blade rose from the Protector's seat to greet her. She held out one of the gourds and he took it.

"I must ask you people to let Swebon and me go for a few hours," he said. "Now we are both chiefs among the Forest People, and must give the Shield of Life to the wounded." He tied the gourd to his belt and picked up the Protector's staff of office.

"Kuka, take this and put it somewhere safe. It's too valuable to leave lying around where anyone can steal it, but I certainly don't want to carry it myself. I—" He frowned, hesitated, then sat down again.

"Blade, are you—?"

"I'm—I'm all right, Swebon. The call—the call has come to return—" He frowned again, apparently in pain. Then he said, "To return to England," in a steady, clear voice—and he was gone. Where he'd been was only empty air, and the staff was gone with him.

Swebon was the first to recover his voice, because he was the only one Blade had told of what was going to happen. "He had a vision," the chief said quietly. "He told me that when Gerhaa was free he would return to England."

Ho-Marn nodded slowly. "Yes, but—did he tell you that the gods would carry him there? It can be nothing else but the work of the gods we've seen here."

Kuka and Meera nodded. Swebon noticed that Meera was shaking, and took her in his arms until she was calm. Then all five of them prayed, each to what he worshipped and each in the manner of his own people.

Chapter 24

The secure telephone in J's office rang. He wasn't surprised to hear Lord Leighton on the other end.

"Ah, J. Good news. Nearly the best, in fact. Richard's not only back, but he had a fairly straightforward trip and a *very* easy transition."

"Both ways?" asked J. He would have liked to be on hand for Richard's return himself, but for once he hadn't been able to make it. As chief of security for the Project, he was still tying up loose ends left over from the Ngaa affair.

"Yes. There wasn't any of the usual psychedelic display on the way out, and no trauma to speak of on the way back. I would say the physiological stress was equivalent to—oh, his running five or six miles on a good track."

J's eyebrows rose. "So—something well within the capacity of anyone in good physical condition?"

"I would say yes. Mind you, I'm only going on the doctor's first report. But it seems as if my hypothesis about the KALI capsule's reducing the stress of the transition may have something in it."

A year ago Lord Leighton might have been claiming complete vindication. But the Wizard of Rentoro and the Ngaa seemed to have taught him what J considered badly-needed and long-overdue lessons in caution.

"What about the trip itself? You called it 'straightforward', I recall?"

"Quite. It was very much the sort of thing Richard once called 'Inter-Dimensional social work'—helping people solve a problem they didn't quite have the knowledge to solve themselves. The sort of thing he can do on his head."

J caught the hint in the scientist's voice and said with gentle firmness, "That doesn't mean anyone else can do the same, Leighton."

"Certainly not. And we can't really expect to predict what sort of problems our people will find in Dimension X until

185

we can predict where they're going to end up. However, I'm quite willing to put off trying to repeat trips until we've solved the problem of sending other people besides Blade.

"I'd like to get started on that at once. This will mean a bit of money—"

"How much?"

"Not more than twenty thousand pounds."

That was small enough so that even the Prime Minister might swallow it. "What exactly do you need it for?"

"To finish assembling the third KALI launch capsule. The one we used this time was the spare. We'd assembled components for a third, to use when we set up a two-capsule rig. It will need a good deal of work before it's operational, though."

"Good enough. As soon as you've delivered your full report on this trip, I'll approach the Prime Minister."

"I appreciate that." *Click.*

J hung up and leaned back in his chair. He couldn't help wondering if Leighton *had* permanently lost some of his old fire and arrogance. Or was it just that the nightmarish battle with the Ngaa had shaken him temporarily, and he'd be back to his old self soon enough?

J swiveled his chair away from his desk and began to think seriously. The could increase the search for another Dimension X traveler now. That meant going back to the personnel records of the various agencies in the British intelligence establishment and the Ministry of Defense. They'd be sticking to experienced field operatives or similar types from the armed forces for the time being. Such people were most likely to have the necessary range of survival skills, and they'd also be easier for Richard to work with.

What about extending the search outside Britain? That might come eventually, but where should they start? The CIA was out of the question. Their security was so full of holes that sooner or later the Dimension X secret would trickle out through one of them. They'd done the Project a good turn during the affair of the Ngaa, but that had been largely on the initiative of a good field man who owed Blade a favor. Their central office hadn't done a blessed thing.

The British Commonwealth? Now that was a real possibility. Their intelligence operations were small, but they had a certain number of good people. And the Prime Minister would probably be enthusiastic. He was always speaking out in favor of revived Commonwealth ties—probably to conceal his inability to do anything about Britain's own problems.

J turned back to his desk and started scribbling notes. Excitement rose in him. He hadn't felt so optimistic about the prospects of a breakthrough in the Project in a long time. As he scribbled, he occasionally wondered what Richard might be thinking now.

Richard Blade wasn't thinking very much. He was lying in bed in the Project's hospital, halfway between waking and sleep.

He really didn't need to be in the hospital. The doctor who'd examined him said as much. "You could go out and climb in the Alps right now if you wanted to," were his words. Then he added, "But just in case there's something that hasn't shown up yet, I'd like to keep you under observation for about forty-eight hours."

Blade took a shower, pulled on a pair of his own pajamas, and went to bed. He started drifting off to sleep almost at once, and as he did so, realized that he felt better than he'd done since the battle with Ngaa and Zoe's death.

The Project was saved, at least for the time being. He'd made a round trip into Dimension X without any real complications, successfully testing the combination of the old computer and the new KALI capsule. J and Leighton could tell the P.M. that things were back to normal—whatever that was. Could you call it "normal" to turn a whole people in a new direction and prevent a series of wars which might have killed hundreds of thousands?

The Protector's staff now sat in the Project's master safe, and it would stay there until somebody figured out what to do with it. That might take a while, since it was definitely more ornamental than useful.

The Shield of Life was very different. The Project biochemists were already hard at work on analyzing it. Blade would be interested in the results of that analysis, but there was one thing he knew already. It would be almost impossible to turn the Shield of Life into a killing weapon. The tranquilizing effect he'd never been able to test might be developed as a riot-control weapon, but that was about it. He'd brought back something for healing, not destruction.

Blade drifted off to sleep, and as he did he realized that for the first time in months he wasn't afraid of the nightmares sleep might bring him.

RICHARD BLADE by Jeffrey Lord

Richard Blade is Everyman, a mighty and intrepid hero exploring the hitherto-uncharted realm of worlds beyond our knowledge, in the best tradition of America's most popular heroic fantasy giants such as Tarzan, Doc Savage, and Conan.

Over 2.5 million copies in print!

☐	40-432-8	The Bronze Axe	#1	$1.50
☐	220593-8	Jade Warrior	#2	1.25
☐	40-433-6	Jewel of Tharn	#3	1.50
☐	40-434-4	Slave of Sarma	#4	1.50
☐	40-435-2	Liberator of Jedd	#5	1.50
☐	40-436-0	Monster of the Maze	#6	1.50
☐	40-437-9	Pearl of Patmos	#7	1.50
☐	40-438-7	Undying World	#8	1.50
☐	40-439-5	Kingdom of Royth	#9	1.50
☐	40-440-9	Ice Dragon	#10	1.50
☐	220474-1	Dimensions of Dreams	#11	1.25
☐	40-441-7	King of Zunga	#12	1.50
☐	220559-9	Golden Steed	#13	1.25
☐	220623-3	Temples of Ayocan	#14	1.25
☐	40-442-5	Towers of Melnon	#15	1.50
☐	220780-1	Crystal Seas	#16	1.25
☐	40-443-3	Mountains of Brega	#17	1.50
☐	220822-1	Warlords of Gaikon	#18	1.25
☐	220855-1	Looters of Tharn	#19	1.25
☐	220881-7	Guardian Coral Throne	#20	1.25
☐	40-257-0	Champion of the Gods	#21	1.50
☐	40-457-3	Forests of Gleor	#22	1.50
☐	40-263-5	Empire of Blood	#23	1.50
☐	40-260-0	Dragons of Englor	#24	1.50
☐	40-444-1	Torian Pearls	#25	1.50
☐	40-193-0	City of the Living Dead	#26	1.50
☐	40-205-8	Master of the Hashomi	#27	1.50
☐	40-206-6	Wizard of Rentoro	#28	1.50
☐	40-207-4	Treasure of the Stars	#29	1.50
☐	40-208-2	Dimension of Horror	#30	1.50